Demonology

The Bond

Kadeem Locke

Demonology: The Bond
Copyright © 2024 by Kadeem Locke

All rights reserved. No part of this publication may be reproduced, distributed, or transmitted in any form or by any means, including photocopying, recording or other electronic or mechanical methods, without the prior written permission of the author, except in the case of brief quotations embodied in reviews and certain other non-commercial uses permitted by copyright law.

Without in any way limiting the author's [and publisher's] exclusive rights under copyright, any use of this publication to "train" generative artificial intelligence (AI) technologies to generate text is expressly prohibited. The author reserves all rights to license uses of this work for generative AI training and development of machine learning language models.

Printed in the United States of America

Hardcover ISBN: 978-1-960876-62-1
Paperback ISBN: 978-1-960876-63-8
eBook ISBN: 978-1-960876-79-9

Muse Literary

CONTENTS

Chapter 1	1
Chapter 2	13
Chapter 3	29
Chapter 4	35
Chapter 5	45
Chapter 6	55
Chapter 7	69
Chapter 8	81
Chapter 9	85
Chapter 10	93
Chapter 11	101
Chapter 12	107
Chapter 13	117
Chapter 14	127
Chapter 15	133
Chapter 16	145
Chapter 17	153
Chapter 18	161
Chapter 19	171
Chapter 20	179
Chapter 21	189
Chapter 22	203
Chapter 23	209
Chapter 24	219
Chapter 25	225
Acknowledgments	233
About the Author	235

For Ina

*Thank you for believing in my dreams when I
couldn't even fathom the reality of them.*

1

I swore the sound of the clock's ticking was growing louder—*tick—tick—tick*. Each second, another tick. The seconds seemed longer, then shorter—something less than a second, just to fuck with my head. It was an alarm, blaring in my ear to remind me of how my life as a personal trainer had reached an Olympic level of boredom. No pun intended. I checked my watch to see if time was moving any faster on it. Same time, same day, same year... same everything. My phone came next. The minute flipped one digit as the backlight turned on. At least it was something.

I leaned over the front counter desk and peered through the dark windows into the parking lot. The music was low with a pop singer I didn't know or care about singing to her heart's content. Apparently, the music was supposed to help get people going in the morning. But after a year-and-a-half of listening, it tends to lull me to sleep. I was working the dreadful 5 am slot, which meant there wouldn't be any real gym traffic for a few more hours. Every day I ask myself why we're even open this early, but then, there's always one more chipper person that walks through the door. I always figured it was a Florida thing. Dave, the head personal trainer, crunched on an apple while walking to the front desk.

Dave was a few years out of middle-aged, but you wouldn't be able to tell. It was probably because of all the apples. "You look tired," he said.

"Look it, feel it," I replied. "Another day in paradise."

Dave munched on his apple again, speaking. I hate when people talk with their mouth full, but at this point, I'd take what conversation I could get. "Eat some fruit," he said between bites. "Will help you stay awake. All that artificial shit gets to your brain."

Normally I wouldn't want to sit around and listen to Dave rant about artificial food but at this point, I was so tired I wouldn't mind it. At least it was something to keep me awake. "It's gonna get us one way or the other, anyways," I said.

Dave nodded. "Ahh, but if I keep eating this fruit and you don't, then it might get you before me." He laughed to himself as he walked over to his desk. Morning people were always a mystery to me.

The red dot on the phone flashed at me as if I didn't hear it ringing obnoxiously loudly for an empty gym. "Heeellooo. How can I help you?" I asked.

The person on the other line, an elderly woman, fumbled around for a bit. "Perfect," she said in the sweetest tone. "I didn't want to call you too early, figured I'd give you a few minutes."

I wasn't sure if that was a joke or not, but I laughed, anyway. "What can I do for you?"

"Can you put me down for the pool, Lane Two?" she asked.

I took her name and jotted it down on the pool list. "Anything else?"

"No, that will be it. Thank you!"

"Anytime!" I hung up the phone, leaning against the front desk and grunting in frustration.

"Pool lady?" Dave asked from his desk.

"Pool lady." I sighed. "Like clockwork."

I glared at the clock. Two minutes passed. It was progress, if nothing else. I stared at the phone for a little while, hoping it would ring again. Had my life become such an endless cycle of mediocrity? When I first graduated, I never thought I would land a good editing job straight out the gate or anything outrageous like that… But I at least hoped I'd get a job somewhat in my career field. When that ended up not working out, my rent payment found me a nice job at the local gym.

I told myself it was a bad market and my master's degree would pay off soon enough, but soon enough hasn't come just yet.

"I'll be back," I said to anyone listening and went to do my rounds.

The good thing about working the morning shift was there really wasn't anyone to mess things up. I got to avoid the chaos in my boredom. The regulars that always waited by the door as if it was a Black Friday shopping sale were already well into their workouts by now. Right behind me, I heard shoes as they slapped against the treadmills.

I envied how happy they were in their routine. Something about doing the same thing every day and seeing the same people every day drove me insane.

I slowly made my way around the gym, putting weights that had been left out where they were intended to be. In the mornings, I didn't mind as much as I did other shifts since it gave me something to kill time. After I put a couple of dumbbells back, I sat on the bench behind me and stared at myself in the mirror. I looked horrible. My hair was a curly jumble of yarn, while my shirt's neck drooped past my collarbone, exposing my brown skin.

I took my time relaxing, not having to deal with anyone. Killing time was the name of the game. After a couple of minutes, a gymgoer struck up a conversation with me, which I didn't want or need—but who was I to not give a little time back? I chatted with the older gentleman before getting up and finishing my rounds.

When I returned to the front, I grabbed my jacket from the back of the stool. When I first started working at the gym, I made the mistake of thinking the building would be survivable without protective gear and paid for it. Since then, my black-and-white Nike hoodie with the name spelled out in big letters across the front, never left the building (besides to get washed, of course). It was my comfort hoodie, some would say.

The thermostat in the building must be broken. Regardless of what it read, it was a snow globe in here. No one seemed to care, though. Everyone that wasn't working out just bundled up like it was time to sit next to the fireplace with hot cocoa.

The Bar was in downtown Union City, which meant it was the only gym of its kind in the area. With it being the central point of the city, The Bar saw a very diverse crowd. I've met the owner maybe once since working here, but I was fine with that. I've heard a few stories about him, none that were good. The Bar was a little way from my house, but it paid a little better than most gyms, which helped me barely make rent each month. Which I'm hoping my next paycheck covers.

I leaned forward and stapled two sticky notes together as Alekka, one of the morning regulars, walked in. Alekka had been going to The Bar since I started working and there weren't as many customers. She was always an overly cheerful person, though it worked for her. "Hey, *Lloyd*," Alekka said, waving. Alekka wore a black hoodie with the hood half up, her large ponytail tucked inside like normal. She was the type of person who would wear a sweater in the middle of a scorching summer afternoon.

"Why'd you say my name like that?" I waved back.

"Like what?"

"Like you're some kind of robot," I said.

"Umm, no, I didn't," she replied. "Maybe it's too early in the morning for someone."

Alekka was probably right. "Never mind," I said. "You're right, it's way too early for me."

"You sure you're okay?"

I nodded. "Yeah, I'm good. Sorry."

Alekka buzzed in. She paused, stepped back, and looked over at me. "How's writing going? I forgot to ask."

I scanned the room as if someone was going to magically appear and give her a better answer than the one I had for her. "About that." I tried to think of a good excuse, but I had nothing. "Honestly... Not great... Not even good, if I'm being honest."

Alekka scrunched her face in disappointment. "Still lacking motivation?"

For a city with a small art community, we ended up finding each other, anyway. Ironically enough, Alekka was a writer as well—only she happened to work for a literary agency like I wished I did. Alekka sometimes asked me about my writing, but I never had anything good to update her on. The only thing I could hang my hat on was that it wasn't for a lack of trying. At least I could get words on a page – though they didn't amount to anything.

"I don't know if I would call it a lack of motivation." I sighed, leaning against the desk. "It's just not good."

Alekka laughed. "Someone's a Debbie Downer." She readjusted her gym bag around her shoulder. "I need to get my workout started or I'm going to end up late for work. You want to get a drink tonight? I have a

DEMONOLOGY

work question for you." Alekka lowered her eyes at me. I rubbed my neck. I can't remember the last time I went for drinks with anyone. "Come on, it's not like I'm asking you out on a date or something."

I didn't take any offense. It wasn't like I was thinking she was asking me out on a date, or better yet, I was in no place to even think about going out on dates myself. And when Alekka asked me about writing, she reminded me of all the nights I ignored writing. "No can do." I shook my head. "I have a few things I need to get done when I get home. Next time?"

Alekka smiled at me as she tossed her keys in her bag. "Suit yourself. Another time, then."

I watched as she threw her hood over her head and walked around the gym toward the locker room. Don't get me wrong, I wanted to meet with her. A part of me was interested in what "work question" she could have. But something inside of me spoke before I could change its mind. Maybe it was a force of habit.

I wasted my time away, making laps when I could and chatting with a few of the usual faces. Once my shift was over, I packed my bag, grabbed my jacket, and made my way out of the building.

The afternoon felt dull—almost dead. It was one of those muggy days that forced you to sleep on your couch after reading a good book. I walked down the sidewalk to the parking lot for our building. My car wasn't anything special. A silver Volkswagen Jetta with as much character as it has miles. It got me from point A to B and never had any real issues. I didn't see any reason for me to get rid of it. Not like I was in a position to go car shopping, anyway. I wasn't complaining, though. It wasn't like I was starving, but I wasn't living lavishly, either.

I pulled out of the parking lot but slammed on the brake as I neared the exit. A small black cat moved by, rolling its shoulders with each step. Clearly, it understood that it owned the street. I waited for it to pass. When it got to the other side, it looked toward the park.

The gloom and dullness of the day thickened. It felt like nothing moved—nothing but the cat and me.

I shook my head and started my drive home.

I stopped at the familiar lights, hearing the same sound of car horns shouting. The monotonous stopping and starting threatened to lull me to sleep in the deep orange sun. I didn't bother turning on any music. It would annoy me more than anything. I'd driven this route enough times to know I would drown it out by the time I got home. The traffic began to clear in the same area it always did; a mile or so after crossing the bridge to the south side of the city. The light turned yellow, then red, stopping me. It was the same light that stopped me every day.

I investigated the car next to me. An aging man dressed in business casual. He looked like he was either fed up with the day or he had just received bad news. There was also the third option. He could be the same as me, stuck in a routine he couldn't escape. He glanced over at me through fishbowl windows. The man nodded, a gesture I'm sure was all instinct. There was a loss in his eyes that I was sure he wasn't aware of.

The light shifted to green. The man didn't move for a second. He just stared at me with lifeless eyes. The car behind him honked as he started to pull away.

My hunger pains caught up to me on the way home, and I knew there was no chance of me cooking tonight—not with this headache. I decided on Chinese takeout, the usual spot a block or so from my house.

I browsed through my phone while I waited but quickly placed it back in my pocket after I opened my bank app against my better judgment. This meal seemed more of a luxury now than it did a few seconds ago. I needed to work as many shifts as possible to make both rent and my survival happen. The glare from the screen made my eyes feel like they were being shot from my skull. I needed to get home. My body hadn't been cooperating with me. I wasn't sick or feverish. But I didn't feel like myself.

The store owner waved at me when my order was ready. She tied the plastic bag together as I went to the counter. I grabbed it, thanking her, and went back to the Jetta.

I pulled into my driveway, exhaling—my head and hands on the steering wheel. Another day down. I grabbed my things and went inside.

My house had a simple layout. After my failed relationship, I had to relocate—and downsize. Luckily, I found a one-bedroom loft on the south side of town at a reasonable price. The owner was a retiree who was going to sell the place. A few years into retirement, she realized dealing with tenants wasn't in her future. Now that she had time for traveling out of the country and waking up with a margarita in hand, that was. She was always telling me stories about the places her boyfriend and her returned from. After talking with her, she decided to let me rent it out for as long as I needed to get back on my feet from moving after the breakup. Either way, it had been over a year since she made the decision, and she never asked any questions.

My head killed me. Before anything else, I made a quick stop to my bathroom and took a couple Ibuprofen. When I returned downstairs, I took the reluctant trip to the mailbox before turning back, locking up the front door, and throwing my keys on the counter. It was junk mail, the usual offers to open new credit cards and offers for internet services I didn't need. I looked at the name that the cards were addressed to: L-loy-d. My vision blurred a little. I dropped the mail; *I'll have to sort through it tomorrow.* Trying to read anything right now would give my headache a reason to grow.

After a nap, and a few hours searching for jobs and browsing the net, I couldn't help but wonder if Alekka found a nice happy hour to go to. It wasn't like I wanted to lie, but I knew there was no way I was going out. Not with the way I was feeling. I knew sleep would be the only thing on my mind when I got home.

By the time I took a shower and settled in for the night, the medicine finally started kicking in. I walked back downstairs, grabbing my laptop on the way. Without it, I felt like I wasn't doing anything. I put my takeout on a plate and brought it to the living room with a glass of water. Another night binge-watching TV. I decided against anything new; I didn't think I could focus enough to enjoy a film tonight. Instead, I turned on an episode of *Detective Cirrus*, a show I saw more times than I could count. Nothing like a good mystery to help me unwind from the day.

I finished my food before long, then lay down watching the show. I got some writing done, but not enough to really make any progress on anything. Somewhere between the beginning and the end of the episode, I fell asleep and woke up to the streaming services screen asking me if I was still watching. It was still a reasonable time of the night, so I finished my water and opened my laptop again.

I tried again to get some writing in. I clicked around until I found the piece I wanted to work on. While scrolling, my eyes locked on the name below the title: Nl-o-xd. I blinked my eyes. They started to hurt as badly as they did earlier. I thought it was because I didn't eat all day, but I guess not. Looks like sleep was the only thing that would help this headache.

I placed my hand on my head. *What's going on? Maybe it's my poor sleep schedule.* My head had to be feeling it. I turned off the television and closed my laptop. *Who am I kidding?* No productive work was getting done tonight.

As I turned off the main lights, I couldn't help but feel like even this space was too much for me. Sure, it was only one bedroom, but having two stories felt unnecessary. I went up the stairs to my room to get some rest for the cycle to start again tomorrow.

I didn't dream as much as I saw things while I slept. I couldn't be sure if I stared at the backs of my eyelids, or if I just slept deeply... It was the first time I'd dreamt of anything in ages. The night terrors never truly left. It seemed I'd only delayed their return.

Tonight, my unborn child tugged at my being. There's not a day that goes by where I don't think of her... or him. I never found out. It was for the best— it would have only made it that much harder. At least that's what I told myself. It was the only thing that made it bearable at times.

I cried for the loss in my dream state. At least I think I did. I cried as I wondered if I would have been a good father. Would I have been able to make ends meet, or even guide someone through the trials of this world? My child shone in a golden light through the darkness. The light blinded me, and I swore I heard something speaking to me. I listened closer, trying to make out the words. But the only sound I could hear was my phone's alarm that screamed at me to wake up and get my day started.

I stopped my alarm and got to my early morning routine. Things felt different as I moved around. I needed to have a better day today than yesterday. Looking out my window, I saw it was still overcast. Weather wouldn't be of any help today—great. At least I had more energy today, and my headache was gone. The weather wasn't doing my mood any favors, but at least I felt better. I washed my face, clearing all the stress from my eyes, and then brushed my teeth.

I'm usually not a big breakfast eater, not because I didn't like it—but more because I was a horrible morning person. And being up before the sun had a habit of holding my appetite back. Today didn't feel like one of my usual mornings, though. I made breakfast while I played music, one of my *chill* playlists, something to relax to. I finished getting dressed before heading back downstairs to eat. Three fried eggs, with toast and apple juice. It wasn't breakfast made for champions, but it would do.

Only the few gymgoers who always waited at the door for it to open at 5 am were there when I arrived. Half an hour later, Dave walked in, biting his usual apple. He walked straight to the desk as the phone rang. He said a few things before grabbing the sheet of paper next to the computer. He wrote the woman's name and which lane she preferred before heading back to his desk.

We nearly sat in silence for another half hour when Alekka walked in with a bright smile on her face. She put her duffle bag on the floor in front of the desk as she scanned in. "Morning," she said.

"Morning," I replied. "Find a good happy hour spot?"

"Of course, and some rich guy there bought the whole bar out," she said, pointing at me. "Annnd, as he left, offered to take me on his yacht." Alekka shrugged sarcastically.

I stared at her, then scoffed. "So, did you go or not?" I laughed.

Alekka shook her head. "Nope, couldn't make it, either, sadly, so missed out on free drinks and a free yacht ride. Something came up that I had to handle. By the time I finished, the hour was no longer happy, so I dedicated my night to a little self-care. You get everything handled you needed to?" She cocked her head to one side. "You seem to be chipper this morning."

I thought back to the lie I told yesterday, feeling more guilty about it now. "Yeah," I said. "All handled now." I tapped my head a few times. "Who knows, it could have been a head cold. But I feel amazing this morning."

"Good. You seemed... stressed yesterday." The phone chimed. "Can't write if you don't take care of yourself." Alekka grabbed her things. "I think someone's looking for you. I'll catch you before I leave."

"Sure thing," I replied.

I went back to my work as the day progressed. Things felt normal—better than normal, to be honest. Before long, the morning clients who understood how good it felt to wake up at a normal time funneled in. I scanned in a couple, while dealing with another gymgoer's late membership fee. Dave sent over one of his clients that was quitting training, and the gym altogether, once the desk cleared a bit. I didn't bother trying to convince them to stay. I felt better, but not well enough to try to talk someone out of their decisions.

I was so wrapped up with clients that I didn't notice Alekka waiting on the side of the desk. "Ll-e-x-us," she said. "Come over here really quick."

There it was again. Why did she say my name like that? Or attempted to say my name, at least... Maybe something was wrong with my hearing? I rubbed at my ears like that would do any good. My head instantly throbbed, pounding like a jackhammer chipping away at still cement. Then the sharp knifing pain came. I fell to one knee, holding myself up on my desk. I panted, anything to try and make the pain subside.

Alekka was suddenly by my side, helping me gather myself. I leaned against the desk, breathing in slowly. There were moments like these when I wished I had health insurance. I needed to check in on that. Welcome to adulting.

Alekka left and returned with water from the nearest fountain in a small paper cup.

I took it from her, drank it, and then sat on the stool, breathing. The room slowly stopped spinning, and the lights stopped hurting my eyes so much. I finished the last drops remaining in the cup before tossing it in the trash.

"You okay?" Alekka asked.

I exhaled. "Yeah," I said. "Not sure what happened, to be honest. But I think it's passing."

Alekka stared at me, then checked her watch. She glowered at me. "Fine," she said. "I have to get to work, anyways, but the offer still stands." Alekka frowned. "It would be nice to have another writer's opinion who I don't happen to work for."

I kept hearing ringing in my ears, over and over and over, until it became so loud, I couldn't bear it any longer. I rubbed at my temples. "Where at?" I needed to clear my mind.

Alekka twirled her keys on her finger. "You choose."

"How about Fernando's?" I asked out of habit, instantly regretting it. It was my usual hangout spot before I stopped going over a year ago. Showing up out of the blue now was the last thing I wanted to do.

"Sure," Alekka responded. "Here's my number. I'll text you when I'm leaving work." She grabbed my phone and saved her contact. "See you later... And thanks!" Alekka pulled her hoodie over her head and exited the building.

I grabbed my phone and studied her contact as if there was something wrong with it. I knew it wasn't a big deal, and Alekka probably just needed a quick favor... But having a woman give me her number still held a level of pressure I wasn't sure I was ready for yet. Maybe a new friend, and another writer at that, was what I needed right now...I just wasn't sure if I was ready yet. Having friends has its own kind of pressure.

I sighed. I couldn't take being cooped in this gym any longer. But I worked double today, which meant I was going to have to head to happy hour right after work. It wasn't like I had any other plans. It might be good to change things up for once. My personal life was as dull as the rest of my work life. From the outside looking in, people might have assumed I had an extensive friend group. On the south side of Union City, I had encountered just about everyone. Whether it was positive or negative, I had acquaintances in every corner of this city, which was also part of why I was such a loner. I was never around any one place long enough to build relationships. After so long I'd become accustomed to it and never questioned it. It worked for me, though. I did better alone, less to worry about.

My love life wasn't any better. I wasn't an ugly guy—I hoped. I kept myself together. I was tallish, 6'1, to be exact. I even managed to stay up to fashion and have enough tattoos that made me look cooler than I was. Truthfully, I lacked social connection as of late (late being over a year now). Sure, I saw people every second at the gym, but that was surface-level bonding. I wasn't about to tell someone I barely knew about my personal woes and troubles. Maybe that's why I was considering meeting Alekka for drinks.

I sat behind the desk, trying to avoid seeing stars. My head ached. I grabbed several aspirins out of my bag and walked into the restroom. Hopefully, this headache would go away by the time I had to get to the bar. I took the pills and drank from the faucet. My eyes went to the mirror. My rough image stared back at me, fair brown skin and curly hair. I leaned closer. My eyes were hazel, there was no doubt about that, but they seemed brighter today, almost golden.

Must be the lighting.

I returned to the front and waited out my sentence in silence. When it neared happy hour, I texted Alekka to see if she still wanted to go (I wouldn't have been mad if she said no). She responded unexpectedly quickly, letting me know we were still on. I had to leave now if I planned on dressing in something other than gym clothes and making it on time. The new shift member walked in, at least that's who I assumed it was. Gyms go through employees like people go through McDonald's fries. After a while, I didn't try to remember anyone's name.

I exited the building and went to the parking lot. A small black cat with golden eyes was at the end of the sidewalk. The animal stared at me while licking its paw. I couldn't help but return its gaze. Something about the cat drew me closer. I got to the trunk of my car and stared at the small animal. It regarded me and then stretched its back before moving. Before I could get close enough to see if it even had a collar, it trotted down a few spaces and underneath another car.

I shook my head, going back to my car. I needed a drink more than I knew. I didn't even like cats. Based on my previous experiences with them, I was pretty sure they weren't fond of me, either. Yet my gut told me it was watching me.

The crazies must have set in. I could have sworn that it was the same cat from yesterday. *Maybe we've picked up a new forever guest.* I unlocked my car and got in before I wasted any more time overthinking useless things.

Traffic in Union City was unbearable depending on the time you were driving. If I got stuck on one of the many bridges in the city trying to get across town, it could easily push me back an hour. It would be testing fate to leave without any prior planning. I sighed, half regretting committing to happy hour. I couldn't remember how long it'd been since I'd been to the beach bars. I wasn't much for crowds—besides the obvious problem of not knowing if I was going to make a fool out of myself in front of Alekka. I hadn't been out in months. At this point I was a novice at "going out" again. Here's hoping a Wednesday happy hour wasn't a zoo.

2

I went home and changed into something I thought would pass as presentable; a gray Henley, black jeans, and a pair of black sneakers. I wasn't much for dressing up, and working at the gym only furthered my remaining in my comfort zone. I entered Fernando's and found the first seat at the bar. The familiar sound of music playing from the jukebox hummed in the background. I was never quite sure if it was really the jukebox playing or if Fernando set it up to look that way.

A handful of visitors laughed while playing giant Jenga near the back of the bar. Another group watched as a guy in his early twenties thought entirely too hard about how to get his ring on the metal post. They laughed as they drank beer and shouted at him. I always wondered if everyone was having as much fun as they pretended to have. Or if secretly they were telling themselves that they were having the time of their lives when really, they'd rather be home in their comfortable beds watching their favorite TV shows.

I looked around, feeling the cool ocean breeze brush against my face. The ocean lapped against itself in the distance. The air was briny. Everything was just the way I left it. Only I wasn't sure if that was good or bad, seeing the circumstances.

"Looook who it is," Fernando said, punching some numbers on one of the registers. "Long time no see." Fernando, though the owner, liked working at the bar. He always said no matter how popular the bar got, nobody could take him away from being with the people. Fernando was a stocky Portuguese man, who sported a full beard that I wish I could grow. His eyes were stern from years of dealing with the bullshit of bar life. Yet he always managed to have a genuine smile.

"Long time no see," Fernando said. He poured me a light beer on tap, then slid it to me. "I was starting to think I'd never see you again."

My stomach dropped. I suddenly felt like I made the wrong decision coming here. I pushed that thought away before it could fester and owned up to my mistake. "Yeah… Sorry. I should have stopped by more." I paused. "I-I just knew if I saw the bar, I wouldn't make it, man. Figured I better stay away for the time being."

"I get it." Fernando wiped the bar in front of me. I met Fernando a few years back, with my ex-girlfriend, Nya. His bar used to be our hangout spot. After the split, I never felt the urge to come back. Knowing I might run into her, or the group we used to drink with, didn't appeal to me. But then again, that was my own anxiety speaking those thoughts. They weren't worried about me.

"Heard she moved," Fernando said. Then he looked at me with a neutral stare before he went back to cleaning. "You, know, in case you were worried about running into her."

"Yeah, she told me, let me know she was leaving. Last I heard from her, actually. Just didn't feel right."

Fernando narrowed his eyes at me. I sighed. "And I didn't want to run into anyone."

First, Fernando's was somewhere we'd come after work, or on the weekends for some of the best blackened shrimp in town to go along with reasonably priced drinks. That changed quickly when we showed up every other day for a week and ended up becoming friends with the owner. Somewhere between the beer glasses, I'd forgotten that friendship.

Fernando nodded. He turned around and served other customers. It was his silent way of letting me know he understood. I'm just glad he wasn't the type to hold onto grudges. I didn't know if I would be so strong if roles were reversed. Fernando returned after a few minutes of tending to the bar.

"So, what brings you in then?" he asked. "Since you aren't here to see my beautiful face."

I checked my phone. An hour has passed since I left work. "I'm supposed to be meeting a friend here," I said. Fernando raised a brow. "A writing friend," I added.

Fernando shrugged. "Hey, no judgment here. Shit, if you're asking me, you need to get your ass back up on that saddle. You don't want to be in the dating world at my age. The battlefield isn't favorable, I'll tell you that." He shook his head.

I thought that over for a minute as I twirled my beer around. I started to speak, stopped, then started again. "I wish I could. I really do," I said.

Fernando gave me a hard stare; one that told me he was serious. "I've been working in a bar a long time now, so trust me when I tell you 'I've heard some stories.' Yours isn't the best, nor is it the worst. But take your time. Things will come to you."

I didn't have time to sit with Fernando's words—or my thoughts—before I heard a familiar voice.

"N e o y s," a voice called from the entrance.

I turned to see Alekka. She looked great, to say the least. She was wearing a short, yellow dress that hugged every curve. The color complimented her eyes and commanded the room's attention. This was my first time seeing her in anything but gym attire. And the first time I realized how… gorgeous Alekka was. Don't get me wrong, I always knew she was pretty. But up to this point, I've only seen her in a giant hoodie.

"Sorry I'm late," Alekka said. "Figured I should change."

Fernando leaned closer to me. "Interesting."

I instinctively looked down at myself. I didn't have business casual attire and working at the gym meant I didn't need any. I planned to buy some if I landed a job after graduate school, but I put that on hold for a bit. Hence, I looked bland as bland could be—dry toast.

If I had any sort of ego, it was killed then.

Alekka ordered me a beer, and herself a double whiskey and Coke. I wasn't sure whether to be impressed or worried about who was driving her home.

"So tell me, you're from Union City, right?" she asked.

"What makes you think that?" I questioned. I drank some more. She didn't budge. "Born and raised."

Alekka used her finger as a mixing straw, then nodded. "So, are you the Southside guy, Westside, or Eastside?" She tasted her drink, barely flinching. "Come on, you know it makes a difference."

I had to agree with her. I remember the first time I had to go to after school activities across the bridge—it changed my life forever. It was where I fell in love with sports and started adventuring the city, for better or for worse. It wasn't like I had anyone to tell me no. Different sides of town had different tastes in music and hobbies. We all lived different truths. While some kids were crying over getting grounded, others were already taking care of their siblings.

"I guess you could say I was raised all around," I said. "But I spent the most time on the Southside."

"So you're a water guy? In-ter-esting." She placed her glass down on the bar top. "You didn't strike me as beach boy at all. I would have guessed you were one of the city boys ten out of ten times."

"Not really. I never really made it to the beach much, either, though. Don't get me wrong. I was either playing sports or locked up in my room reading and writing." When everyone my age was heading to the beach, I was cooped up in the house, or in some organized sport I wasn't really in the mood for. Sure, I ended up enjoying the games and comradery, and it kept me out of trouble—but I would have much rather been near a body of water with a book in hand. I was never one for the groups and crowds.

"Hmm. A smart jock, I see. Learn something new every day." She tasted her liquor. She made a thinking face, then finally settled on a question. Before she asked it, Alekka gave Fernando a slight wave to let him know we were moving, then beckoned me along. We moved outside near the two cornhole boards. She leaned her arms against the railing. The wind was stronger out here, blowing her hair about. The night was warm, but not overbearing, a perfect fall evening.

"Sorry, figured it'd be easier to hear out here," she said. She pointed at me. "But, back to my question game."

I stopped her before she could continue. "If this is a game, I think I get to ask questions, too, right?" I asked. "Seeing as I'd have to be playing with you."

She tapped the tip of her glass with her nail. "Correct," she said. "Make it good."

I nodded. *Well, there goes my mouth again.* In truth, I was being a smart ass saying that. There was never a follow-up. I drank some more beer. It'd been a while since I'd done the whole "socializing" thing. I was forgetting small talk as fast as I'd learned it. I ended up going with my gut and spewing the same thing Alekka asked me back to her.

"I don't think you're from Union City," I said. I shrugged. "But I also don't have a clue where you could be from. If I was betting on it, I'd say you were born in one of the big cities."

"So I'm guessing you aren't a good better, then, either?" Alekka asked. "I'm a Midwest gal, or whatever you folk here call us. I grew up in a small town, no more than fifteen hundred people. We'd always joke that we had more cattle than people living there. Hell, I can name off my whole graduating class if you put me up to it." She stared at me. "Only if you want."

I shook my free hand. "I'm good, actually, maybe another time." We both chuckled.

Alekka tapped her foot on the ground. The air chilled as the breeze from the sea skated across the bar. "I came here for this," she said. "I'd always have my head in a book as a child, normally geography and history books. For some reason I always had a fascination with the coasts, didn't matter which, if I'm being truthful." She moved a piece of hair from her face that must have come loose from the wind. "It was only natural for me to move to writing when you think about it. So when I landed the job here in Union City, I jumped at it and moved immediately." She paused, then finished with, "I'm still not sure if I'm more of a reader or writer, and it drives me insane."

"Wow," I said. "You have me beat. I would have never guessed that."

She shrugged. "My flight to Union City was my first. I think my stomach left my body when we took off."

I laughed with her, mainly because I still hadn't taken my first flight. Hopefully, by then, I would have worked on my fear of heights more.

"Your family still live out here?" Alekka asked. I heard the words before I registered what she asked me. Or maybe I didn't want to process it. The life in the air between us died, but I did my best to try and revive it by at least smiling. I didn't want Alekka to think she'd done something wrong in asking. It was a valid and normal question to ask in a regular situation—none of which was mine. I didn't have any taboo against speaking of my family situation. Family was rarely a thought of mine. It was easy since I've never seen them, heard them, or even met them, for them to matter. I was more familiar with the four walls of my boarding school's dorm room than my parents.

"Never met them," I said. "So what did you want to ask me, anyway?"

Alekka respected my wishes and continued without missing a beat. "Ohh, yeah, I almost forgot," she said. "Sorry, I'm a bit of a scatterbrain. Speaking of reading… I work for a publishing company, Hometown Press. We have a department here in Union City."

"And?"

Alekka fumbled with her drink, not making eye contact. All of a sudden, she seemed… nervous. "Well–it's just… It's hard to explain."

"How about we start at the beginning?"

Alekka sighed. "Remember how I can't figure out if I'm a reader or writer?" Alekka gave me a second to process what she said and acknowledge her. "Well, it's just that. I know I'm a good writer, sure. But is that it, or am I more than good? Which is where I need your help."

"Help with what?" I was still as confused now as I was when she started.

Alekka sighed in frustration. "I work in the 'industry' now. I couldn't get an honest opinion if I paid for it," she said. "I finished writing a short story recently and I want your honest thoughts on it. Andddd… I want to read one of your stories. You always talk about writing, let me see what you got… If you want to, of course."

I blinked at her a few times, though she didn't budge. Holy shit, she was serious. But it made sense. I could see it being harder to get honest critique the closer to the work you got, which in retrospect should make no sense. Lending a hand couldn't hurt, though it felt like forever since I had anyone read any of my work. But I'm sure I could find something to send to her.

Who knows, maybe reading Alekka's work might spark the flame of inspiration that dwindled. "Yeah, no, of course," I said. "Email me. I'll take a look at your piece and send one of mine over. I'll warn you; it might be kinda old at this point."

Alekka smiled. "Perfect, which means there should be growth since then."

I sighed, though I agreed with her in theory. "And now we've arrived at the crux of the problem. I haven't written anything of any worth since graduating. My writer's block is worse now than ever." It was the first time I had openly admitted those thoughts aloud. I had spent months sitting and staring at my computer, night after night, yet I could never write anything worth keeping. More useless words I've long but forgotten. And if I was being completely honest with myself, I felt I've regressed since graduate school—but that was a problem I would shelve for another time.

"Ever thought you just haven't lived enough yet or you're living the wrong life?" Alekka asked.

"I do plenty of living," I lied. Alekka didn't need to know this was my first time out in months.

Alekka led us back to the bar. She ordered us two bottled waters and two shots of tequila. "I believe you," she said, smiling.

She didn't believe me.

Alekka pulled out her phone and clicked around for a second or two. "There you go," she said. "Gotta love technology. I emailed you." Alekka stared at me. "I'm guessing working the front desk at the gym isn't your dream job?"

What about, "What's your favorite color or desired location to live?" For the first time hanging out, Alekka sure didn't pull her punches. I fiddled with my beer for a moment. "You know, the usual. Always wanted to be a writer. I've had this vision of being in a bookstore, doing a signing and someone telling me they read my novel in one sitting. The same way I would have told my favorite author if I saw them." I took a sip of my beer. "Maybe it's just a dream, but it feels so real sometimes."

Alekka nodded with approval. "Honestly," she started, "I respect it. I've always known I wanted to work in the publishing world. So I'll figure it out on the way, I guess."

"I thought I'd want to work for a publishing company out of grad school, too," I said. "But as you can see, that didn't work out as planned."

We continued, laughing as we genuinely enjoyed each other's

company—which I have to say was becoming a dying art. I started feeling bad for judging Alekka too quickly.

"What about you?" I asked. "What's the major plan?"

"Before or after I take over the world?" she replied.

"Let's go with before, to be safe," I said.

She shrugged, then sighed. "That's where you and I differed. I know I want to work in literature. I've been obsessed with novels for as long as I can remember—I even turned out to be a decent writer, some would say. But I don't really have a big dream or plan like you I figure I'd get in the door and everything else will figure itself out. It has so far. No use in changing my tactics now." The water and shots appeared in front of us. "Either way, I'll end up doing something great." She lifted her shot.

I lifted my shot and regretted it immediately. Tequila was my fated enemy, the one I could never beat no matter how many times we fought. The Ash to my Gary. At one point, I accepted my fate and decided never to fight it again. Each time we saw each other now, we only politely nodded and waved.

We drank the shots. I gave it a reasonable amount of time, then drank half the water bottle. There seemed to be clarity in the unknown for Alekka. And I believed her when she said no matter what, she'd be great. Living that close to the edge would have driven me off the cliff in a second—but Alekka appeared to relish that unknown. I envied her in a lot of ways. Everything had to be planned with me. If I couldn't see it in my future, then it didn't belong there. Having that level of unknown in my life terrified me, it made me feel like I didn't do enough upfront planning. And that only led to issues. Balance in life was key and I was in desperate need of it. Alekka seemed to understand that balance, or not care what anyone thought either way. I might be able to learn a thing or two from her.

We sat talking while people came in and out of the building. For a Wednesday night, the bar was busier than I expected. Fernando's must have started attracting more of a crowd than it did previously. Being so close to the ocean, it didn't get as much attention as the bars closer to the main street and parking. A couple left the bar top for the dance floor, showing the patrons their moves—I respected the confidence. It took a certain person to be the first to the dance floor, and I knew I wasn't going to follow. I would much rather blend in than stand out. An empty dance floor meant all eyes on me, and I was never the one to seek attention.

The song switched, slowing the tempo. The woman reached her arms around the man's neck, and they danced as they held each other. I averted my eyes before I found myself thinking about the times Nya tried to get me to dance with her in that same spot–and the times that I told her *no*.

Fernando came over to us and asked if we needed anything else. Alekka looked down at her phone and frowned. She shook her head. "I actually need to get out of here before it gets too late," she said. "As much fun as I'm having, I'm going to have to cut. Sometimes we have to be responsible." Alekka handed Fernando some cash, then turned to me. "Keep your head up, *Neous*," she said. "I doubt you'll be down for long. Who knows, you probably just haven't found your niche yet." She gave me a warm smile. "Don't stay out too late now. Can't have you tired at work. Call an Uber if you get too drunk. Remember, time and water." She laughed as she waved to me, then Fernando, before leaving.

My head suddenly hurt, and here I was thinking I was feeling better. I tried to pay it no mind, and nodded to Alekka and gave her a goodbye hug. I sat back down and drank the remainder of my water. The drumming slowed.

I paid, ignoring Fernando's eyes. They'd say more than I wanted to hear right now. I knew he had questions. But I had no answers. Why couldn't two adults with similar interests get drinks together without people ballooning it into something it wasn't? I let Fernando know I was leaving while he was too busy to talk.

As I left, I turned my head to the sky. I still had a few hours to get some writing in if I hurried. I needed to decide which story I was going to send Alekka. Writing used to come to me so easy. I would put a movie on, and then let my thoughts roam through the depths of my mind. But now it was like there was a constant roadblock refusing to let me push by it.

I listened to the sound of the beach as it echoed in the distance, along with the garbled sound of music from the various bars. A set of friends exited the bar nearest to me. They looked down the row of bars that lined the street, wondering if they should call it quits or not.

I continued walking along, trying to think of what I would send to

Alekka. Ember lights led the way back to my car. As I followed the lights, a feeling of unrest overcame me. I wasn't a paranoid person, but something felt off.

I glanced over my shoulder but didn't see anything even remotely close to me. When I turned back around, there was a black cat that sat in front of me. It spun its head, moving like some sort of rotary. It had golden eyes; the same as the cat from earlier, only this cat seemed larger. The feline turned and started walking. It turned back to me and gestured as if beckoning me to follow.

A sense of unease fell upon me. Was this the same cat that I saw the other two times? And if it was, why was it on the beach, almost forty minutes from the gym? I began to question myself. There was no way this could be the same cat—right?

The cat motioned behind a nearby restaurant. If it weren't for its eyes, I wouldn't be able to keep track of it. Every few seconds the cat peered back at me, then continued. The cat's dark fur blended into the darkness, almost becoming a shadow. It allowed me to close the distance as we made it past a dumpster. It rounded its shoulders gradually, slowing down its stride. The cat stopped, as did I.

The sound of lips smacking, slurping, and the occasional burp came from down the alley. I listened closer, trying to make out what I was hearing. I've heard of bad manners, but this was an entirely different level of disgusting. The vulgar sounds reached me, making me want to gag. The world around me felt heavy. It was as if my boots were glued to the ground. Something felt different—wrong. Yet I had no clue what or where this feeling came from. My instincts told me to pack up and leave as fast as I could get my things, but my body wouldn't cooperate. This murky feeling of malice and sadness filled the tight space.

The cat jumped on the dumpster and sat, looking aimlessly. It turned its eyes to a shadowy figure in the distance. I stepped closer. My legs felt like cement blocks. I peered down the alley into the night. The noises ceased. The figure cocked its head toward me. Its eyes were bright red, large, like grand rubies. Blood dripped from its gaping mouth, large, jagged fangs gleaming at me. It rose from the ground, stepping over what was left of the corpse beneath it. I felt my heart skip, then race as everything around me lost focus. That person was dead. No, they were murdered... *What the fuck did I just walk into?*

I stared at the body. There was nothing left of their eyes, only darkness. Deep claw wounds traced the victim's face like an Etch A Sketch doodle. The *thing* settled its fangs into the corpse's neck and ripped a chunk of flesh from it. The skin stretched, then snapped off along with muscle covered in deep liquid. Then it snapped its jaws around the flesh and forced it down with more garbled burps. I forced myself to look away when I saw the body of the victim, or what would have been the body. *What kind of psycho is this person?*

I looked closer. This thing's arms were too long to be human. And its legs were much too short. Everything about it was wrong. The human-like creature cracked its fingers, then shrieked. It felt like someone shoved needles in my ears as I covered them from the wail. This was insane. What the hell could scream this loud—and why the hell would they?

I wanted to run, but fear weighed me down like an anchor in water. The beast licked its lips. Then it was upon me.

Its mouth widened as it went to snap at my neck. I screamed like bloody hell as I got my legs to cooperate with me. I would be surprised if I had a voice tomorrow with how loud I cried. The creature missed my face, and its fangs ended up in the wall behind me. It struggled, trying to break free. Then it bit down and crushed the wall in its mandibles. I backed away slowly. "H-hey, look," I said. "I don't know who, or what you are... or even what you want. But how about we both just get out of here? Is it money you want, because I don't have much of that." I grabbed my wallet, pulled the rest of my cash out, and chucked it ahead.

It didn't respond. There seemed to be no reasoning with whatever the hell this was. I stared at the figure's form, blinking. Its skin looked worn, leathery, a faded gray. In several places on its arm, its skin was completely torn, though no blood fell. No human would act this way, *nothing* could. Then that would mean there's some face-eating, body-mutilating, beast running around Union City. And out of everyone in this city, I somehow stumbled upon it.

Shit, shit, shit.

It roared, eyes cutting through me. The way its neck swiveled from side to side, while its tongue hung from its mouth, blood trailing from it —the movements seemed unconscious. The thing's hair was long, though it matted itself to the being's face. My throat tightened.

Again, it came for me. There was nothing I could do but watch as death bulleted for me. Its mouth gaped open, its teeth an army of knives. The thing crashed into me, its hands crushing my shoulders.

I wasn't the strongest man by any means, but I did work out. I work at the gym, for Christ's sake. This is all to say that my strength did nothing against the thing. I was helpless against its power, no matter how much I fought back, it was fruitless. Was I really that hopeless? There had to be something I could do, anything. My eardrums screamed as it roared again. It leaned closer. I closed my eyes—hopelessly. Its tongue trailed my face, tasting my fear.

It was subtle, but I felt a surge of energy—like the first cup of morning tea, piled with sugar and creamer. I did all I could and kicked it with everything I had. It spit up some other liquid from its mouth that I didn't want to take the time to learn about. It stumbled back, its hands going to its stomach. I didn't wait for it to tell me to leave to run. I sprinted for freedom, though the lights seemed farther away than they had earlier.

I never had a chance to escape—or to think I'd make it to safety. By the time I got a step in, it grabbed my foot with its tongue extended. Its tongue slithered around my ankle twice before latching on. I screamed as I tried to pull my leg free. Its body came closer with its tongue. I held myself against the force and kicked it in the face. Another pull, another kick—the beast's head snapped back and forth like a bobblehead toy.

But it still held on to me, no matter what. Its eyes were lifeless, glowing with a demonic rage. It slithered closer as it let out a low groan that sounded like a train horn. What the fuck was this monster? I kicked again. Tears of anger and fear consumed me.

"Get! Off! Of! Me!" I kicked it one more time, but this time, it grabbed my leg before I could land the blow. It stared at my leg as if it was foreign currency. Then it cocked its head to the side, its scarlet eyes devouring me. My heart couldn't have raced any faster than in this moment. I watched the thing retract its tongue, though it still held onto my other leg. The creature hovered over me. It smelled foul, of dried blood and rotten meat.

A bitter gust of wind blew through the alley. I threw my arm against the force. A frozen second passed. Then a whisper cut through the night. The sound was pure, clean. Warm liquid splashed against my face.

My eyes shot open. Inches from me, the creature fell to the ground. Its body was now only a split lump of flesh. I stared a lifeless gaze at the thing. Its body spasmed for a few seconds, then finally went still.

I could feel the blood as it coated my body in giant splotches. I trembled as I tried to rub it away, though I knew I was only making it worse. My skin was stained as if built of rust. Perhaps it was the rotten corpse, or the blood, or the dumpster behind me, but the air had become a soup of wicked stenches. I gagged, managing to keep the drinks down, but I knew the inevitable was coming. I halted, then swallowed. If the thing was dead, that means something, or someone, had killed it.

I looked to the edge of the alley.

A woman stood far off where the alley met the parking lot. I couldn't make out her features in the darkness, only her silhouette. Tall and strong, her hair draped down her back. I'd never forget the weapon she carried, either. A large glaive. The blade jutted out. Blood stained its metal, dripping to the ground in a pool. Around the shaft of the weapon was white fur. And tied near the blade, a long fang hung. The glaive shined white with angelic power. She glared in my direction. Even from this distance, I could see her eyes, glowing a frozen white. Her back faced me as she walked away, her footsteps echoing in the night.

Maybe I should have called the police. But the only thought on my mind was safety, and how quickly I could get to it. Besides, I could count on the police wanting answers to questions I didn't have.

So, I did what any sensible person would do. I sprinted to my car. I got in the Jetta, locked the door, and then sped out of the parking lot. My body shook with fright. I gripped the steering wheel so tightly my knuckles hurt.

What the hell was that? I checked the rearview mirror every other second as if someone was behind me. *What. The. Fuck?* There was no way that happened. Yet when I looked at the blood on my hands, I realized it must have.

I wanted to speed down the road so I could get home in record time, but instead, I drove the speed limit, creeping ahead at what seemed like sloth speed. Something told me Union City Police wouldn't take well to finding out the man they stopped for speeding was covered in blood and who knows what else. Every so often, I would catch my reflection in my rearview mirror and feel sick to my core. I managed to keep myself together long enough to make it home. I drove over the speed bump and let the gate scanner tag my sticker. The gate was grand for our little community. The arm went up as the two metal sides parted ways. I went through impatiently, tapping my shaking hands against the steering wheel. I could see the security guard as he drove his golf cart around while he did his nightly checks. Luckily, he wasn't near my street. I couldn't risk him seeing me like this. Then another thought came to the forefront. A guard stood no chance against what I faced. He didn't even have a gun.

I parked in my single-car driveway, and sat still, hands on the steering wheel holding tight. I screamed. Then screamed some more. Then screamed again to make sure I'd gotten it all out. It was over. No matter which way I turned it, flipped it, twisted it... I should've been dead. The pressure of that thought alone made me want to vomit. Then I saw my hands and really did barf. I opened the car door and puked in the bushes. More threatened to come, but I held it down.

Trying to open the door when you're in a frantic rush was exactly how hard they made it seem in the movies. I fumbled inside and immediately felt the cool air of what would have been my welcoming home. Instead, I felt sick to my stomach and stumbled to the half bathroom downstairs.

The room spun. The smell of blood resonated in my nostrils. I slumped over the toilet, my mouth a waterfall. I threw up, then threw up again, and then once more before my stomach finally became void of anything. My mouth tasted like I drank a battery-filled smoothie. I'm sure the tequila helped with that. Minutes passed as I rested on the cold ground. I pressed my face against the frozen tile. It was the most comfortable position I could manage right now.

Images of that thing flashed in my mind. And the woman who had killed it. *What are they?* I lowered my eyes to see the blood staining my arms, then attempted to peel myself from the floor. At the least, I had to get myself cleaned up.

I took my shoes off before heading upstairs. The railing assisted me along the way while it held the brunt of my weight. It felt like ages from the bottom to my room. I went to the bathroom, turned the shower on, then found myself staring in the mirror. I didn't only feel like shit, I looked like shit, too. Blood covered my face in uneven dried splotches.

My dark, curly hair was matted down with bodily fluids that weren't mine—disgusting.

I climbed into the shower and let the hot water run over my head and down my body. Red-orange liquid slithered down the drain. I felt filthy. No matter how much water washed my body, no matter how much soap, no matter the shampoo, I still felt the blood sticking to me. The strength in my body disappeared, leaving me on the floor as I clutched my knees. I remained there until my skin pruned.

It had to have been past midnight by the time I made it out of the shower and back to my room. My laptop sat open on my computer desk, staring at me. I almost laughed. After the night I had there was no chance of anything productive getting done. My mind was too much of a foggy mess right now to think clearly.

I turned the lights off. My eyes remained closed, though I knew it'd be impossible to get any rest. Still, I could at least pretend. If I didn't have some sense of normality, I would go crazy. Although, once I closed my eyes all I could see was that thing staring at me. It brought its red eyes closer, until they were bright, burning in my mind.

I drew my comforter tighter.

3

I was wide awake before my alarm went off in the morning. There was no way I would have been able to sleep after living through that. The sound of the garbage trucks picking up trash reminded me that I had forgotten to take mine to the road. It also reminded me of the way that thing wailed. I'll never forget that screeching.

I took another shower, though it didn't make me feel any cleaner. My normal morning routine consisted of making a cup of tea, watching my favorite sports talk show, and eating breakfast. This morning was different. I dressed in something comfortable; it wasn't like I was trying to impress anyone. Before leaving the room, I went and grabbed my laptop and placed it in my bag. I felt lost without it. I would always have the *What if I could write?* thoughts that would nag me all shift. Truthfully, I should be happy nobody said anything to me.

I went downstairs and started the teapot. I turned the TV on but instead of watching my normal sports station, I flipped on the local news. The newscaster went on and on about weather, traffic, and a tropical storm we may need to keep an eye on. But nothing of that thing, it being killed, the person it had murdered, or the woman who spilled its blood all over me. I saw its eyes in my mind as they stared into my soul. The feeling of its tongue on my body sent frost down my spine. How many people had it murdered before it had finally been killed?

I melted into the couch, placing my hands over my face, and exhaled. Did I doubt my own thoughts? Was I going insane? There was no way. I knew what happened. So why wasn't there anything on the news about it? A sliced-up corpse by a dumpster should've been found by now, right?

The teapot hissed from the kitchen.

I poured the scalding water over the teabag into my travel thermos. Why wasn't there anything on the news? I took out a tablespoon and put more sugar in the cup than should have been legal. I added a few Splenda packets to perfect the cup. I took a taste test. Sure, I could have used a bit more sugar, but the tea lacked the *kick* it normally has. It'd have to do.

I grabbed the keys to my car lying on the counter and then headed out the door. I got in the Jetta, still in deep thought. My body moved, while my mind raced with thoughts on what could have happened. As I left the neighborhood, I stopped at the intersection that led downtown, with the gym one way, and the beach the other.

My eyes shifted to the clock. I was already running behind and didn't want to wait in morning traffic. A few more minutes wasn't going to make a difference. I turned right and drove away from work, toward the beaches. Even if I went to work now, my thoughts and suspicions would nag at me too much to get anything done.

I turned right, heading away from work and to the beach, back toward Fernando's. There wasn't any traffic heading this way. I passed through light after light without being stopped. *Figured. Nobody went to the beach to work. Not this early, at least. Must have a nice life.* Being from Union City, people would think I'd love the beach. Honestly, I could care less about it. I went once a year, if I found time. Something about getting sand in places it didn't belong never appealed to me. If it was up to me, I'd live in a loft in the middle of the city—with a pool, of course. Union City had its own kind of flair. I sighed, shaking my head—if only it was that easy.

I parked my trusty steed and made my way to the back of the restaurant. A couple casually jogged by me. They nodded and pressed about their merry way. The man was in his early fifties. He wore no shirt and had small earbuds in. The woman looked a few years younger. She wore athletic gear and over-ear headphones. Something inside me hated that they could casually jog as if working wasn't necessary. But then again, here I was, skipping out on work as well. Hey, sometimes the pot must let the kettle know it's black. Besides, they'd likely earned the right to slack off.

I took the way along the back end of the restaurant near the beach—the same path I happened upon yesterday. As I neared, the subtle hum of the ocean waves grew louder. I was having a heavy case of déjà vu. The salty smell touched my nose. I swallowed.

A part of me feared what I could possibly see. Or not see. I slipped down the alley, taking a few extra glances around to make sure nobody followed me. After the night I had, I wasn't willing to take any chances. It didn't take long to find my answer. The alley was cleaner than my criminal record. I went to the ground my back had been pressed against. Nothing. There wasn't even a single speck of blood. I investigated the entire surrounding area, even going into the trash to make sure nobody got funny and discarded the remains.

Something was off—it had to be. *There's no way...* I was going crazy. *Is there? No. I know what happened.* I remembered that thing's face. I still felt the way its blood coated my skin like some thick ooze. Yet there wasn't even one cop or reporter in sight.

"You won't find what you're looking for until you're ready to see. Those who don't want to never do," a voice said. I spun around, looking every way possible in a frantic panic. There wasn't anything in the vicinity, not a person in sight. Was I hearing things? The hairs on the back of my neck stood at attention. *I need to get out of here.* I wasn't about to wait around and to see if *something* appeared.

I dragged into the gym an hour late—my mind still cluttered with thoughts I didn't know how to process. The other front desk employee gave me a brief turnover before heading out the front.

"You're tardy," Dave said, his apple in hand, from his desk.

He was right. But I couldn't think straight enough to comment back.

Instead, I regarded him as anyone should their elders. "You're right," I said. "I need to do better."

Dave narrowed his eyes, then continued eating. Thankfully, someone grabbed his attention as they were leaving before he could press more. I went back to work, or I tried to, at least. No matter how much I tried to keep my mind off yesterday's big surprise, the more I circled back to it. If Alekka didn't text me, saying, "Hope you're not hung over!" I would have forgotten I needed to read her story.

I grabbed my laptop and booted it up. I opened the document, not knowing what to expect. It had been a while since I read someone else's work. Suddenly, I wondered if I had ever asked Alekka what college she went to, as if it mattered.

The words appeared on the screen. I read the first line, then the next, and after that, I was sure a customer watched me read the next paragraph or two instead of helping them. I laughed harder than I had laughed in a long time. There was a comedic element to it that felt natural. The scene with the woman going to an interview was hilarious. At least I could give Alekka an honest opinion about her work when I saw her.

Now to my other issues. If I was going to send Alekka something, I wanted to make sure it was the right piece. Only nothing looked *right* now. Then I thought about what Alekka asked of me. Alekka wanted honesty, which likely meant she would be one to give it in return. I double-clicked on one of my favorite stories I had written and gave it a read-through.

I fixed a few errors, changed a couple of lines, and then checked out a customer who wanted to buy bottled water. Before I could talk myself out of my decision, I attached the file and emailed it to Alekka. I waited a few minutes before sending Alekka a text, letting her know I sent her an email. I put my phone back in my pocket. The quicker I could forget about the email, the better. If not, I would spend every moment anxiously waiting for the text. I went to my email inbox. There it was, at the top, the story Alekka wanted me to read.

I shut off my computer and went through my normal checks before coming back to the front and manning my station. Whenever my mind wasn't occupied with something, my thoughts would circle back to last night, unable to think of anything else. Dave came to the front and leaned his arm against the table, eating another apple, though I didn't pay him any mind. My eyes stared out into the distance, not focusing on anything.

"Now that's a face people want to see when they walk in the gym," Dave said.

I exhaled. "Sorry, man. Just got a lot on my mind." As I gazed out of the dark windows, I saw a small cat sitting outside the entrance. A patron walked right past it, opened the door, and scanned in. As the door closed, the cat leered at me with bright golden eyes.

"Do you see that?" I asked, pointing.

"See what?" Dave squinted, trying to get a closer look.

"That cat outside," I replied. "I saw it yesterday in the parking lot."

Dave folded his arms. "Now I know my eyes aren't the best anymore, but I don't see anything. You sure you're okay?"

I shook my head. "Can you watch the front for me for a bit?"

Dave shrugged. "Why not? But make sure you—"

Before Dave finished his sentence, I started for the front. As I moved, the cat rose. It stretched its back, and maybe my eyes were playing tricks on me, but it seemed to grin at me. My mind begged me to stop. I knew what would happen if I followed. Things would only continue to spiral out of control. Yet every bone in my body moved with a sense of purpose I didn't know I had.

The cat sat on the other side of the glass. It had a small, smug smile on its face. It waited for me to open the door, then led on.

4

I've done a few questionable things in my life (none that I want to speak about now) but following a cat through downtown Union City must be the most bizarre yet.

The cat took me down the sidewalk. It managed to cross the street at the crosswalk a few blocks away. It was safer and more responsible than me. I would have crossed anywhere on the road, considering no one ever drove downtown.

"Where the hell are you taking me?" I asked. Now I had lost it. Not only was I following this cat as if it knew the answers to whether a writer should self-publish or go the traditional route—but I also tried to have a conversation with it.

The cat didn't stop. Instead, it turned to me and nudged its head as if telling me, *We'll be there soon.* I tapped my face enough to feel pain. Something's been off ever since my first encounter with this cat. I wasn't going crazy. But what was it trying to show me?

We arrived at Midtown Park, right on the Johnston River. It was one of the best views in Union City, though people rarely cherished it for what it was. It was a shame, honestly. The downtown area was beautiful, though on most days it was a wasteland, empty of a body—poor city management made sure of that. I scanned the area. Not a soul in sight.

The cat stopped near a park bench and plopped over comfortably. I was losing it. Why had I followed this cat all the way to the park? I slapped my face harder this time, then checked my cell phone. I needed a good night's sleep desperately. Dave was going to think all I did was slack off if I didn't get back soon. He wouldn't want to man the front desk for too long.

I started heading back to the gym, when a force pulled at me, as if I was on the end of a lasso. My body snapped around.

The force grew stronger. Malice and grief, hatred and agony, colliding emotions struck me—all fueling whatever was before me. It pulled me nearer, drawing me in—dragging me to where the weight was crushing. I could barely remain upright under the invisible force. Meanwhile, the cat lay on its back, pawing the air as if it was an infinite ball of yarn.

The other sensations vanished, and the only thing left was an abundance of fear. I followed that sensation as I traveled across the park to the entrance to the fire museum. A red mailbox sat to the right, while two fire hydrants showed my path. My class had come here once to clean as volunteer service when I was in grade school, but I hadn't been back since. Now it looked... sad—lifeless. I passed the half-circle stone seats that were near the entrance.

I halted and looked at the structure. The brick building towered over me. I went and put my hand against the thick glass to look through. There were small trinkets of fire engines, helmets, and other items on the other side of shelves that people could buy as memorabilia. I wondered how long those items had been there, collecting dust and taking up space. There was no doubt about it, the sense of fear I felt came from here... But where... and why? I took my hand off the cool surface and stepped back.

There was a sense of unease about the structure. No amount of paint could hide the true nature of the old and withered bricks. The longer I stared at the building, the harder it became to make out the details of it. It looked distorted as if I was staring at the building through a raindrop. I rubbed my eyes, blinking. I glanced at the mailbox and stone seats behind me. It all seemed normal, or at least I saw it—normal. But when my eyes returned to the museum, it was again blurred—like my eyes had been doused with water.

Then, like a zipper, the building... opened, and a dark void appeared. Darkness covered the building like paint. I stared. I heard a loud groan, followed by something that sounded like metal clashing. The noise grew louder. I saw the claws of the creature first. Then its glowing blue eyes followed. A sudden rush of heat came from the opening—then the same groaning from before, only much louder. A giant pincer that looked like a crab claw appeared and dug into the ground. I felt the ground rumble beneath my feet as the creature on the other side pulled its body through. Or maybe my legs just shook with fright. Behind the beast, the void vanished.

The creature resembled a giant scorpion, or at least, that's the closest being I could relate to, except for the fact it was large as a tiger with fur as bright as headlights. It had pincers on either side of its body, legs, and a stinger that nearly matched its body in size. It glared at me with wanting eyes. All the emotions from before funneled into me.

I stared in disbelief. A gaping hole in the space before me opened, and if some sort of bag. I wasn't seeing things. Some giant scorpion was clamping its pincers at me. Its mouth widened, heat billowing from it. I took a calculated step to the left. Something told me if I ran, it would pounce on my back immediately. The scorpion's blue eyes followed me. When I stepped back, it slid in a half circle, so it had a clear view of me. That at least confirmed that whatever this was, I was its target. I felt the same fear, but this time I could pinpoint exactly where it was coming from, which in all honestly made no sense. This scorpion-thing was a clear predator in this world—why would *it* be scared?

It snapped one of its pincers together. There was no warning before it bounded toward me faster than I could gather my thoughts. I fell to my side in a horrendous attempt at a dodge. I scampered up in a dead sprint, back the way I came. My eyes met the cat's as I passed the bench where it sat. I lost my footing and slammed into the earth. The sound of the scorpion closing in on me grew.

I turned to the cat. "Get out of here!" I yelled. Who was I kidding? I was no hero, but I wouldn't be able to live with myself if the cat died too. Though ... there was no telling if I was going to survive, either.

The cat licked at one of its paws while it gazed at me. The black of its eyes waned, becoming slits. It didn't move. Never once did it even turn to acknowledge the scorpion creature. Great. The scorpion scurried toward me. The way its body moved made my skin crawl. I needed to run. I had to get out of here. What the hell was I going to do? What the hell was even happening?

"Looks like you're finally *seeing*," a voice said. I whipped my head around. I was the only person in the park, besides the giant scorpion… and the cat. Everything seemed to freeze around me. Time stopped as I locked eyes with the feline sitting on the bench.

"You," I said. Piece by piece, the picture came together until it was as clear as polished glass. This wasn't a coincidence. None of it was. There's no way it could be. In every one of these *situations,* this cat was there. "What the hell are you trying to do? Kill me?"

"That wouldn't do either of us any good," the cat purred. "Now, would it?" It turned to the scorpion. "But if you can't figure your way through this, you'll be no good to me, anyway." The cat turned around and curled into a tight ball.

"What the hell does that even mean?" I asked. The cat didn't respond. *Man, I hate cats.*

The scorpion's pincer came within inches of me and almost snapped my left leg from beneath me. I jumped back to escape being chopped to pieces and sprinted for my life through the park.

The sound of destruction exploding in the beast's path reverberated behind me. Running seemed the only plausible choice initially. Now, it felt like a longer journey to the inevitable end. There was no way I could keep this up. First the alleyway thing, now this… I'd die from exhaustion before anything else.

Survive. It was the only thing I could do right now.

It covered any sort of distance I gained before I could catch my breath. The only way I stood a chance at keeping space between the scorpion and me was sprinting at this pace (and I mean *sprinting*, sprinting). I cut across the park, back toward the river. Wrong idea. The open field only made it faster. And running toward the river gave me less room to work with. Out here, the only thing it could crush was my body.

I turned back toward the empty road. Even if I did run that way, what would that do? Get people killed by whatever this was. I came to a stop at the edge of the park overlooking the river. I spun back to the scorpion inching closer and closer, clamping its pincers. Great. I didn't really like my odds in this one.

I always thought it was unrealistic when the characters in scary movies fell the moment the villain started chasing them. Until now. The scorpion lunged at me, and I dropped immediately—without an ounce of grace. I half rolled, half crawled out of the way of the scorpion's oversized stinger. It stuck to the ground, embedding itself in the earth. I tried to gain distance as it pulled itself free, but it only bought me one, maybe two, seconds. The monster attacked again when I rose. I barely managed to escape its aculeus.

My eyes quickly trailed to the segments that missed my body. I didn't know what I was thinking. To be completely honest, I couldn't have been thinking. Before the beast could retract its tail, I reached down and grabbed around the segment with my arm, clenching tight. The monster groaned again, the voice deep and oily. It took everything in me to hold it down, but somehow, I managed.

Fear struck me once more. I planted my feet again and maintained focus. The scorpion pulled harder against my grasp, but it was off balance and couldn't regain footing. I pulled it another inch closer. Then I heard what I had blocked out before—the Johnston River's waves hitting the wall behind me. Whatever this thing was, it was scared and there were only two things out here that could cause that—me, or the water. I was going to take a quick guess at which it was.

"Looks like… someone doesn't like— the water," I said, finally.

It tried to pull away, but I held on tight. I drove my feet into the ground and widened my stance. That worked for a second, before I was thrown in the air several feet. I crashed and tumbled away on the dewy grass on the side opposite of the river.

"Yeah, someone definitely doesn't like the water. Noted."

It came for me again; its movements were sloppy as it destroyed the park. I ran around as I watched the movements of the scorpion. It seemed almost… robotic. As if it was programmed to follow me. Whether that was the case or not, it was my only option that possibly saw me getting out of here in one piece.

I waited near the center of the park, panting. No matter where I went, it was going to follow. I wished I was home on the couch with a good book in hand right about now.

It didn't give me much time to prepare as it charged at me. I bolted to the right, circling its body. The beast screeched to a halt. Its blue eyes watched me as it turned to keep its body square. I waited until I had a straight shot for my goal—the river.

I didn't look back once. There was no reason to. If it caught me, I was dead. So, I did the only thing I could: kept my head down, pumped my arms, and ran like my life depended on it. I sprinted faster than I've ever sprinted in my life, adrenaline siphoning through my veins. I felt the ground as it trembled beneath the creature's large legs. I pushed harder. When I reached the edge, I used it as a springboard and jumped as far out as I could. I flailed my arms forward, then turned to see the creature jump out after me.

It followed, splashing into the water next to me. I fluttered away from it. It groaned, then stopped altogether, as if it finally realized what had happened. It thrashed around in confusion, sinking quickly. One victory I could be happy about later. Now for the real problem—I couldn't swim, either. Yeah, yeah, yeah, trust me—I know.

The plan was almost flawless. Everything lined up, but now I was half choking on air, half calling for help. But who the hell would be out here? I fought a freaking giant scorpion in the middle of Metropolitan Park and nobody saw me. My chances of being saved were grim, at best. At least I knew that creature wouldn't be roaming Union City doing whatever the hell it pleased. There was no telling how many people would have been hurt.

I swallowed a mouthful of water and my arms felt like hot metal. I couldn't keep whatever the hell I was doing up much longer. After the fight with that giant scorpion, I had nothing left. More time passed, and I couldn't feel my body any longer.

"He-Help!" I gasped.

I remembered my body sinking, then everything went dark. Yet in that darkness, someone asked me, "What's your name?" And the only name that came to mind was *Nexus*.

I woke up in a panic. I scanned the darkness as my hands traced my body. What the hell was going on? I felt my face again, and my chest.

Everything was... real—and alive. The last thing I remember was jumping into the Johnston River. I couldn't hold on any longer, and I thought there wasn't anyone out there. I scanned the darkness. How the hell did I end up in my own house? No matter how dark it was, I knew my home.

The longer I thought, the more puzzled I became. I took a deep breath trying to concentrate. All I was wearing was underwear and socks—both dry. I rose a bit and looked out my blinds to see the fountain water funneling out into pigtails before splashing into the pond. Call me crazy, but a part of me wanted to believe I'd just fallen asleep the night prior and dreamt the whole thing—but I knew that was not the case.

It was all too real.

I'd gotten lucky. If that scorpion hadn't jumped into the river behind me as if possessed, I would have died in the park. I didn't understand why it wanted me dead, but it was clear that I was its target. I took the blanket off my body and placed my feet on the ground. I wobbled and fell to my knees. My body felt weak. It was hard to keep my eyes open. I took another deep breath and then tried to move.

I dragged myself out of my room, using any surface for stability everywhere I could. My stomach burned as if I'd just received a flurry of punches from a boxer. How could I even be alive after what happened? My head spinning, each blink made me want to keep my eyes closed. I slapped my face, gathering myself. My arm slammed against the door as I slid around the frame.

The stairs proved to be a more formidable foe than I anticipated. I made sure to turn the lights on and searched my surroundings. I grabbed onto the handrail and went down slowly. The quickest thing I could find was a protein bar and a glass of water. I finished both, then repeated the process twice. Before I finished drinking the last of my water, the toilet in the downstairs bathroom flushed.

I dropped the glass in my hand and went for the steak knife. "Come out slowly with your hands up or I will filet you, I swear!" I yelled. Normally, you would have thought I was full of shit, but after all I had been through, I really would.

The sink turned on, and I could hear someone washing their hands. Like personal hygiene mattered right now. I didn't know whether to be happy they cared or be mad that they made a point of it.

The door crept open. "Cool it, Chuck Norris, before you get yourself killed." A man with brown skin around my height, but in way better shape, came from the bathroom. To be frank, he was terrifying. Not terrifying in the sense of appearance, but he carried himself with a demeanor that said he'd done and seen things that I couldn't imagine. He had his dreads tied into a tight ponytail and wore a black windbreaker. His jeans were more fashionable than anything I had in my closet, and his boots probably cost more than the TV in my living room. When he turned his face to me, I could see a scar of what looked to be claw marks that ran from the top of his neck to below his right eye.

My intruder walked into my kitchen. He grabbed a few paper towels and dried his hands. Still ignoring me, he threw the towels away, then came and leaned his body against the counter across from me. He pulled a water bottle out from his jacket and drank a third of it before he placed it down.

"First of all, I don't suggest jumping in the river if you can't swim. Won't look good having you die out there. But... It was probably your only choice in that situation." He raised his hands and outlined an imaginary TV. "Local man dives in river but can't swim." He nodded to himself. "Or Union City Police will arrest you after saving you. We both know they're dying to do anything but serve the community."

I glowered at the man. "Who the hell are you?"

He tossed me my wallet first, then my keys. "A thank you would be nice," he said.

I kept the knife pointed in his direction. He did everything but tap his foot while he stared at me. "Thank you," I said slowly. "Now, who the hell are you?"

"Much better," he said. "Name's Gyle." I hated that he was leading this conversation. I had the knife pointed at him, but he didn't seem frightened at all. At this point, it was more for the show of force than anything.

"And you rescued me from..." I thought back to the scorpion. And to me in the Johnston River, drowning. "How'd you find me?"

Gyle took a seat at my high kitchen table, his back pressed against it —one of his legs crossed over the other. He gave me a pensive look. "You have any water?"

I stared at him with confusion. He just took a bottle from his jacket and finished it in a short amount of time. And he really had the gall to ask me for water after he broke into my home. "You being serious right now?"

"My bad... Please?"

This situation couldn't get any weirder. Now I was hosting my intruder? I carefully maneuvered through the kitchen, avoiding any glass on the floor. I kept my eyes on Gyle and made sure he didn't move. He leaned with his arm against the table—getting comfortable. I fiddled in the fridge until I grabbed a water bottle and tossed it at Gyle.

He drank most of it before I could safely travel back through the glassy terrain. "Can a man not do a good deed while going for his daily run? I just so happened to hear your cries for help and figured I hadn't done anything good in a while. You know, need to keep my karma up."

"Don't give me that bullshit," I said. I stepped toward him, the knife still at attention. "I'm really starting to get tired of your sarcastic game. Start speaking the truth... Now."

He finished the water. Before he threw it away, he turned to me. "You recycle?"

My patience was so thin right now it could have sliced through thick metal. I inhaled slowly, then exhaled. "It's out the door," I said, pointing behind him.

Gyle put his hands up. "Let me," he said. I watched as he slipped out the door and tossed the bottle. When he returned, he propped his body against the counter.

"What's this burning question you have?" he asked. "You know, since you're asking the questions here."

There were so many thoughts, so many questions. How could I pick one? Where would I begin to start? I ended up staring at Gyle with my mouth almost open.

He clasped his hands together and nodded. "Exactly," he said. "So, like I was saying. Heard you calling for help, came to help, no biggie."

"A good Samaritan would have taken me to the hospital," I said.

Gyle's eyes flashed violet. He sighed, then grinned. "At least you're not dumb," he said. Gyle reached into his pocket and then pushed a folded piece of paper into my chest.

"Meet here tomorrow. Don't make me come find you." He pointed to the door. "If I were you, I'd change these locks out. Locks like these are way too easy to get into." Then just as quickly as Gyle came, he left.

5

I barely slept that night, there was no way my thoughts would allow it. I had a billion and one things on my mind. For instance, who the hell was Gyle, and why in the hell should I listen to him? I played by my own rules. Or at least that was what I would have liked to think. Nobody would move me. I was from Union City; I'd been in plenty of fights in my day. Though Gyle didn't strike me as someone who'd engage in a fistfight, let alone lose if he was to get in one. Something told me if he wanted me dead, I'd be dead already.

And why had so many weird occurrences happened so suddenly? Maybe I was cursed. Hopefully, I wouldn't lose my job over not showing back up to work after everything that had happened.

I cleaned up the glass in the kitchen. My brain rattled as I tried to sort through the slush pile of my mind. So I did the only thing I could at this point. I went to my bedroom, grabbed my laptop, and then returned to the living room. Some people stressed over the little things—I was some people. But I've learned to calm myself, or at least divert the stress, over the years.

I wasn't what people would call the prototypical writer. There wasn't some big routine to how I wrote or a method to the madness. In all honesty, that was probably part of why I had nothing to show for my writing. I'd put "create positive habits" on the ever-growing list of things to do. For me, it was simple. I turned on something I could listen to in the background. Sports, an anime I've seen more times than I could count, or really, any noise would do. It didn't matter where I was, the time, or even the day—if I wanted to write, I wrote.

Today wasn't one of those days.

No matter how much I tried to get my ideas flowing, all I could think about was the possible chance that that scorpion made it out of the river and was heading straight for me. Or the fact that a mystery man found me, who then proceeded to take me to my home and tucked me in for the night. In all honesty, that was creepier than the scorpion. After watching *How to Get Away with Murder*, I should have thrown red flags all over this situation. I covered my face with my hand and laughed. It was comical. I was almost murdered—twice, and I was sitting in front of the computer screen hoping I would create magic.

Several hours and episodes later, I finally got something on the computer, though after reading a bit of it over, I deemed most of it as garbage. But it was better than nothing. I got something down; more than I could say of my previous attempts, even though it took me greeting the sun for breakfast to get it. I stretched, letting each bone in my body crack with relief.

My phone buzzed multiple times before settling. There were four unread messages from Alekka. The first message said, "Holy shit!" And the most recent said, "Meet me at work ASAP!" My phone hadn't been a priority, with my life being in danger and all. Today was my off day, and I didn't want to go back to the gym and face what could have been. I noted the address and then texted Alekka back, letting her know that I'd be by later.

I got dressed and checked the news again... just in case. Nothing—again. This time, I expected it. Of course, nobody would have noticed a giant scorpion attacking a man in the middle of Midtown Park. Sometimes I wondered where the good taxpayers' dollars went. I grabbed my keys and wallet before leaving the house. I double-checked the lock to the door. A bit of healthy paranoia never hurt anyone.

Hometown Press was only a short drive from the gym, located in downtown Union City. The publishing agency was housed in an old brick structure that had long seen its most energetic days. It was one of those buildings that would outlive its tenants and still be there long after anyone ever rented out the space. I parked the Jetta in one of the many open spaces in the lot. The sun was barely visible rising over the beach in the far distance. It was going to be another foggy, overcast, Union City morning. There wasn't anything about rain on the news, but in Florida, you always had to know and expect that could change at a moment's notice. Luckily for me, this weather fueled me. The more miserable the day, the livelier I was. It was probably the artist in me. Go figure.

The bottom floor of the building reminded me of a hotel lobby more than anything else, though the inside resembled something out of an outdoor pool in the winter because of how barren it was. I chose to take the stairs instead of the elevator. Alekka told me the office was on the third floor, and I couldn't justify the wait. I exited the stairwell to a long hall with double glass doors at the end with frosted letters on the door that read: Hometown Press. I didn't know whether to be jealous or impressed.

I went to the end of the hall and opened the door to the office. The receptionist at the front greeted me with a smile. "Welcome to Hometown Press. How may I assist you?" she asked. It felt odd being on the other side of this encounter. Normally I was the one doing the greeting.

"I'm here for Alekka," I said.

"Loooook who it is!" I heard Alekka yell from a cubicle a few paces away. She approached, wearing a navy blue blazer and gold earrings. Alekka thanked the woman manning the front, then pulled me off to her cubicle. She stacked a few papers together while organizing her desk as much as she could. "Please, make yourself at home."

I leaned my body against her computer desk and let it hold my weight. Alekka stared at me with wondering eyes. "Everything okay with you?" she asked.

I put my hand over my face and exhaled. "Sorry," I said. "I'm a bit on edge, I guess." I thought about telling Alekka the truth and talking to her about what happened after I left Fernando's the other night, and not to mention the scorpion. But... telling her the truth would only make me sound crazier than I looked. Where would I even begin to explain what was happening? I didn't even have a concept of what was going on.

Alekka brushed it off and sat in her rolling chair. "Don't worry about it," she said. "Look, I'm going to get straight to the point. I liked your short story. So much so that I had my boss, Tara, take a look, and she liked it as well."

"Cool," I said. "I'm glad you both liked it."

"So, question. Do you happen to have a full-length project you're working on?" Alekka asked.

"I guess so. Don't we all?" I joked.

Alekka let me sit with my failed attempt at comedy before speaking again. "First, no. We don't all have a novel we're working on, hence why I asked. Second, if you do, I think you should submit to the contest we're running right now."

With everything happening there was no way I would be able to concentrate long enough to finish something. "When's the deadline for submissions?" I asked. It couldn't hurt to ask. Maybe a deadline was what I needed to get writing again.

The receptionist handed Alekka a sticky note and then walked off.

Alekka laughed a little. "Next week," she said. "But if I talk with Tara, I can get her to extend it a day or so for you."

"Fuck." I didn't even know where to start. "I think I can get something to you—maybe."

"Perfect," Alekka shouted, before quickly reeling it in. "Good thing, too. I already told Tara you'd be submitting," Alekka smirked.

"Essentially, you lied." I folded my arms.

"Kinda sorta, but who's talking essentials? Speaking of essentials... Did you read my story? What do you think?"

"Honest opinion?" I asked. I waited long enough for Alekka to get anxious.

"Stop playing around and tell me," she said. "This is valuable information."

"My honest opinion is that I enjoyed it," I said. "And you're mad funny."

Alekka's face dropped. "It wasn't supposed to be funny. I thought that was very apparent."

"I-I.,," *Well, I sure knew when to put my foot in my mouth.*

Then Alekka started laughing. "Naw, I'm giving you shit, but your face told me everything I needed to know."

I loved how she laughed at almost having to call the ambulance to her work office. Once I picked my head off the ground, I asked, "What does that mean?" Had my face said something that I hadn't realized?

"Nothing bad," Alekka said. The receptionist walked up once more.

I pointed toward the front with my thumb. "So, what, you're like the boss or something?" I asked sarcastically.

"And what if I am?" Alekka said, raising a brow.

"Wait… Your boss left *you* in charge?" That sounded harsher than I meant it to.

"Sure did." Alekka dangled a set of keys in front of me. "For lack of better words, I run this bitch." She spun the keys around her finger, grinning. "Tara has a bunch of video calls with the big boss today. Figured she wouldn't have enough time to come in. I love the support."

"Holy shit, you're serious." It's not that I couldn't see Alekka running Hometown Press—it was just until recently, I've only seen her at the gym. And nothing screamed literary lover. Either way, Alekka was in the driver's seat. I wish I had something good to write to go with all of this motivation.

Alekka threw a finger up as she reached into her pocket and answered her phone. She uttered a cluster of words so fast that I lost track of what she was saying—then she muted the phone. "I swear, I've been up for three hours and two of them have been updating Tara. She's on a mission to drive me crazy." She unmuted the phone, said a few more acknowledgments, and then muted it once more. "I don't know how she keeps up with everything. This woman has to run on coffee and sugar." Alekka said a couple of words, then hung up the phone.

"Does it look like she's gonna let up?"

"It never does." Alekka leaned her back against the wall and deflated like a balloon.

One of the lights flickered. I felt a dark, looming sense of death. A faint sound, like glass cracking in the distance, the same sound as when the scorpion appeared yesterday. My shoulders suddenly became heavy as if someone was standing over me, pressing down with all their weight. Something was out there; I was sure of it. Only I didn't know what or who—or why I could even tell.

"Have you ever felt like there was something else out there?" I asked. The words came out naturally. Alekka didn't react. I drew my breath in and cursed to myself under my breath. *Who says shit like that?* "Never mind, it's nothing." I tried to play it off.

"Something like what?" Alekka grinned. "Is this your way of asking me if I believe in aliens? Because the answer, of course, is a giant YES!"

"I'm not joking," I responded. I shook my head in confusion. "I don't know. But things have been weird lately. I'm sure I'm not losing my shit. We're not the only people out here." I stared back toward the entrance. "Even now, I can feel something's presence out there. I can't be sure where or what it wants, but I know it's out there." I rubbed my curly hair, frustrated. I hated not being able to piece this together. It was like getting to the end of the puzzle and not being able to find the last piece to finish it.

Alekka folded her arms, pouting a little. "I wasn't joking, either." She laughed. "Thought I found a fellow alien lover." Alekka's demeanor became slightly more serious. "You know… You're an interesting guy. Definitely need way more sleep. But very interesting." Alekka frowned as if she was worried about something. I stopped speaking. Whatever was going on, I didn't want to get Alekka wrapped up in it. And I could already tell she would pry it out of me.

The sensation that was weighing me down earlier disappeared. I scanned the office, but nothing had changed. Of course nothing had. I felt like the boy who cried wolf. My paranoia was slowly rising every day. I heard the creaking of the building's walls with how hard I was listening to my surroundings. *But what would that even do? Give me enough time to see my killer before it offs me—great.*

I shook those thoughts from my mind and turned back to Alekka. I stood. "Sorry, don't want to keep you," I said. "Some people have regular jobs. Not that I don't have a regular job…" I shut my mouth. "I'll see you later."

Alekka chuckled. "You sure you don't want a tour before you go?"

I thought about it genuinely, then shook my head. "Not today, thanks," I responded. I left the cubicle, waved bye to the receptionist, and then went down the stairs into the hotel lobby. As I walked out of the elevator, a stocky man approached me. He looked around as he tried to place himself while on the phone. He looked important. And he prob-

DEMONOLOGY

ably felt that way, too, when he didn't look where he was going and bumped into me, knocking my phone out of my hand. I prayed the screen wasn't cracked, then picked it up.

"Sorry about that," the man said, with the voice of a car salesman.

"Don't worry about it," I said, picking it up. The screen was intact. Crisis averted.

The man's phone rang, and he immediately answered. He said a few words, then turned to me. "You know how to get to Hometown Press?"

I nodded. "Take the elevators right there, third floor."

"Thanks." He walked away, talking more business, I presumed.

Anxiety crept in. I wanted to go home. If I could start my weekend and get back to normalcy—then maybe things would be okay. But who was I kidding? Was that even possible at this point? Every logical part of me told me to head home. It was the right choice—the only choice. Nothing would be the same if I didn't. But then I envisioned Gyle's voice whispering, "Don't make me come find you." I shuddered.

I shoved the front door open and went back to the Jetta. Maybe it was the thought of what Gyle would do to me *if* he did have to find me. Or maybe it was just foolish curiosity. But I placed the coordinates Gyle gave me in the GPS and began my drive to the destination. My gut was screaming so loud at me that I had to crank the music up to drown it out.

I ended up on a side of town I wasn't very familiar with. It bore the name Riverside, since this section of the city outlined the Johnston River. It was a wonder how I never frequented this area. It was only a short drive from the gym, even though you had to cross a bridge or two to get there. And it was also the part of town known for highlighting the artists in the city. Though artists from the city have always had a love or hate relationship with Riverside. That mostly had to do with the recent flood of new people who frequented the area. Some were drawn naturally to the art and the energy of the subsection, while with others, it was clear they were there to fit a role. Did they really love the arts, or were they only out here to perpetuate a standard they thought would allow them to fit in with certain crowds?

I parked on the street down the block, then followed the directions further down the street. I passed by a rooftop bar and a few other restaurants, one being a crystal shop with a giant sun stained on the front glass. The GPS took me to a side avenue, which opened to another road with a warehouse that was tattooed in a myriad of artistic expressions.

I walked to the building. The GPS pointed straight ahead, so it had to be the warehouse. Something about it felt... off. It was in an open dirt lot, yet in this growing area, it was left untouched. There was no way the city hadn't tried to buy the land from whoever owned it to turn it into some nightclub. I crossed the street toward the warehouse. When I stepped into the dirt my body became heavy, then a vibrating sensation pricked at my skin. I looked down at my hands, turning them over so I could see both sides. They looked normal enough.

When I turned back to the street, everything looked different. Behind me, the area appeared distorted. The buildings appeared foggy as if I were crying. Several pedestrians walked by on the sidewalk, yet none even bothered turning my way, despite me staring directly at them with a confused look. The ground seemed like an undeveloped version of what was only several feet from it. I even waved my hands and shouted at the next group—nothing.

I knew the right response would have been to run like hell and get out of Dodge. But I also knew I wanted answers more than anything right now, and Gyle was somewhere I could start to find them.

I went to the warehouse at the end of the lot and stared up at its metal structure. I had to respect the artwork. Some of it was graffiti that was clearly professional work, and on the other side was an anime character even I wasn't familiar with. I knocked on the metal door, then stepped back and waited. It felt odd waiting like some door-to-door salesman trying to sell the newest product. I put my hands in my pockets and rolled my ankles with impatience. Maybe I was a bit nervous.

While I waited, I watched each person that passed the warehouse. Not even one person turned in the direction of the building. With it being so large and covered in spray paint—I doubted that was actually the case. There was no way anyone would have passed by without glancing over for a second.

The slat opened. A pair of violet eyes stared at me. "Name?" a voice said.

I knew my name; how couldn't I, it was my birth name, the only one I've known. It was what my friends, teachers, and everyone called me. Yet another name, so foreign to my own, spewed out, as if attached to a fishing line being dragged from my body. My lips moved on their own, uttering the name, "Nexus," in a low, calm tone. The slat closed, and then a murky stillness took control.

Several seconds passed. Then a minute. I began to wonder what the hell I was doing—when the locks clicked on the other side. Lock after lock turned until finally, the door began to slide open. It moved, screeching with every inch. The door had to weigh several hundred pounds. No residential home would have steel that thick and durable lying around.

"Looks like you made it," Gyle said. "And here I thought I was going to have to come find you. Smart choice."

My eyes went to the scar on his face. I didn't move. There was too much uncertainty, too much confusion. I wanted—no, needed to know just what the fuck was going on. "Who the hell are you?" I threw my hands to the side, frantic. "What the hell is this place? What do you know about what's been going on with me?" The words kept pouring out; word after word, all spilling out of the holes of the net I called a mouth. "Why..."

Gyle brushed one of his dreads from his face. "Follow me," he said. "Trust me on this one. If I start throwing information at you now, your head will explode. Besides, there's someone I want to introduce you to." He went behind me and nudged me ahead. Then Gyle slid the door shut behind both of us. Any chance at freedom I had closed with it.

6

I followed Gyle down a narrow hallway. There was only a crack of visible light coming from small windows high above. The large windows next to me were all covered with thick maroon curtains. The walls felt like they were collapsing on me, making me feel tiny. Gyle unlocked yet another door, finally coming to another hallway, but this one was well-lit. The room held an orange glow, the type you only got from the daytime sun. I stopped and gazed at the wooden arches that led the way. The interior of the warehouse differed vastly from the exterior. It had grace, whereas the outside looked like something the city would talk about tearing down at board meetings. It smelled of leather and aging bark and had intricate paintings that looked to be from a museum hung on the walls. Multiple large windows were spread evenly along the way. I stopped, gently brushing one of the curtains out of the way, and peered out the window. Like before my view was distorted, as if I'd taken one too many shots of whiskey.

"I'm surprised you've made it this far without having any encounters with the Otherworld," Gyle said.

"Otherworld?"

Gyle tapped his foot against the ground as he thought. "Well, there's the real world, the place you're used to. Your normal friends, your normal city, your normal life." Gyle paused. "The Otherworld is sort of like the ocean. Nobody knows for sure how deep it goes, or how vast it is—or what lives there. In some places, Union City will look as it should. In others... Well, I wouldn't be able to tell up from down, or left from right. That thing that attacked you in the park was a lesser demon from the Otherworld."

I laughed. "You have to be fucking shitting me," I said. "How gullible do you think I am?" I walked in a semi-circle near the window. "Look, I know things have been getting weird lately, but the Otherworld... That can't be real."

Gyle stared at me. He cracked his neck, turning it to either side. "What, you think that demon just appeared from nowhere?" he asked.

"Well... No, but still, that's things you hear about in books. Someone would have to be crazy to believe that."

A chunk of cement broke off from the wall, the sound crumbling in my ear. Gyle's body stood a hair's length from mine, his breath hot against my face. Debris struck the ground with soft patters. "Do I look crazy to you?" Gyle's eyes shifted to something dark, terrifying. The whites of his eyes turned black, and the irises glowed with a violet hue. He brought his hand back to his body with a sigh. Rubble covered his hand.

I reeled back as much as I could. "I didn't mean it like that," I said. I swallowed, my body shaking.

Gyle's eyes returned to their normal state. He rubbed at his temples. "Just come on." For a moment, he froze with a look halfway between somber and irritation. Gyle led without speaking the rest of the way.

We arrived at a set of steel double doors. He pushed them open with strength that I knew was impossible for any man to have possessed. Once the doors were cracked open, he paused, then turned to me.

"Look... I'm not telling you to believe me," he said. "You don't have to listen to anything I tell you. But I have nothing to gain from telling you lies. What you believe is up to you." From Gyle's jacket pocket, an animal appeared. It scurried around Gyle's arm until it was on his shoulder. As I observed it closer, it was clear the animal was a ferret. The ferret's two-toned fur was slick from the jacket's material pressing upon it. It turned to me and cocked its head, staring. Its eyes glowed violet, the same shade Gyle's had. Another ferret emerged. This one was the exact opposite of the first. Where the first had black fur, this ferret was white. The mustelids appeared odd. Just looking in their direction suffocated me, my breathing becoming heavy.

"Will you two shut up already," the first ferret said. It yawned, then adjusted itself on Gyle's shoulder. "Can't get any sleep with all the yapping." Gyle rubbed at the ferret's head, enticing a soft purr. "Now hurry up and get in there before I get pissed."

I didn't answer, though I listened. What was I supposed to do? Nothing made sense, but lately nothing had. It was one thing after another. Anything was on the table at this point. Maybe I was the one who was crazy. But I was not going to find out what happened if I pissed off a talking ferret.

I felt a set of eyes lock on me as soon as I walked through the doors. The common area was massive in comparison to my little townhome. In the center of the room was a giant black leather couch, one of the kinds you only saw online and wondered who the hell needed that much space. Across from it was a projection screen, most likely to go with the projector that was hanging from the ceiling. The room had its own bar with liquor upon liquor bottles that filled the shelves. It felt like I was on a new episode of one of those rich and wonderful HGTV shows.

I looked up to see the grand chandelier that hung low, lighting the room. The giant fan above hummed as it cooled the room. I heard a familiar sound in the distance; the score from a video game song I couldn't place. Who the hell was funding this whole operation? Gyle walked to a young girl who sat in the corner gaming on a PlayStation. There was no way she could be a day over nineteen. She looked up at Gyle, then at me, before going back to her game. Her hair was tied into a long blonde ponytail, and she wore a pair of denim overalls with a long-sleeved shirt beneath. Unlike Gyle, her aura seemed different—pure, yet peculiar. I couldn't put my finger on exactly what it was.

"Where's Voss?" Gyle asked. The girl ignored him and focused harder on her game.

I crouched to get a better look, then the excitement took control.

"*Trails of Cold Steel*? I love that series. I put in over a hundred hours on this one alone. Had to platinum it." I reeled back in embarrassment. "Sorry, I'm a big RPG fan. Just got a little excited there."

The girl glowered at me, then went back to playing the game as if none of us existed.

Gyle went to the bar. "That's Quintyla, but she goes by Quin," he said. He grabbed water from the mini-fridge and finished half of it before taking a breath. "She's not much of a talker. Kinda just sits there playing her games all day. Stays to herself. But she stays out of trouble, so can't be too upset."

"Any idea why she doesn't talk?" I asked, taking a seat at the bar. I glanced back over to the slim teen.

Gyle shook his head. "No clue. She's never so much as uttered a word around me. To be honest, I don't think anyone's heard her speak before." The second ferret from earlier climbed from Gyle's jacket and placed itself on the bar.

"I'm telling you, it's something that damn demon of hers did," the woman ferret said. "Probably hexed that poor girl's throat." She turned and licked at her white and black fur.

"Not our problem." The male ferret yawned. "We don't even know who her partner is. Can't say for certain what's going on. And I'm not about to stick my neck where it doesn't belong. A quick way to get it cut off."

I watched the two ferrets go back and forth. There's no doubt they were speaking, and with just as much personality as any human. I took that back. They had more personality.

"What are they talking about?" I asked.

"*They* have a name," the male ferret snarled.

"Shut it, Symon," the woman ferret said. "Don't mind him, honey. He's a bully. Forgets he has manners when he's tired." She stretched out across the bar. "The name's Claudette, but you can call me Claudy. And that meanie over there is Symon."

"Sorry about that," I said, looking at Symon. "I didn't mean to offend."

"None taken," Claudy responded. Then she sat up and stared at me, her eyes little violet orbs. There was a sudden change in her demeanor. "Not all Hybrids have a relationship like we do with Gyle."

"Hybrids?" I'd never heard the word before in this context, and I wasn't about to start guessing what it meant. Hell, I was talking to a ferret. Expect the unexpected.

"Half-breeds," Gyle said. "Humans that share their hearts with demons." He finished his water bottle. "Usually, Hybrids don't make it. When a higher-level demon decides to take control of a source, the human usually dies. They can't complete the bond. Other times, as in my case, the host has a connection to the Otherworld." Gyle rubbed at Symon's head. "Luckily, these two took a liking to me and let me keep my body. Though it's ours to share now."

I glanced at Symon, Claudy, and then at Gyle. "What do you mean, *share?*"

"What do you think?" Symon questioned, his voice laced with sarcasm. "You seem like a smart guy. What do you do when you share something?"

"My body is theirs; their bodies are mine," Gyle said. "Simple as that."

I tried to wrap my mind around the concept, but the more I thought it over, the more ridiculous it seemed. How could any of this be true? Yet Gyle stood in truth next to me with his demon ferrets. All the proof I needed was staring me in the face.

The metal double doors to the common area opened before I could throw myself into endless thought. A man maybe an inch or two taller than me walked through the door. His hair was blond, fine, and pulled into a bun atop his head. Truth be told, he looked like a character out of a mafia movie. The man opted for a clean, yet flashy look. He wore a charcoal-gray vest with a tight-fitting short-sleeved shirt underneath, and a watch that cost more than my townhome. There was a sense about him, dark, yet almost enticing, that drew me in—while simultaneously pushing me away.

At the man's side was a fox. Its fur was orange-black and its eyes, like Claudy's and Symon's, glowed bright, though it glowed in an ember hue. The fox's fur flickered either way as if it were a flame. Much like the man, the fox strode ahead with a sense of confidence that I knew had to be justified. It turned, and then its eyes turned to Gyle. Even from where I sat, I felt the rumble in its chest, a deep bellow filled with power. I rose—it felt right in this moment.

The blond man walked over to me. "Voss," he said. He stopped in front of me and offered me his hand.

I shook it, and the name, Nexus, left my lips. I glared at him in confusion. "Sorry, I didn't mean that. My name is, Nexus." Again, I said that alien name—one that I didn't know, or ever heard before a day ago. Annoyance took control of my body. I inhaled and said, "Nexus. Nexus. Nexus!" I covered my mouth.

Voss raised a brow at Gyle. Gyle laughed, way more than I thought he should have at that moment. The fox stared at Gyle with an annoyed expression.

Voss took a pack of cigarettes from inside his vest pocket and popped one in his mouth and lit it. "You didn't say he was this fresh," he said.

I scanned the room, locking eyes with Quin, who turned back and continued playing her game. I felt anger welling up, like a kettle ready to explode. There was no way I was going to attempt to say my name again and risk looking more idiotic than I already did. Instead, I asked, "What's so funny?"

"Don't worry, honey. We're not laughing at you," Claudy said.

I scanned the room. "Well, seeing that I'm not laughing, you can't be laughing with me."

"When did you start forgetting your name?" Voss asked. He pulled the cigarette from his mouth, and a billow of smoke followed.

It wasn't something I wanted to think about. The more I tried to remember, the more I felt like I'd lost something that I'd never get back. "I guess it started a few days ago," I said.

"Possession," Voss said. "You belong to the Otherworld just as much as you belong to this world. In their world, your name is Nexus."

Possession... The thought of it gave me an empty feeling. If I couldn't claim my own identity, then who the hell was I?

"Hybrids have a connection to the Otherworld," Voss said. "Think of it as having one foot in the real world, and one foot in the Otherworld. The same way you exist in Union City, you also exist in their world."

"I'm not really following," I replied.

"If a human becomes a Hybrid, they're as human as they are demon," Gyle interjected. "When their connection with the Otherworld forms, a name is given to a human by their demon, binding them for life. When the bond is formed, your old name disappears, and the name given to you by your demon replaces your old one—none the wiser." Gyle shrugged. "Couldn't tell you my old name if you had a gun to my head."

I gazed at the fox that sat at Voss's feet, then at both Claudy and Symon. "So you mean to tell me you're all these Hybrid things?"

Voss nodded. He reached around the bar and started pouring a glass of dark liquor. "Not only us," he said. "You're one, too." Voss tasted the drink, letting out a satisfying sigh.

I laughed awkwardly. It was my reaction when I was under too much stress, a defense against the unknown. I wasn't much for confrontation. This was a different level of stress. My ears began to ring. "Look, maybe we're all missing something here," I said. "Sure, I can't remember my name. Weird shit keeps happening to me. But I have no idea what any of you are talking about." I stared at the fox. "Besides, if I'm a Hybrid, I'm pretty sure I would remember a demon trying to take control of my body. Right?"

I started to feel idiotic for even coming here. What the hell was I doing? These people were insane and were trying to get me roped up in their weird games. Something must have happened to me at the bar the other day. My head throbbed and it became hard to breathe. I stumbled into the barstool.

Gyle grabbed another water bottle and slid it across the bar to me. "It's a lot to handle all at once," he said.

"A lot to handle... This goes way beyond that," I said. "I almost died after leaving my favorite bar. I can't shut my eyes without seeing that *thing* or the scorpion from the park. Either one could pop up at any time to come and finish the job." I shook my head. "No. Ya'll are crazy... I don't know who—or what you people are. But I want you to leave me alone. Let me go live my normal, boring life. I just want to write..."

Voss came closer, resting his elbow against the bar. "I'm not the one who invited you here, for one," he said. "Besides, reality is what it is, whether or not you can understand it." He leered at me with eyes that burned red-orange embers.

Voss continued as if he didn't just scare me shitless. "My job isn't to make you believe us, nor is it to protect you. The only reason you're even here right now is because Gyle vouched for you." Voss didn't break eye contact, though he smirked at me. "Besides, do you think I'm talented enough to come up with this guy here?" He pointed at the fox at his side. It turned its head. Its face had metal jutting out of it in several places like some sort of motherboard.

Voss was both terrifying and charismatic. But above all, it was clear he was a man who held himself to a high moral standard. Convoluting some elaborate scheme against a gym employee didn't seem like his thing. And for what?

I thought about Alekka's deadline—and about the work that I hadn't made a dent in yet. I envied those whose ideas spewed from their minds like a broken levee. When I made the decision to write, I gave up all chances of stability. Expect the unexpected. But I needed to figure out what the hell was going on if I planned on getting back to writing and meeting Alekka's deadline. And to do that, I needed the answers I drove here to get. Someone needed to make sense of this or I was going to go insane.

I forced myself from the chair. The fox watched me as I moved. I took a few steps over and knelt next to the beast. It couldn't be fake. There was no way something this... *real* could be fabricated. Its eyes were a furnace. A deep flame that surfed in the darkness.

"What do you want, child?" it growled.

"Y-Your name." I glanced back at Claudy. "Names are important, right?"

The fox dampened its lips. There was a long pause. It looked at me with ember eyes. "Knives," it growled. "And yours?" The fox opened its mouth, showing me its deadly, sharp fangs. It was clear they were sharper than any blade, at least anything I had ever seen. The pumpkin-colored beast rolled its head toward me, showing me its chin.

Being this close I could see his fur for what it was. I brought my hand ahead, hesitant. The beast's fur gave way in certain areas, though in others it seemed solid, as if steel grating—as if his fur was fluid.

"Nexus," I finally said.

Knives didn't speak. The large fox took a few steps away, then found a spot on the floor and laid down. He also got in perfect striking distance, I noted.

Something appeared off. I didn't know why, but my instinct (though I had no point of reference) told me I shouldn't have so readily told Knives my name. If names were so important, then was the Otherworld like Union City? Was the world huge, but at the same time tiny? Though Union City was the largest city land mass-wise in the United States, everyone knew everyone, or of everyone. If you heard a name, you likely knew someone who knew someone who knew them—or knew them yourself. You never gave someone your name, not until you knew why they were asking.

"Question?" I asked as I looked at Voss and Knives.

Voss tapped the end of his cigarette, letting the ash drip off into the glass tray on the bar top. "I might have an answer," he replied.

I had to make sure I worded my thoughts how I wanted. I barely knew what was going on. Trying to ask logical questions almost felt impossible. "In the Otherworld, are all... demons connected?" I asked. "You know, so did Claudy and Symon know of Knives before your meeting in our world and vice versa?"

Knives eyes lowered. "For the most part, that could be seen as a true statement," he said. "Of course, there are some higher-level demons that slip through unnoticed. But any demon strong enough to reach higher-level is known in some capacity."

I thought. "Then couldn't the same be said of their humans?"

Knives grinned, though he never responded. I took the silence as the answer I was looking for. If that was the case, I had to be careful who I gave my name to. If they knew my name, they knew who named me, and we could both be in danger... Which brought me back to square one with the large, looming questions. Who named me, why, and when? I watched the room.

I turned back to Voss who was taking another slow sip of whiskey.

"So I'm guessing the cat was with you guys then, too?" I asked. He placed the whiskey down.

"Cat?" Voss lit his cigarette, his eyes lowered to me.

"Yeah," I replied. "Whenever things first started getting weird the other day, there was this cat. I ended up following it to the alley where I was attacked." I remembered everything so vividly. My heart sped up. "I just remember its eyes, golden, like nothing I've ever seen before. It was there in the park, too."

Voss glanced at Knives with what I assumed to be a concerned look or maybe it was something else entirely. He packed the box of cigarettes in his hand. "Interesting," he said. "What do you think?"

Knives lay on the floor, getting comfortable. "Not sure. I don't know the name Nexus. And I don't know of any demons attached to a human named such." Knives closed his eyes, and his body rose and lowered slowly with each breath.

"So do you know the cat or not? I'm confused," I asked, pressing.

Gyle shook his head. "Not a clue," he responded.

As soon as I thought things were lining up, another curve ball was thrown at me. I would have put my last dollar that they had something to do with the creepy cat. I guess it was a good thing I wasn't a betting man. But if they weren't the ones who it was with… Then where the hell had it come from?

Voss's phone rang.

He took it from his pocket, turned his back to us, and answered it. Smoke still billowed above his head as he nodded a few times and gave a few words of understanding. His voice was steeled as he responded. Whatever was said on the other line couldn't have been good, but his outward appearance remained calm. Voss tapped his cigarette on the ashtray before he hung up the phone.

"What was that about?" Gyle asked.

Voss checked his watch. "More of the same," he said. "I need to check on a few things. More activity." He turned to me and tapped me on the shoulder. "Everyone's story is different, but that's why it's your story." He smiled genuinely. "Or something like that."

"Wait, what's going on?" I scanned the room, confused.

"Would you believe me if I told you?" Voss ground his cigarette into the ashtray. He started for the door and waved his hand at Knives. Voss pointed at Gyle. "Be on standby."

Gyle nodded.

I slumped back in the chair. "Can you pour me a drink?" I asked. "Whatever you have."

"Whiskey it is," he said. He grabbed a bottle from the middle shelf of the bar. "Voss's preferred, so the place is stocked full of it."

Gyle walked behind the bar and poured a glass a third of the way with a brand of whiskey that was normally too expensive for me to think of drinking. I gulped enough to burn my throat and everything it touched on the way down. We didn't speak for several minutes. I thought over everything that'd happened—everything I'd seen. I took another drink, rubbing my eyes.

"You vouched for me?" I asked.

Gyle waved a hand. "I didn't really do much," he said. "I just told him the truth. You don't remind me of any Hybrid I've ever met before, And at the very least, you can be trusted."

"What do other Hybrids act like?"

"Hmm, good question," he said. "Now you're getting it." He chuckled a bit as he thought. "Well... To be honest, they're paranoid, introverted, and scared. A lot of them have been hunted for years, always looking over their shoulders. Eventually, they get so paranoid they tend to lock themselves away from the world. Or on the other, they become so aggressive anything that gets near them dies." Gyle rubbed at his dreads. "But you on the other hand... Well, you're as harmless as a bee in a glass cup."

None of those fates sounded like options I wanted for myself. Yet Gyle stood there, smiling as if things were normal. "How can you be so sure?" I shook my head. "At this point, I'm not even sure how any of this happened. I wouldn't trust me. I can't even trust myself right now."

He rubbed Claudy's head. "This little lady right here. Her eyes see more than our eyes could ever hope." Gyle grabbed another bottle of water. He leaned against the bar, cracking his back. "Trust me, I didn't want to believe half of this shit either when it first happened to me."

My hands were glued to the cup. "Say I do believe you, then what? I'm supposed to keep letting all this weird shit happen to me?" I glared at Gyle. "What do you guys even want with me?"

Claudy jumped onto Gyle's shoulder. Her violet eyes flickered around the room, before fixating on me. "Hybrids have become targets as of late," she said. There was a level of concern that came with her words. "Over the last two months, two Hybrids have been killed in other cities. Hybrids are a rarity in the first place, so if someone decided to start hunting us, we'd go extinct quickly. Here in Union City, Otherworld activity has picked up recently. And then there's you."

"And then there's me? What's that supposed to mean?"

"Like I said, you're harmless," Gyle said. "So that takes away any thought that you're the one causing the trouble. The safety of all the Hybrids in Union City is our top priority. I said we can trust you, but that doesn't mean your situation isn't alarming. Finding out what the hell is going on comes next." He crossed his arms across his chest, thinking. "Voss is keeping tabs on Otherworld activity in other cities as much as he can, and it hasn't been looking good."

I looked around the room. "So we're all the Hybrids in Union City," I said as I drank more.

"Just about," Gyle said. He shook his head in disappointment. "There's one more that we've been trying to get a hold of, but they're not really the type for group projects."

I placed my head against the bar top. "Shit." No matter how much I wanted to believe this was all a dream, I doubted Gyle was the type to blatantly lie. Voss seemed more of the same. I finished the rest of my drink, grabbed the bottle, and poured myself another round. I finished the next round faster than the first. For several minutes I drank, then drank some more, then placed my head back on the cold bar top.

An hour later, things became foggy.

Gyle poured me a shot and a bottle of water and said, "Drink both." He did that more than once, but I quit counting after the third. When I finished the water, Gyle handed me one more bottle of water, this time alone.

"No shot this time?" I asked, surprised.

Gyle shook his head though he looked more like a mirage at this point. "You're cut off," he said. "You had your time to drink yourself into a wreck." He shrugged. "You had me to supervise you. As far as I'm concerned, everyone gets a freebie. Now finish that water or you're gonna hate yourself in the morning."

I couldn't comprehend Gyle at the moment, but I got the gist of it. In the end, he was looking out for me or something like that. Which, to be honest, meant a lot, seeing as he didn't know me in any way. Call it intuition, but something told me he wasn't someone who I should be on the defense about. Even if he did scare me half to death when I first met him. I drank the water in a daze. I remembered trying to move, but my body didn't respond how I envisioned. Gyle came to my side, helping me walk. "Whoa, there, champ," he said. I wished he would have stopped me three or four drinks ago. But who was I kidding, I wouldn't have taken his advice. Hell, I didn't even remember getting this drunk.

"Th-Thanks," I said, slurring. "You know... You're much nicer than your appearance will give you. Maybe you aren't such a bad guy."

"You know, that's exactly what I needed to hear," Gyle said.

Holding my liquor wasn't one of my strongest attributes. Yet I got through most of the whole bottle. I stumbled along with Gyle's assistance. He took me down a hall across from where Quin sat playing her game. There was room after room on either side of the hallway leading down to a final door at the end. I wanted to puke as I gazed down the hall, the length of it ballooning and deflating every other second.

"Holy shit. There's a... ton... of rooms," I said eventually.

"Yeah, this is Syler's safehouse, and he built it to accommodate as much space as possible, sort of like a hotel."

I burped. "Or like a boarding school." At least that's what I thought I said.

"What?" Gyle leaned in a little closer to me. When I said nothing, he kept walking. "Don't worry. The rooms will be nice, trust me."

We came to a room, past a couple of others, on the left. Gyle opened the door to a bed in the center of the spinning room. He tossed me down before heading back to the door.

"Get some rest," he said. "We'll talk in the morning."

I grunted a response. The spins took control for a few minutes, tumbling over and over and over, in the washing machine of life. Somewhere between the end of the wash and the spin cycle, I found myself in a whiskey-filled slumber.

7

I blinked my eyes open, groaning. My head throbbed, my mouth was a desert, and my body felt like it had been used as a crash dummy. My eyes felt like they had needles poking into the back of them. I sat up and placed my hand on my head, rubbing at my temples. My body was covered in sheets that felt too soft to be affordable, and a bed too big to be mine. It was low to the ground, a floating bed. The moonlight illuminated the room enough for me to make out figures. There was a bathroom to my right, a small sofa (like that was even needed in a room with a bed already), and a work desk with a lamp.

When I gazed before me, my body became ice, frozen in time. A set of golden eyes stared into my soul from the edge of the bed. I knew those eyes; they were the same ones that belonged to the cat that decided to plague my life.

I scampered back and slammed into the headboard. I tried to scream, but there was a force holding my mouth closed, or maybe it was tightening my throat. No matter what I did, my lips wouldn't part. It was as if my lips were sewn together, and a rope was tied around my throat. A lamp in the corner of the room lit up, letting me see the cat that sat at my feet licking its paw. "I'm going to say this one time, and one time only: if you scream, I'll rip out your throat."

The cat made a gesture with its paw. I felt the force that bound my lips release its hold. Almost instinctively, I screamed. It wasn't my smartest decision, and it could have very well gotten me killed—but I was terrified and not thinking clearly.

"And you're an idiot," the cat said, disappointed. I drew in my words and held them for ransom. The cat continued. "You humans *really* are as dumb as you look. Aren't much of the listening type, either, I see." The cat examined me for a minute, then purred deeply. "Do me a favor now, will ya?" The beast waited patiently until I acknowledged him, nodding. "You being here must be some sort of mistake. I'm looking for a man called Nev Nox. Where is he?"

That name would forever be burned into my mind. Though it wasn't one I ever thought of or wanted to think about. I would cheer the day I could finally rid myself of it and move on. Yet here I was, brought face-to-face with Nev again. It wasn't every day that I heard my father's name. Though my response would have been the same no matter the situation. "Sorry, I can't help you." My life being in danger didn't matter any longer.

The demon cat stepped closer to me, his eyes lowered, then sat once more. "So you do know him," he said, missing the "can't" in my sentence. "Go ahead and point me to him, and I'll be out of your way."

Maybe it was my petty nature, but I enjoyed what I said next more than I should have. "He's dead," I said. The words came off my tongue like syrup, yet they felt like poison to utter.

"Dead?"

"Dead. Deceased, in the ground, not coming back up." My face said more than words ever could. "Get it?"

"Save the melodrama." The cat put a paw up to me as if putting me on hold. He pondered over a few thoughts, then turned back to me. "But you do know of him, though? Who is he to you?"

"Why does it matter?" I asked.

A force gripped at my throat, making it hard to breathe. I clawed at my neck, but the grip only got tighter.

"Now I'm going to ask you this again, and I want you to tell me the answer. Simple." The cat swiped the air with a claw. The force loosened. I gasped, taking in all the air I had once taken for granted. My body finally relaxed after a coughing spell. I tried to regain my composure.

DEMONOLOGY

"H-He's my father," I said reluctantly. By this time, I was thoroughly pissed.

The kitten cocked its head to the side. "You've got to be shitting me," the cat said. "You're Nev's brat? Has it already been that long?"

Nev's brat... I hadn't had someone mention my father's name, let alone associate me with him since I was a child. As far as I was concerned, that name had nothing to do with me. I gripped the blanket, ready to make my move, but then the cat chimed in once more. "If I was you, I wouldn't do that," he said. "It would only annoy me. Let me think in peace."

I let go of the blanket, feeling more useless now than before.

I reached for the lamp on the nightstand next to the bed and fumbled around until I pressed a button that turned the light on. The room came into view. Voss had fine taste. I take back my previous boarding school statement. There would be a waiting list for boarding school if the rooms looked like this. This place was *pinkies-up* fancy. But now that the lights were on, I was even more terrified, not because the cat's appearance brought me fear but because it didn't. He was as cute as any other black kitten roaming the streets. I wasn't the pet guy, but I can acknowledge cats are cute when they aren't destroying everything you love.

The cat inched around the bed, finally jumping onto my legs, then thighs. "The link... It's been gone for as long as I can remember," he said. "It's already been decades. It's faint, but I can feel it now." The cat reached its paw toward my chest. Its paw pads cooled my body through my clothes, though something inside of me swelled with a warm embrace. The cat put its paw on my left pec and then traced my body. Its claw dug into my skin. I panicked at first, but then I realized I felt no pain. My body didn't brace against the claw, nor stood in its way. Instead, the claw slid through my body as if it were air.

"Nexus." The cat purred. My body was entrapped in a sensation far beyond anything I had experienced before. Everything turned cool as if I sat under a waterfall—yet it burned with an ardent flame. I felt weightless and motionless; my body was not my own any longer. It was his to do what he wanted, and he knew it.

I stared into the golden orbs of the demon cat, then said the name. His name. "Nyx."

The demon purred once more as it pulled its claw from my chest.

The world around me returned to whatever normal was. "So, you're the boy from that day," Nyx said. He paced back and forth on the bed. "Well, this solves the most pressing issue. I don't need Nev after all. You're the one I've been looking for."

I touched my chest where Nyx's claw had been. "You're looking for me?" I asked. "Why?"

"You heard correct," he said. "Seeing as your father broke the bond between us, I've been searching for you ever since. When I realized it was impossible, I went to find Nev to hopefully get to you."

"Well, he's dead," I said. I swung my feet off the bed and got to my feet. Maybe it was foolish, but I didn't feel like I was in any immediate danger. Which also meant I didn't have to sit here and put up with shit. I wasn't under arrest. "Look, I don't mean to be rude, and honestly, I'm really starting to believe the whole demon and Otherworld thing. But if you aren't going to kill me, I'd like to go. All this talk about my father and Hybrids has got my head jumbled up."

A low-toned alarm with a steady wailing hum echoed through the warehouse. *Perfect, now what?* I walked to the door. Whatever this sound was, it got its point across. Annoying as hell—check. My head pounded, my body ached, and I was dehydrated beyond belief. All I wanted was a cold Gatorade and sleep. I opened the door and looked outside. Quin peered down the hallway, though she didn't seem as worried as I was. She took one glance at me, yawned, placed her earbuds back in her ears, then closed and locked her door.

Nyx walked from between my legs into the hallway. He poked his nose into the air, sniffing around. "Ahh, looks like we have some company," he said. Nyx traveled down the hall as if he hadn't a bit of a care in the world. I waited. Were they here for me again? If there was something out there, where the hell would I be safe? Shit. I ended up following. No matter what the case was, I needed to get to my car and get the hell out of here. *Hopefully, I can get out before whatever Nyx was talking about arrives.* We came back to the large common area where the sound of the alarm was louder.

I caught a glimpse of Gyle striding toward the sliding door that led to the front. It seemed he was too concerned about what was occurring to even notice me walking in his direction. I followed him through the main hall that led outside. The closer I got, the more I had an uneasy feeling—one like the night at the bar and at the park.

Nyx turned his head to me while keeping a steady pace. "You feel it too, right?" he asked. I nodded but didn't speak. The sensation was dark, muggy, like being submerged in a swamp amid the night. There was a thundering scrape against the large window to my left. I fell back in fright, hitting my body against the adjacent wall. Nyx rolled his eyes. "Get moving."

I hesitantly pushed myself from the ground and stumbled after Nyx. We passed through the first door and back into the small neighboring hall. Nyx stopped in front of the steel door and pointed his nose toward it. "Open it," he ordered.

"How?" I asked. I looked around. "I don't see a button or anything to open it."

Nyx sighed. "Slide it open," he said.

"I think you have way more faith in me than you should," I said. "There's no way I can open that door." Who did Nyx think I was? I went to the gym, but nobody would mistake me for a bodybuilder. This door could weigh a ton. There was no way I could move it.

"Do it!" Nyx ordered.

A force commanded me. I couldn't quite make it out. When I moved, it wasn't against my will. It was almost like I was being pressured into opening the door—but the sensation felt exhilarating. I gripped the handle, planted my feet into the ground, and yanked with everything I had. At first, nothing happened. But then, I heard metal turning. I pulled harder. Inch by inch, the door reacted to my pull, until it opened enough for Nyx and myself to pass through. I placed my hands on my knees, breathing hard. Nyx licked his lips as he walked through.

"Your strength will grow as our bond grows," he said.

I rose and looked at my hands. Wait... *Our bond?* Did he mean he was *my* demon, like Knives was to Voss, or Claudy and Symon were to Gyle? I should know my own strength better than anyone, yet my body felt alien. Even now, if I was being honest with myself, for the liquor I drank, I should have felt much worse, unable to fully function until the late afternoon. But I was weirdly all right.

Nyx stalked through the door with feline confidence, knowing I was close behind him.

Midnight darkness filled the sky. Gyle stood a few meters from the building, Claudy and Symon on either shoulder. He turned to me, his eyes bright violet. "What the hell are you doing?" he shouted. "Get back inside."

"Quiet, human," Nyx retorted. Gyle froze. I half expected Symon to respond, but he remained silent. Only the wind spoke, whispering quiet remarks in our ears. Nyx scanned the area and then looked at me. "Rise, Nexus." His bellowing voice pulled me. With the call of my name, I felt something inside of me rising to the surface. A force full of malice pulled at my being, telling me to let it engulf me—and trying to take control. And everything inside of me wanted it to.

I relished the sublime, letting it do what it wanted with me. It was like I was drinking from a pool of unlimited malice. Could something harbor this much hate? It made my chest tighten just thinking of it. The sensation weighed me down as much as it lifted me up. It felt like I just scored a touchdown and found out I didn't get picked for the basketball team all at the same time. I couldn't pinpoint any one emotion; they flipped as fast as I could process them.

The feeling brought me close, tempting me to draw on its power more. I had no idea what it was, that foreign energy that wanted me to take it as my own. I followed it down that path, letting the pool take me further into its depths. A figure appeared of a thick midnight miasma, though I knew it was Nyx. I could feel the bond he had spoken of that connected us. Nyx walked on top of the pool as if he wielded the waters. His paws rippled but they didn't sink.

Nyx didn't speak. Instead, he watched me silently. My body floated there somehow, even though I knew I couldn't swim. Nyx circled me. I tried to speak, but nothing happened. More silence. Then Nyx kept walking over the hate-filled waters until he was out of sight. Darkness. I was left alone in the darkness with nowhere to turn. Unless… I wasn't supposed to turn from it at all. Or better yet, it didn't want me to turn from it. The energy was mine to do what I wanted. That power excited and terrified me. What was I supposed to do with it?

This power was mine, that was the one thing I was very certain of. Every drop of this pool would be mine if I so desired. I shut my eyes as a fiery sensation touched my skin. As my body warmed, I let my mind wander of thoughts somewhere between destruction and possibilities.

But then that annoying voice in my head, the one that chimed in when I happened to be having too much fun, called out to me. It made sure to let me know how much of a dumbass I was being, and that I was making a mistake. Oh, how I wished that voice wouldn't interfere in my life. I fought against the darkness instead of letting it swallow me whole. My body rose inch by inch until I was sitting on top of the water. I sat alone, listening to the silence. The ghastly form of Nyx returned until it was across from me, as if we were pawns in our own chess game.

When I opened my eyes again and realized where I was, Gyle was standing in front of me waving his hands. "Yo, you good?" He continued shouting until I finally grabbed his hand and responded, "Yeah."

Gyle stepped away from me. My eyes traced his every move. Every subtle twitch became another note.

The sensation from before grew. I could feel some energy—foul, sloppy—navigating around the building. "What's that?"

"Demons," Gyle said. "Not sure how many."

Nyx twisted his body through my leg. "Three. All Seed demons."

I raised a brow. "*Three?*" I questioned "Seeds? What the hell is going on?

"Demons without purpose," Nyx said. "They live in search of *voltage* they can absorb in hopes of becoming a Germs to Synth demons." Nyx waited for me to process that bit of information.

"And voltage is?" I asked.

"Power, energy… or voltage—volt for short," Gyle chimed in.

"Similar to the demons you've encountered thus far," Nyx said.

"They will attack anything with voltage they think they can destroy. Easy prey."

"Or more simply put, *me*," I said. I thought back to the times I'd been attacked in the recent days.

Nyx grinned. "Ahh, now you're getting it. Though they might come to realize you aren't such easy prey any longer."

Gyle's head shot around the area as he chased something in the distance with his eyes. "They're here," he said. He walked further into the lot, then turned around toward the building. Gyle cleared his throat, then held up three fingers. "Before I tell you the deal, I'll preface it with the fact that I will only give this offer once!" he shouted.

From behind the building, two figures appeared. One of the fiend's bodies was much larger than it should have been in one area. Its upper body had muscle upon muscle, while its legs looked like it missed more than a few days at the gym. Thick cord-like veins ran from its neck, going in every direction. Long hair covered its face, but I could vaguely see a murky, green hue appearing from where its eyes should have been.

The other demon resembled a snake, somewhat, at least. Its body was seven to eight feet tall, with plated scales covering every inch. That's as far as its snakelike appearance held. When it opened its mouth, it was more akin to a shark than any snake. Its teeth jutted out in a cascade of rows, filling any available gum space. Near the front of its body were two legs, like a lizard, though it didn't have any back legs. The beast's tongue flapped out, licking its filmy eye as it blinked at me.

"Wow, you two really need to work on your skincare," Gyle said. "If you need any help, go ahead and call me." The misshaped demon made a clicking noise that sounded like a chipmunk carving the outer layer of a nut. Gyle used his other hand to point back to his three fingers. "Annnyyyway, back to the point... If you guys go ahead and get out of here before I get pissed, I'll let you survive. No questions asked. I'll give you three seconds."

Neither of the demons moved.

"One!"

They stepped closer.

"Two!"

They came closer again, only this time they both angled themselves better on Gyle.

"Three," Gyle said. Gyle hissed his teeth as he shook his head. "And I thought we could solve this without violence. Bad choice. Symon."

Nyx sat back and licked his paw, watching.

"Yeah, yeah, yeah," Symon huffed. "Don't rush me." Symon scamped about on Gyle's shoulder. The ferret rose to all fours and wailed, his black-and-white fur standing. A violet light filled the night sky, then darkness returned. Symon disappeared, but now, Gyle held a pistol in his hand. The weapon was black-and-white, with what looked like little hairs covering the entirety. Gyle clicked the hammer back and placed his index finger on what would have been the trigger, though it looked more like the bottom of a tiny paw.

"Make this quick," Symon echoed.

Gyle rubbed the barrel of the pistol, drawing a subtle purr from Symon. "Plan on it," he said. Claudy stood atop Gyle's left shoulder, her eyes flipping from demon to demon. My eyes moved to the heavy breathing of the humanoid demon. It was then that the snake demon slithered ahead.

"To the right," Claudy said without removing her eyes from the other foe. After a few seconds, Gyle pointed the pistol to the right without turning his body and pulled the trigger.

Violet light sprung from the barrel, and a bullet pierced through the back of the snake's mouth and curved into his body. The snake slammed onto its side, twitching as it flicked its tongue at Gyle one last time.

Claudy raised one of her small front legs. A small translucent purple barrier rose above Gyle's shoulder. The venomous liquid the snake shot splattered on the barrier. It crept down the shield slowly, dripping to the ground, burning into the earth. Gyle turned his head to the reptilian creature and pulled Symon's trigger twice more. More purple shots struck the snake demon, drawing blood and then the creature burst into a blackish-red mist.

The bad-bodied demon sprang into action. It swung its massive arms at Gyle, though it seemed off balance. Gyle placed his arms in a cross-guard, taking the heavy full brunt of the blow. He took the attack and chuckled a bit. I heard how heavy the strike was from here, yet Gyle's body barely moved an inch.

"Ohh, so you're supposed to be the strong one, huh?" Gyle said. He let the weight of the demon shift, then kicked at its right knee. I heard the bone shatter into puzzle-like pieces that'd never find their way together again. The demon fell, bringing its head almost level with Gyle. Gyle shoved Symon into the skull of his enemy. "Shoulda took the deal." He pulled the trigger. The demon cried out as blood spewed from its head.

Something felt off. The hairs on the back of my neck stood stiff. That uncomfortable feeling that I had earlier hadn't left—it only grew. A sense of cold pricked my skin, enough to make me shiver. I looked at Nyx. "You said there were three, right?"

Nyx stared at me with irritated eyes. "I prefer not repeating myself."

I turned my body and scanned the area. Then I saw it, standing atop the building, watching us. It was a tall creature, its skin a grayish black. Its arms swung below its knees and its back hunched over. It didn't make a sound. Instead, it jumped from the building and scurried swiftly to the humanoid demon. It reached its long arms down and gripped the head of its fallen brethren. My stomach knotted as I watched the Otherworld's natural order put on display in front of my eyes. It wanted easy and accessible voltage. Before it even thought about coming after us, it was going to finish the easiest prey. Agonizing roars filled the night, then soon, more silence. The demon's throat expanded as it devoured its meal. It went for more as if we weren't there, scarfing down what used to be part of a neck. The long-armed demon licked its bloodstained jaws as it turned its head to us.

Before our eyes, it changed. Joints cracked and bones broke as the demon's figure restructured. Its arms twisted around before curving, its bones shattering more. Blood and another liquid oozed from the demon's arms as they morphed into long scythes. Its eyes grew brighter and held a different light than the other demons. It opened its mouth and spit at me. I only reacted enough to move my head a few inches. The saliva solidified, cutting my cheek as it grazed my skin.

"Fuck," I screamed, holding my hand against my cheek, feeling warm liquid. "No. I have to get out of here!"

Nyx stepped ahead. "Come," he said. "It's our turn. Time to see what we can do."

My body warmed with a refreshing sensation. I took my hand from my cheek, expecting to see it coated with blood, but it was clean of any stains. I touched my hand to my cheek again, but no blood came. In fact, there wasn't even a trace of where I'd been cut. I knew I wanted to go, but I couldn't. The situation wouldn't allow it.

I watched Nyx. He was serious. How the hell had I gotten myself into this position? Our scythe-armed foe let out a shriek of its own. *Shit, shit, shit.*

8

The fur on Nyx's body stood. His tail puffed as it shot up. It was faint, but I saw a goldish-black miasma rising from his body and felt the gathering of voltage. When Nyx released his volts, I realized how dangerous he was—and how much it affected me. My body temperature rose. I glanced at my hands to see the same miasma emitting from my body. Or better yet, Nyx drew it from my body. He roared, which shattered nearby windows and set off car alarms. I covered my eyes momentarily. When I lowered my arm, I barely recognized what stood where Nyx had.

Nyx's small form had vanished. Now, a large black jaguar stood in his place. His legs were thick, strong, and ready to propel at any prey. Nyx's tail whipped back and forth before he turned to me, yawning. His face was ferocious, and the lovable look he once had was now gone. His new form was made for killing. His fangs gleamed as if daggers, and his golden eyes stared into me.

"It seems I can take my true form once more," Nyx said. He stretched his body out in front of me. I heard every bone cracking as he let out a pleasurable purr. Nyx plopped on his side, staring at the scythe-armed demon. His tail swept the ground. "Come now, don't make me wait all day."

The demon hesitated, if only for a second—but it was enough for me to notice its fear. Nyx, while relaxed, made this demon think twice before it attacked. It came at us, swinging its scythe arms at Nyx. The blade chimed as it struck earth and reverberated through the demon's body. I stepped back. The demon's dull, emerald eyes shifted to me.

Nyx reappeared a few feet to the left as if he ripped a hole in the world itself. He licked his lips, inching closer to his prey. "That one is mine," he said. "I suggest you take your filthy eyes off of him."

There was more hesitation in the demon's actions. But still, its primal instincts took hold—violent greed. It came towards me with sluggish moves. Its actions were simplistic. It swayed as it watched me. It only wanted one thing—to devour me. I wasn't about to sit around and let it have its fill. I darted to the right, trying to gain distance. My body felt weightless. I wasn't slow by any means. My days playing football made sure of that. But my normal speed was nothing compared to how fast I could run now.

A scythe arm cut me off. I stopped but fell, unable to control my own speed. Holy shit. I never would have imagined going that fast. My heart raced. I watched the demon's bladed arm rise and whisper death as it sliced through the night. Red-blue sparks flew. Nyx stood over me, his large paws pressed into the ground—his tail, now a large black curved blade, pressing into the demon's bladed arm. I watched it in terror. My life had almost ended. So easily everything could have been done. No more gym, no more dreams of selling my novels—game over. I couldn't move. I couldn't collect myself enough to make any sort of reaction.

Nyx roared. The demon chose the smart option and backed away, at least until it could assess the situation. "Pick another time to feel sorry for yourself," Nyx said.

Any fear I had was replaced with anger—relentless, uncontrollable rage.

I felt the fury piling up on itself. Everything from this week, coupled with the mention of my father, all my emotions threatened to engulf me. I gazed at the demon.

"You know," I began. I loosened the top button of my shirt. "I'm getting real pissed off. I think I need to blow off some steam."

Nyx grinned, his feline excitement rising. A part of me knew what I was doing. Nyx's emotions were the same as mine. They were linked. I felt it as much as Nyx. My anger fueled him, while his violent excitement threatened to push me off a cliff.

"Don't become too hasty," Nyx said. "This one's mine."

There was no point arguing. I would become mincemeat if I jumped into the fray prematurely. It was better for me to leave the stunts to Nyx for now. But that didn't mean there was nothing for me to do. I felt our voltage. I knew the power we shared. And I was going to make sure this demon knew it, too. I let all the malice, all the anger, all the rage fuel my words as I spoke death. "Nyx," I said. The demon black jaguar glanced at me over his shoulder. "Kill it." I pointed at the lesser demon.

Nyx licked his lips. It all happened before I could take a breath. Nyx planted his paws, spun on his front legs, then swiped his tail at the demon's arms. Instead of colliding, Nyx's curved tail cut clean through his enemy's weapons as if they were nothing but straw. The fiend shrieked in agony—blood showering the ground. Nyx swiped again, this time slicing its arms where the forearms should have been, then to the elbow. I could see the fear in its eyes, telling it to run, to get as far from this place as possible.

That excited Nyx or maybe me. Our emotions had intertwined so much already that I couldn't tell which. I didn't have to speak my thoughts; I knew my emotions were reaching Nyx. This demon wasn't leaving. It would die here with that same fear illuminating its eyes.

Nyx pressed his right paw into the ground. The demon fell under an invisible weight. Its body squelched as if it were a deflating balloon. Nyx strode beside the demon. He sat down, licking one of his paws. "Filth," he purred. His tail whipped around and settled on the neck of the demon. Its head lopped off, and then the demon's body burst into a black-red mist.

My thoughts returned to normal as the rage left my body. My lungs felt cold, and my breaths were heavy. I blinked as the world returned to normal around me. What the hell was that sensation?

Nyx walked until he was near me again. "Order me like that again, and that demon's head won't be the only one that comes off," he said. There was a golden flash, and Nyx reappeared in his *cute* form.

I scanned the aftermath. Gyle crouched where one of the demons was slain. Claudy pointed and said something in his ear. I couldn't begin to wrap my mind around what just happened. The world around me was breaking apart. This wasn't a simple difference between real and fake. There were things far beyond my understanding occurring—whether I wanted to believe it or not. What mattered now was finding out as much as I could about whatever the hell was happening. I couldn't handle being left in the dark any longer.

"Tell me," I said. Gyle continued a conversation with Claudy and Symon. "Tell me what the hell is going on."

Gyle sighed, adjusting his jacket. "Believe me now, huh?" he said. "Sure you don't want to write it off as some cheap trick and run to the cops?"

"First of all, the cops would probably do more harm than good if they came here." I took a deep breath. "Besides... The way that I feel right now is no trick."

Gyle's expression hardened. I stared at the scar climbing from his neck to his face. "You know, there's three kinds of people who encounter the Otherworld. The first person is one who avoids it and acts like it isn't real. They always have some sort of explanation for what they see. The second person goes mad and is consumed by their own paranoia. How is someone supposed to process finding out all their biggest fears are real? That at any moment they can be swallowed whole by their own nightmares?"

"Who's the third person?" I asked.

"The third..." Gyle tapped my shoulder, smiling. "The third person realizes the threat and looks like a fool to the rest of the world, trying to protect them from it."

"Not many good options," I said. I followed behind Gyle.

"Not many choices at all," he responded.

9

I sat and stared at Nyx and the rest of the demons in the room. Learning from my previous mistakes, I drank some water as I gathered my thoughts. A piece of me wanted to become the person who acted as if everything I had seen was all some elaborate joke—but I knew that was impossible. I'd end up turning into the second type of person Gyle described, going crazy from looking over my shoulder.

After several minutes of sitting in silence, I asked, "How common are demons and Hybrids?"

"Depends on what you mean," Gyle responded. "Sort of a two-part question." He tapped his fingers against his face as he thought. "First things first. We're not dealing with scary movie exorcist-type stuff. All of that is still fake. Even if that movie franchise will outlive cockroaches. But if you mean someone whose body is taken hostage by a demon, it is very common. Much more common than you'd think, truthfully. Though if you talkin' like a Hybrid, like you or me—rare." Gyle's eyes hardened, though he still seemed entirely calm. "Demons aren't much of the haunting type More of the slit your throat and drink your blood type. Cute, right?"

His words were heavy, as if there was no way to deny the truth in them. I nodded. That's what I had thought. Looking at the recent events, there was no way most demons could ever manage to make a bond with a human. I shuddered thinking of it. They would devour and feed upon a person until there was nothing left.

My eyes turned to Nyx. Something told me he would have done the same to me if he had the opportunity. Whether I wanted to or not, I felt Nyx's emotions—his hate, his disgust for the demon even thinking he was prey... It all poured into me when we fought.

Which made me wonder why he hadn't devoured me already. There was no way I would have been able to protect myself against him. "When we were fighting, I felt different, like my body wasn't my own."

"Your body isn't your own anymore, honey," Claudy said. She crawled to the edge of Gyle's shoulder before sitting. "Think of your body as a hub for both you and your partner; a hub to draw upon your voltage. Your body is no longer your own to do with as you please."

That piece of information was unsettling, but no matter how badly I wanted it to be untrue—I knew it wasn't. Before, I couldn't have fathomed such a concept. Yet now, I couldn't help but feel the bond between Nyx and I. Something so foreign, so strong. Why did it choose now to finally rear its head?

"What if something...What happens if I—"

"If you die?" Gyle said. "Like Claudy said, you're the hub. Something happens to you, and it's over for both of ya." He rubbed Claudy's head. "Which is why I have to make sure I'm in tip-top shape. Can't have nothing happening to these guys here."

"I was actually going to ask how I'm ever supposed to have sex if we're connected. I feel like it could probably get a bit awkward, you know, with us feeling each other's emotions and all." I rubbed at my temples. "But I put two and two together about what happens if one of us dies a little while ago. It only makes sense."

Gyle laughed. "You aren't wrong," he said. "The odds are stacked pretty high against us. But good news for you. The stronger your bond, the better you'll both get at filtering what needs to be there and what doesn't. So you'll be able to enjoy your 'alone' time, to an extent."

Nyx opened one eye slightly, he peered at me from a resting position. I fiddled with the water bottle before drinking some more. Minutes of silence passed by. It was clear Gyle didn't want to press. He had let me ask all the questions, answering them as they came. There was probably merit to his tactic. He was once in my shoes. I was sure he understood how I felt. Plus, if he bombarded me with more facts than I could handle, I might feel like I'm drowning. Hell, I was drowning.

"What do you guys do?" I asked.

Gyle came around the bar and sat in the chair next to me. "We're the fools that protect those that don't believe," he replied.

"So, what, you're like some demon-hunting Power Rangers of Union City?"

"Don't get the wrong idea It's not like we don't have any stake in this, too. Demons follow voltage. When they feed enough, they grow, as you saw. Better for us to kill them when they're Seeds than to let them evolve. Pretty simple decision, when you think about it." Gyle sighed. "Or at least, it was simple, until recently. These doors to the Otherworld keep opening, and we can barely keep up with it. And it's not just Union City. Voss's in contact with Hybrids in other cities, and it's much of the same."

Selfishly, my mind was still on the troubles in Union City. With my encounters, I've been lucky to make it out alive. What if those situations had involved someone who couldn't protect themselves? Or someone who couldn't move quickly enough to get away? Would anyone even believe what happened or would the murder of so many innocent people be bottled into a simple missing persons case? It horrified me to even think of how often this occurred. How many lives were lost to Otherworld beings that the cops or city just deemed to be unsolved cases? If I was too stubborn to believe, I doubt the cops or anyone in power would be so ready to jump on board.

Gyle reached into his pocket, pulling out his cell phone. "Fuck," he said under his breath. He rubbed at his temples. I wondered about the last time he got a good night's sleep. "You think you're up for a little trip?" he asked.

I checked my own phone, which I hadn't looked at since I arrived here last night. Nothing. God. I needed to enhance my social life. I finished my water. "I guess I can move my plans around," I said. Gyle didn't laugh. Maybe he didn't get the joke.

"Come on, you can practice your comedy act in the car." Gyle pulled his keys from his pocket.

I paused before we headed out the entrance. "What about Quin?"

Gyle continued. "She'll be fine. This building is protected by wards. It'll take a Synth demon comparable to Knives to break in here. She's safer here than with us."

No matter what Gyle said, that answer was unsettling. After what we just dealt with, there's no way I would feel at ease knowing Quin was in this building alone with whatever the hell was out there lurking about.

"Don't worry, we'll be back before long." There was a sense of reassurance in Gyle's tone that wasn't previously there. "She knows the routine. Believe me, you need to worry about yourself more than Quin. She's been with us for a few years now. This is nothing new to her."

As much as I didn't want to admit it, Gyle had a point. I have myself to worry about. I was still the one the most in the dark. The best I could do was try to learn as much as I could as quickly as possible. I looked at Nyx who opened one eye lazily at me. "You coming?" I asked.

Nyx rose, stretching. "It'll be much harder to lose you if I'm with you," he said. "I'm sure you'll be killed if I let you out of my sight." Nyx hopped from the table and walked toward the entrance. "Make sure to keep the car cool for me."

Gyle didn't speak. I'm not sure why, but I had an unsettling feeling watching their interaction. Maybe it was the pure fact that I knew Gyle wasn't the type to let anyone speak to him in that manner. His silence was deafening. Just what the hell was going on?

Gyle's car was parked at the edge of the lot, near the sidewalk. He drove one of the new Audi A5's. It had the image of something straight out of a sci-fi film. The car beeped unlocked as the engine revved to a subtle roar, and its white lights shone on the wall across the way. Of course, the car was also all white and managed to avoid a single blemish. The rims, and much of the interior, once I opened my door, were white leather. Nyx hopped into the back seat of the car and circled in place until he made himself comfortable.

"So slaying demons pays well, I'm guessing?" I asked.

Gyle jumped in the car, closing his door. "Slaying demons?" Gyle chuckled. "Hell, no. This isn't some video game where we kill demons and money drops out. I work in marketing. I help new companies grow in Northeast Florida. Social media, website creation, door-to-door if needed. All that type of stuff."

I nodded. That made sense, or at least more sense than anything else thus far. Gyle seemed like he had always been cooler than most. He probably never had that awkward phase where he didn't know where he'd fit in. Instead, he most likely was the person everyone tried to fit in with. Though he didn't strike me like the normal asshole that type of attention created. He had a neutrality about him, one that said he would've acted the way he did whether anyone liked him or not.

"I can see you as a marketing guy," I said. "Suits you." I glanced out the tinted windows once Gyle pulled out of the lot. "Where are we heading to?"

"The door that demon came out of at the park the other day opened back up," he said. He shifted gears. Of course, the car was a manual. I wouldn't have expected anything less. "We're going to head over there and close that bad boy up… Hopefully for good this time."

I checked my phone again. Time was ticking, and I still hadn't written anything for Tara. What's worse, I still didn't know where to start. No beginning. No end. Shit, I didn't even have a thought of the main character at this point. Nothing. My mind was such a jumble right now I would have been surprised if I could form a coherent sentence, let alone finish writing a novel to submit to Alekka.

We merged onto the highway leading toward downtown Union City. I watched as tawny lights passed by like little fireflies in the nighttime.

"So I have a dumb question," I began. Gyle glanced at me out of the corner of his eyes. "If that demon ate another one and got stronger, does that mean Nyx and—?"

"Don't be foolish," Nyx scoffed. "We're Synth demons. We can only gain power from killing other Synths. Feeding on that filth would do more harm than good."

In a way it made sense. Once you've made it so far in life, going back was always a hard thing to do. I guess it was similar when it came to feeding demons. The car's engine hummed a quiet tune as we coasted down the highway. I tapped my finger against my knee as I stared out the window.

"What did you want to be when you grew up when you were younger?" I asked.

"Huh?" Gyle stared at me with a confused gaze.

"You know, like, as a kid, what was the one thing you wanted to do when you grew up?"

Gyle tugged one of his dreads loose from his ponytail. "Shit... Man, I don't know. I never really thought about it much. I sort of just went with the flow my whole life. Guess you can say I sort of just ended up where I am. Flipped a coin and went with my gut." Gyle tapped his hand against the steering wheel. "Now that I think about it, probably not the best advice."

"Robert Frost would have been proud," I said. Gyle didn't budge. "The poet. He was a firm believer in his whole theory behind guessing and luck. Funny. One of the most famous poets in the world, and he made it seem like it all happened by simple chance."

"And that has to do with all of this, how?"

I shook my head, then shrugged. "I have no idea what I want anymore. Since I was a kid, I always dreamed of writing the next big fantasy novel. But honestly, now I wonder if I'd even be happy if I got there." I rested my head against my arm as I got lost in whatever was out the window. Sometimes I wondered if it was because I was an only child. I always wanted to create worlds, friendships, and unbreakable bonds—but that could very well be because those were all the things I never had growing up.

Don't get me wrong, it wasn't like I was upset about not having a family. There was a time a few years ago when I could truly say I was happy—and that came crashing down harder and faster than the whole thing started. But I was the only one to blame. You can't put your happiness in others. They will always let you down—or at least, that's what my jaded mind wanted me to believe. I knew at the core that wasn't true, but it made me feel better about the way everything ended. A sort of "fuck you" to anyone who's ever let me down, including myself.

Gyle leaned back in his seat with one arm still gripping the steering wheel. "A lot has happened in a short amount of time. Don't let it overwhelm you. You have to take it one step at a time. Trust me." He turned to me, grinning. "I don't know much about your fancy poets, but I do know a thing about marketing. You write something good, and I'll be sure the world sees it."

"Calm yourself," Nyx purred. He glared at me with cold eyes. "You let your emotions get out of control and you put us both in danger."

I reeled myself in and investigated the back seat. "I'm fine," I said.

"The stronger our bond becomes, the more our emotions intertwine. And honestly, at this time, I'd rather neither of us fall into depression."

I had a few words about my body being my own and being able to feel what I wanted with it. But in all honesty, it wouldn't change anything—and hell, Nyx was right. I remembered the emotions I felt during our fight with that demon. If it was anything like that, Nyx probably felt overwhelmed by my feelings now, too. Knowing something else could feel my emotions made me uncomfortable. My thoughts weren't sacred anymore. If there was one place that I never wanted anyone to travel to, it was the depths of my mind. Years of mandatory therapy finally equipped me with the tools to travel somewhat unharmed. Now, Nyx was living there rent-free. I took a few deep breaths and focused on the road again.

Gyle took the next exit, winding around the loop until we stopped at a red light. Downtown was always quiet but being down here before the sun rose seemed... wrong. We went down an alternate route that avoided the main road. As we neared, I knew something was off. There wasn't that nagging sensation I always felt recently when I first encountered demons. This time, there was nothing. I glanced out the window scanning the area.

As we neared the park, I turned to Gyle. "I don't feel anything," I said. "I don't have much to go on. But normally, whenever there are demons around, I get this weird uneasy feeling first."

Gyle tapped the wheel a few times, letting out a long whistle. "You can already sense voltage, huh? I couldn't even tell anything out of the ordinary for months after my bond first formed." He slowed the car down to a light cruise. His brow scrunched like a caterpillar. "But you're right. I don't feel anything, either."

We stopped a street over, across from the park. Gyle cut the engine before he opened his door. "Where did you come in contact with the demon?"

"Fire Museum," I said, getting out of the car. Gyle nodded as he took the lead, his head on a swivel. When we arrived at the museum, I went to the building and placed my hand on the bricks. They were warm like some sort of heating pad. Claudy jumped from Gyle's shoulder, sniffing around the ground. She zigzagged, going from one concrete square to the next. After a couple of minutes, she returned, climbing Gyle's leg onto his shoulder.

"The door's closed already," she said.

"Closed or been closed? Come on, Claudy, you know I'm a bit slow," Gyle said.

"It's been closed," Claudy said. She kissed Gyle on the cheek softly.

"And the difference is?" I asked.

"One means the door closed on its own," Gyle said. "The other means someone else closed it." Gyle tapped his foot, his hand to his chin.

"Keep thinking so hard and you might bust a blood vessel," a voice said. The voice was soft, yet direct—every syllable had a purpose. I stepped back and leered into the dying moonlight. From atop the museum, they gazed at me, a cosmos of their own, a pair of eyes as white as the moon itself.

I lost myself in that gaze, my body a statue.

10

"If you're looking for the door, I already closed it," the woman said. "You're a little late, per usual." The temperature dropped several degrees. After a few seconds, my breath became visible. The woman jumped from the top of the museum, landing a few inches from us. In the moonlight, her face was clear.

I stepped closer. "Alekka?" I asked, confused.

She turned her head, her frozen eyes capturing me. "Nexus? Holy shit, what are you doing here?" She pointed at Gyle with her thumb. "And with *this* guy, of all people?"

"What do you mean, *this* guy?" Gyle scrunched his face and opened his palms to her.

"Creep. Slouch. Loser." She pressed her finger into his chest. "Should I add more? Or do you get the point now?" Alekka rolled her eyes.

"Dear God," Gyle began. "I asked you out on *one* date a year ago. Thought we were over this by now."

"One!" Alekka turned her body from Gyle, facing me. "Why does every nice guy have to align themselves with pigs." She threw her hands in the air in frustration.

"Okay, maybe two or three," Gyle said. "But I mean, could you really blame me?"

"Yes. Yes, I can," Alekka retorted. "You know, people figure the first 'no' would be enough, but not in pretty boy Gyle's world. Never thought there would be a girl in this world who wouldn't fall for his shit."

My eyes went from Gyle to Alekka, and then back to Gyle. "Anyone care to explain?" I asked.

Gyle sighed. "Remember the other Hybrid in the city that I spoke of? Here she is." He moved to the stone bench. "When Voss was trying to meet with all the Hybrids in the city, Quin was first. He found me next. We tried to get Alekka on board after, but you can see how that turned out." Gyle opened his palms and shrugged. "And I also may have asked her on a few dates during that time. What can I say? I have a shooter's mentality." Gyle simulated shooting a basketball.

Alekka palmed her face. "Looks like you need to learn how to keep work and pleasure separate."

I couldn't care less about Gyle and Alekka's quarrel. I was just shocked to see Alekka here. But at this point, expect the unexpected. Shit was going to happen, even if it was the weirdest of them all. Gyle ignored Alekka's comments. "Anyways, what are you even doing here?" Gyle asked. "For someone who wants no part in creating a Hybrid network, you sure have been in our business a lot lately."

"Don't flatter yourself," Alekka said. "I can do as I please. This city is just as much mine as it is yours." Alekka glared at me, her white eyes small snowballs in the night. "Besides, I couldn't get any sleep. I've been working overtime taking care of the press while Tara's busy. Ended up doing an overnight workout that turned into cleanup duty." Alekka peered at Nyx for a moment, then came back at me. "So, this is your companion?"

Nyx didn't move. The temperature dropped once more. From behind Alekka, a small animal approached—shrouded in what looked to be a dim white aura as if coated in snow. It was another cat, only this one held an angelic appearance: a small snow leopard. Its beauty was beyond anything my eyes had captured before. Its fur was powdery white with small black spots that ran down its body in random positions. Right above its right paw was a blue bracelet wrapped in a coil. The cat moved with grace as it curled its body around Alekka, purring. It turned its head to me as if I had just entered the room, its eyes frozen, whitish-blue.

My body locked itself into a trance. The demon's eyes drew me in, bringing me to a snowy field where a flurry danced around like mist filling the sky. This trance was different from what I felt with Nyx, though I knew it was akin. It took control of my body and made me want to fall deeper into the ecstasy that I was being fed. My lungs became icy. Everything inside me told me to look away, to break the spell. I didn't remember how long I'd been staring when the snow flurry died abruptly—or better yet, melted.

"I suggest you take your eyes off of my human unless you want me to rip them from your skull," Nyx said. He sat at my feet, his expression mute. The cold vanished. Nyx gazed at the other demon, but I knew Nyx was still watching me. They seemed to be having some sort of internal battle, one that would have passed without my notice if not for the feeling of pride and arrogance Nyx was exuding.

"Eira!" Alekka shouted. She reached down and tapped the snowcat on the head. "He's a friend. Play nice." Alekka lifted Eira, which the cat seemed to hate and love all at once. "Sorry about her, she's a bit standoffish at first. This is Eira, my other half." Alekka shook Eira gently and held her out toward me. "Say hi, Eira!"

The cat turned her head from me and Nyx, then said, "Hi," under her breath.

I couldn't help but grin. "Hey, Eira, the name's Nexus." I waved at her. "And that's Nyx."

Eira's eyes shifted to Nyx. She narrowed her eyes, looking closer, then hopped from Alekka's arms.

"Can I talk to him alone for a second?" Alekka asked, looking at Gyle.

He shrugged sarcastically. "Do you actually care what I say?"

"Perfect." Alekka grinned, then turned to me. "Come with me."

We strode along the museum path toward the river. The constant crashing of the water in the distance was soothing, bringing a calm to the evening. "If this is about Gyle, I honestly just met him the other day," I said. "I don't even know if that's really his name, or what the hell he wants with me. But... I guess he doesn't seem like a bad guy."

Alekka turned around. "No, no, no, this isn't about Gyle," she said. "Yes, I find him repulsive and never want to be within ten feet of him. But he isn't the worst. He's tolerable." She squatted down briefly, touching her partner, Eira. The leopard pressed her body against Alekka's hand and purred. "It's about this. Eira. Nyx. You."

I pursed my lips together. Of course, the one thing I didn't want to talk about. "I'm still trying to process everything." I bit my lower lip. "I don't even know where to begin, you know?"

"I thought something might be going on the other day," she said. Alekka smiled at Nyx. "But I never thought you'd get caught up in all of this. Who would have guessed this would be your companion?" Alekka looked at Nyx, then Eira. "Hopefully they can be buddies." Both cats scoffed at the thought. Then Alekka's demeanor hardened. "How much do you know about the Otherworld?"

"As much as I know about calculus—nothing," I said.

"Lately, Otherworld activity has spiked." Alekka exhaled. "It could all be happenstance, but I doubt it." She stared at me for a moment. "Then out of nowhere, you pop up as a Hybrid. I don't know, maybe I'm overthinking things."

"Gyle said the same thing," I said. "Or at least, something along those lines." I tried to stay calm. I'm already so far in the dark, adding this layer felt overwhelming. "What does this mean for me?"

Alekka shook her head. "Right now, nothing," she replied. "Until I can piece this thing together, I'm just as clueless as you. This is about two things." She put up two fingers. "First, under no circumstance whatsoever will you disclose that you're a Hybrid."

She stared at me until I felt the need to repeat what she said to me. "I won't tell anyone I'm a Hybrid," I said.

"Good, you never know who you can trust out here," she said. "Also, you could possibly give that information to a demon ready to sell it to the highest bidder."

I rubbed my face. I wasn't ready to jump into the thought of the Otherworld's black market. "But wait... Since demons can see other demons, won't they know I'm a Hybrid?"

"No," she said. "You're on the right line of thinking, though. Most demons don't readily choose to live in the natural world until they're ready to feed and collect voltage. So, for the most part, you won't have to interact with them, anyway. Seed and Germ demons try to feed on as much voltage as they can get, but they're also survivalists. They'll avoid other demons at all costs unless they know they can kill and feed on them."

"That sounds horrible," I said.

"Tell me about it," she continued. "For someone to know you're a Hybrid, they'd have to be watching you, to put you and Nyx together multiple times, and that would take thought and planning, which can only be done by a Synth demon. You should be safe if you keep your mouth shut and don't start blabbing." Her eyes narrowed at me. "That means girlfriends, too. You compromise one of us, you compromise all of us."

I laughed a bit. "Trust me, you don't have to worry about that."

"This second one is the tricky one, and the one I'm not so sure about myself." Alekka glanced over my shoulder to where Gyle sat. Her eyes then met mine. "When I spoke of Gyle, I was only speaking for him."

Nyx opened one golden eye when he heard her words. "What do you mean?" I asked.

"I don't know how much I trust the guy he's working with, Voss," she said. "I've only met him once, but there was something dark about him. It was so… heavy. I barely could be around it. I don't know, call it intuition, but I'm not a fan."

I thought back to my meeting hours ago with Voss. I wondered why I didn't feel the same presence. Was I that naïve, or did he display different sides of the same mask to Alekka and me?

"He is an intense guy," I agreed. "Wouldn't want to see what happens to someone who gets on his bad side."

"You met him?" she asked, somewhat surprised.

"Briefly. Only introductions, really. He had to leave right after arriving."

Alekka sighed. "Just be careful," she said. She rubbed the back of her neck. "I would tell Gyle the same, but he wouldn't listen to me."

"What makes you so sure?" I asked.

Alekka laughed. "Come on, you're smarter than that. Please, I can see through all that sarcasm."

I nodded. "Thanks for the heads up," I said.

"Probably should head back before he starts complaining," Alekka said. "Let's go."

I put my hands in my pockets while heading back to Gyle. Nyx trailed behind me, staring out into the distance. "You feel something?" I asked.

He shook his head. "No. Nothing at all."

Gyle stood as we approached. He yawned. "If the door is closed, I guess we have no reason to be here," he said. "I'm exhausted and would like to sleep in on a Sunday, for once."

Alekka laughed. "If you're looking for sleep, better keep searching," she said. "This amount of activity isn't normal. Only Synth demons should be able to open doors to this world, yet here these Seeds and Germs keep popping up. And they're growing, getting stronger, smarter... Something feels off with all of this."

"Voss is already working on figuring out what's going on," Gyle said. "We should have some information soon."

Alekka frowned, nodding. "Keep your eyes open. Something tells me things are going to get worse from here. You're repulsive, but I'd much rather have you alive than dead." Alekka turned to me while Gyle went back to the car. "How are you holding up? You know, with the change and all?"

"It's all still a lot right now, to be honest. It's like someone waking up one day and learning they forgot how to speak their primary language. But I'll survive. Give me some time and I'll learn it back." From the look in Alekka's eyes, I could tell she wasn't going to press. More than anyone, she knew what I was dealing with. She also knew how fragile I was now. I appreciated her holding back. There was too much I was trying to figure out. I was beginning to feel like a failure trying to keep up as is.

I stepped toward Alekka and rubbed my hand through my hair. "Thanks."

"For what?" she questioned.

"Saving me the other day outside of Fernando's," I replied. "I wouldn't be here if it wasn't for you." As I thought about the situation, everything made sense. Alekka leaving, Nyx's appearance, it was all coming together. With the door opened, Alekka and Nyx most likely followed the trail, yet I ended up there as well—and nearly died for it. Who knows, maybe I was drawn to the door as well. When I saw Alekka on top of the museum, with those eyes, I knew immediately it was her. I felt like a fool for not realizing it sooner.

"Holy shit, that was you?" she shouted. "Man, you haven't been able to catch a break. That must have been horrible."

I pursed my lips together and sighed. "Tell me about it."

"Don't worry about it," she said, and added, "Looks like you owe me one now, though." Alekka tapped me on the shoulder. "Glad you're safe. Get home. And try to get some rest, though. I'll see you at work Monday." She waved at me and then left with Eira close on her heels.

I walked back to the car and got in after Nyx. Gyle grumbled, then said, "She's an asshole, right?"

I shrugged. "That's a ya'll problem."

11

I chose to follow Gyle back inside the warehouse. More than ever, I wanted to be home in my own bed for whatever bit of the night I had left. But I also had more questions that I needed answers to—and had a bit of time to think things through. We went back to the common area. I took a seat on the way too big sofa, while Gyle grabbed water. Quin sat in a nook on the other side of the couch playing on a handheld device, her knees tucked in her chest. She leered at me out of the corner of her eye, then went back to her game as if I didn't exist again.

"Don't you have schoolwork to do or something?" I asked.

She didn't respond, or even react. Gyle hopped on the couch near me. "Quin's taking a gap year before she starts college." Claudy walked across his shoulder, her white and black fur meshing. Symon must have been sleeping.

"Besides, in the case of IQ, Quin is easily the smartest person in this room. College would be more of a formality than anything for her." Gyle took a sip of water. "Since you didn't get in your car and get some sleep yourself, I'm guessing you want to talk. You got me for a little before I fall asleep on you."

Lately, the thoughts had surrounded me any chance they had, like a gang of bullies trying to catch their target off guard. This was the first time I had a chance to sit down and catch my breath. I went with the closest question to mind. "What exactly is a door?" I asked.

Gyle thought and then he thought more. He rubbed at his light beard. "I couldn't tell you."

Claudy sighed. "You're hopeless sometimes," she interjected. She turned her little head to me. "To make it simple, it's a collection of voltage that forms in the same spot in your world and the Otherworld. Demons are attracted to that large gathering of voltage. But the worlds become one in that spot letting Otherworld beings cross over through a door, so to speak. Of course, Synth demons can open doors between worlds at will, but that would also attract other demons."

"Wouldn't that be a normal occurrence?" I asked.

"Depends," Claudy said. "Voltage gathering in the same place isn't uncommon. Gathering enough to open a door… that's nearly impossible. But there are limits to the crossover of dimensions and that includes where you can travel. The Otherworld is endless. For the two to meet is a miracle."

"Which is why it's so weird that so many doors are opening in different cities." I said the words to myself, somewhat understanding the scope—though not the severity. "With this 'bond' that Nyx and I share, I'm as much demon as I am human, correct?" My eyes trailed to Nyx, who slept on the couch.

"Bingo," Gyle said. "You and that guy share a heart. You're all wrapped in two. You can put a bow on top if you like."

I touched my chest as if I knew something was different with my body. Nyx and I had been connected for however long and I had no clue. Still, knowing my heart wasn't mine anymore scared me. "How long do demons live on average?"

Claudy gave me what I imagined was a shrug. "Depends. Some live hundreds of years—others can't make it past a few years. The strength of a demon's voltage and how long they go without running into another stronger than them are the biggest factors. Or if the two's voltage doesn't mesh and it ages them tremendously. A Hybrid is still half-human. When you die, Nyx dies. Though your body is still held by human constraints, voltage will preserve your body longer. Some Hybrids have been known to live to be two hundred."

My heart sank. If you told most people they would possibly live to be two hundred, they would be ecstatic. But something was wrong about that. I wasn't sure how to process doubling or tripling my lifespan. I leaned back on the couch and stared into the gaping ceiling.

My life had been invaded; privacy taken away. It was all done under my nose, without me having a clue. I was going to have to do more soul searching than I wanted to in the future if I was going to figure any of this out. Gyle petted Claudy's nose with his finger. He reached into his pocket and pulled out a tiny treat that Claudy took with excitement. He grabbed another one. Without saying a word, Symon reached his little arm out from Gyle's pocket and swiped the treat.

I sat up, watching. Gyle drank more water, then let Claudy drink some out of the cap. "Have you always been so... friendly," I asked. "You know, with Claudy and Symon?"

Gyle shook his head. "Claudy and I for the most part always understood each other and could compromise," he said. "But for the longest time, Symon and I weren't on the same page. He always had a problem with anything I did. So he wouldn't cooperate with me. Made conjuring voltage hell."

"Demons have no business sharing a heart with humans," Symon said from inside Gyle's pocket.

Gyle tapped his jacket. "He's still rough at times, but at the end of the day, they know how I feel about them. Having a bond makes it easier. Less speaking, more feeling." Gyle frowned, his scar curling down his cheek. "You and Nyx will come to an understanding, eventually." He shrugged. "Or you won't. But hope it never comes to that."

I blinked. "What happens if we don't?" I asked. "Have you ever seen a situation play out when they didn't?"

"I only know of one instance, and even that was a story from Voss," he began. "Long story short, if the two parties continue to fight, they'll eventually destroy themselves from within. Their minds break, and they end up becoming a berserk channel of demonic voltage. No telling what kind of destruction they'll cause." Gyle waved his hand. "But don't worry about that. If something like that ever happened, we'd step in and handle it."

I lowered my head, staring at Gyle. "Do you really believe that? Who knows what the hell's out there? Do you really think you all are strong enough to handle it?" My voice was low but cold—hard.

Gyle smiled. "You'll go crazy trying to rack your brain about what's out there. Truth is, we don't know. But whatever it is—if it comes, I'll do everything I can to stop it."

How could I be mad at that answer? "You know, I'd think having our hearts connected with demons would make us... you know... *evil*," I said, sighing. "Don't get me wrong. I know I'm no saint or anything, but in stories, demons are normally associated with the vilest creatures. Yet here you are risking your life to protect the people of Union City from their deepest fears."

Gyle laughed. "You find out you share your heart with a demon, and you're worried about if you're evil or not?"

"Wouldn't you be?" I asked.

"Never really thought about it, I guess," Gyle said. "Good or evil doesn't matter to me. It's always been simpler than that. Knowing me, the second I try to step in and deem something good or evil, the next day I'd be a hypocrite."

He was probably right. My head hurt at the thought of it. Besides, there was nothing I could do about it now. "Voss's the boss around here, right?" I asked.

"Yeah, something like that," he replied. "He's the one who funds this place, at least." Gyle leaned in. "Pretty sure he trades on the stock market. Either way, he's loaded. And a nice guy, two things that make a great boss, I would say."

"Boss?"

"I helped one of his side businesses get off the ground, and I was able to become an independent marketer after that." Gyle drank from his bottle.

"Why do you think he's doing this?" I asked. "Why gather all the Hybrids in the city and give them a place to stay? It doesn't really make sense when I think about it." I scanned the warehouse. "All demons have a goal. That would mean Hybrids do, too, right? What are yours?"

Gyle folded his arms. "Don't know how to hold back any, do you?" He rested his forearms on his knees. "What do you want me to tell you? That we have some righteous reason for banding together, that it's something bigger than just any one of us? I don't know about Voss. Maybe he wants to keep tabs on us. It's better that he knows who we are and what our capabilities are than to have us out there alone. Turns what could have been a foe into a friend." Gyle placed his hand on the couch. "But for me, at the end of the day, it may be as simple as increasing my chances of survival." It was clear there was more on his mind than he was letting on. "I'm not sure what Voss has planned, but he's a calculating man if nothing else. If he says he needs me, I trust his word. It's the least I can do after all he's done for me."

Gyle seemed a very loyal, trustworthy person. I doubt he'd put his faith in someone he didn't fully believe in. If I was going to get anywhere, I would have to have a conversation with Voss, one that could give me some insight into what he was attempting. I doubted he was creating a Hybrid network for nothing.

I relaxed. More thinking would only lead to a stressful life, and I didn't need that. "Guess I should get out of here," I said. "It's way past my bedtime."

"Same," Gyle agreed. He walked with me to the entrance. Gyle opened the door and looked at Nyx and me. "Don't sweat all the details right now. The most important thing is making sure you understand each other and letting your bond grow. Everything else will find its way together eventually."

I absorbed his words, shaking his hand. "Thanks," I said, venturing back to the Jetta.

It took me longer to drive home than I wanted, but the last thing I needed was a speeding ticket to cap off my perfect week. We arrived at my townhouse. I unlocked the door and turned on the light. "Make yourself at home," I said.

I thought about going to the fridge, but I didn't want to see how much food I didn't have. My bank account wasn't ready for the blow a trip to Lix would be. It still hadn't recovered from the last excursion. It looked like I was going to have sleep for dinner. It was probably for the best. I was exhausted.

I started up the stairs.

"Eat something," Nyx said in an iron tone. "I'd rather my companion not be weak and frail."

I stopped, blinked at him, and then went to the fridge slowly, my eyes still locked on Nyx. I made what could pass as a sandwich and grabbed a Gatorade. Without saying a word, I ate the sandwich at record speed. "Happy?"

"It'll do for now," he responded.

I went up the stairs, glancing back at Nyx. The cat jumped on the kitchen counter and moved about, sniffing at objects as he passed. No matter which way I flipped it, Nyx still acted like a cat, even if he really was a large demon cat. I left the downstairs light on and continued to my room.

My room was cool, just how I liked it. It smelled of lavender, from the new diffuser I set up last week. Glad to know home at least felt like home. Sleep was the only thing on my mind. I changed into my nighttime clothes. My bed called me over, enticing, alluring. I listened to its call and became one. Believe it or not, for once I didn't have an issue sleeping.

12

The next day I woke up with more energy than I should have had, considering last night. I felt better when I hit the snooze button, knowing I could sleep in. And that was only after having got four hours of sleep.

When I got up, I showered first. Then I put on a hoodie and got in the car. When I set out, I didn't have a goal in mind—I knew I needed something. Something to make sense of things.

I avoided the highway and chose to cruise down Beach Boulevard; no light stopped me this early in the morning. The sky seemed sad—a deep sullen gray. I couldn't remember the last time the sun was out. After I passed under two major highways I decided where I was going.

The shopping center housed a discount supermarket, a pawn shop, and a game store. What I found out years ago was it was also home to another shop, one that was behind the main buildings. I turned and found the nearest parking spot. There was one other car parked outside, a weathered red pickup truck. It had more life than it had years left in it. I got out and stared at the sign at the foot of the building: *Graff's Bookstore*.

The bell chimed as I entered the store. A voice yelled from afar, "Restrooms are for paying customers only!"

I walked to the front desk on my left and called out to the small office behind it. "Keep talking to me like that, and you might lose your only paying customer," I replied.

Books fell in the back, and I could hear the owner, Graff, hopping down from his stepladder. He stumbled from the back and stared at me through thick frames. He was wearing jeans, a polka-dotted collared shirt that was too loose, and a beige blazer with elbow patches. Graff was a man of average height, with a full head of salted hair, in his mid-sixties. He was a skinny man, almost skeleton-like. If I were to guess, I would imagine Graff missed many meals while lost behind the pages of a book.

"Nexus?" He took his glasses off and cleaned the lenses.

I didn't like the way it sounded, but I nodded. "Yeah," I said. "I was wondering if I could have a look around."

Graff came to me and slapped me across the back of my head. Luckily, my thick hair softened the blow. He huffed, then went back behind the desk, sat down, and waved me off. "You know my shop is always open to you." He shook his head. "But you go that long without checking in again and you'll get more than that. Was beginning to think you ditched town."

"Sorry, haven't gotten out much lately." I touched my hand to the desk, feeling the aged wood. "Stopped doing things I like, I guess."

Graff gazed into my eyes, and it was as if he instantly understood. Wisdom had its way of doing that. "Well, if you're back here, that means you're at least dreaming again." He smiled. "What brings you in?"

"Not sure, to be honest," I said. "I have a lot on my mind and need somewhere to sort through things, you know?" I gazed around the store.

Small bookshelves grew to larger ones as the store traveled back. Though the place looked more like a hoarder's mess than anything. Some books found their way on stools or put on nearby glass tables— though never on the floor. Graff had a rule about putting books on floors: Never do it. Simple.

I tapped the desk. "But I think I'll know once I find it."

"Suit yourself," Graff said. He clasped his knees, rising. I heard his bones creaking. "Let me know if you need any help." He stretched while heading back to his office.

I traveled to a familiar space. It still smelled of sage and withered pages. I first came to Graff's once in high school when I wandered over here after leaving the game store. If I hadn't been waiting so long for my ride, I would have never found it. Sometimes I wondered how Graff even kept the store open. It wasn't in a visible location to be seen by any passersby. And honestly, I doubted Graff would want them, anyway. I've seen him turn down one or two clients, so who knew however many there had been before that?

I went to the left down the second row. Graff didn't organize the store by regular author names. Instead he did it by series and genre. For those who did standalones, he titled their series that name. Mysteries go with mysteries, nonfiction with nonfiction, and so on and so forth. It wasn't a perfect system, by any means, and sometimes, it made no sense. It was a bit of a pain at first, but once I got the hang of it—I honestly found it hard to go back to the more traditional route. I headed down the nonfiction aisle and checked the spines as I moved.

I stopped and picked up an autobiography of an author I wasn't familiar with. After turning the book around I noticed the author was a writer of horror. No wonder. I wasn't a complete chicken, but I didn't believe in raising my blood pressure when I was trying to go to my happy place. I placed the book back, eyeing the one right next to it.

The next book, like the last, could be considered horror in a sense. The summary told of a local Union City actor who was called crazy by those in the media and Hollywood after they started *seeing* things. I opened the front cover, reading the text.

I vaguely remembered hearing this story when I was in grade school. Union City wasn't home to many celebrities past the local sports team members. So when a local actor, Joanne Freehling, started talking about hearing voices and spirits, it caught wind fast. I don't think I had seen her in a movie since her first hiccup. Almost all wrote her off as being mad. They even sent her to an institution to get help. There wasn't much more ever said about her. At the time, it meant nothing to me. But now... I wasn't so sure.

I read several pages, then opened the middle of the book and did the same. Maybe this was just another story about some nutcase, but I wouldn't know until I took that journey.

I closed the book and took it with me as I proceeded down the aisle. The smell of pages read and unread filled the shelves. These shelves used to keep me company day in and day out when I was dating Nya—

when I was at my happiest. Everything felt like some romcom. I'd come and read anything I could get my hands on, anything that Graff put on these shelves. I'd bring Nya a novel or two, and we'd clear out sections of the store like it was sport.

I turned to go down the mystery section I'd become acquainted with over time. There weren't many books in this section that I hadn't read. Graff's was only stocked with novels that Graff had read himself. I continued along but stopped near the end of the aisle. There was a book, bright green with gold lettering, which stuck out like a tiger in a pen of chickens. I grabbed the book: *A Night to Remember*. There was no summary on the back. I turned toward the front of the store. "What's *A Night to Remember* about?" I yelled.

There was shuffling from up front. "Ahh, that's a good one," he called back. "Protagonist sees a murder but wakes up in another world... or do they? Worth a read."

I nodded. "Wow, Graff's stamp of approval—that's high praise." Graff had never steered me wrong before. "Thanks," I added, taking the book with me.

After a minute of reminiscing and looking through books that I had viewed hundreds of times, I came to the fantasy section. My childhood lived here. Even before I knew Graff, or came to his shop, I was always an avid fantasy reader. I'd spend hours escaping to worlds where things made more sense. I took a seat on the little gray stepladder and stared up at the bookshelves. Since finding Graff's, whenever I felt unsure about something or needed answers—this was where I came. And like clockwork, here I was again, lost.

Even if I took the time to talk to Graff about what was happening, I risked ending up looking like a lunatic. Or a storyteller, which I wouldn't mind—though I'd be telling the truth. Or even if he did believe me, I wouldn't want him wrapped up in all this mess. The more I thought things through, the more alone I felt.

I sighed into my hands, then turned back to the books in front of me. No matter how crazy I seemed, books never judged, only gave me more of themselves without asking for anything in return. I leaned in, pulling a novel off the bottom shelf: *Victory*—a classic. It was one of my favorite novels, one I'd gone back to more than a few times.

Yet I couldn't remember what it was about. It was vague, like seeing

DEMONOLOGY

an outline of an image without the detail that filled the contents. I could remember the way I felt about the story, that it was one of my favorites —but why couldn't I remember the substance? I touched the tip of the book until it was free and brought it in close. The book was an all-black hardcover, with little red stitching along the border. I opened the front page, reading the blurb:

Two brothers, a war fought together. Is it love, or is it hate? Only through grueling battles and heartache will they find out.

Nothing. Why couldn't I remember? Had it been that long? I stared at the familiar, yet unfamiliar book. Maybe my memory was foggy from everything. Reading it through one more time wouldn't kill me. I added it to my pile, while I scanned the shelf.

I knew Nyx was awake by now. I doubt he was asleep when I left this morning, but I assumed he was tired. There was no way he wasn't, after the night we had. How was I supposed to act? Should I let him know when I'm leaving? Did we have to always remain attached to each other's hips? Would I ever have privacy again? My thoughts were a ball of yarn, too entangled to reach the end. Maybe I became accustomed to being alone. It was all I knew. That loneliness wrapped its warm blanket around me and pulled me closer. I shook the familiar feeling off and stared back at the shelves.

I went through the rows, looking over titles I was familiar with. Once I finished the shelf, I rose and continued, but stopped when I noticed a smaller shelf behind me that I hadn't seen before. On it was one book— yet another I hadn't seen before. It really had been too long. *One.*

"Find anything you like?" Graff called out to me.

I placed the book with the rest of my things and rose. "Yeah, think I found a few things," I called back. I traveled around the shelves, going back to the front of the store. "Looks like you've done a good bit of reading since I've been gone."

"Only thing that keeps me sane," he said.

I put the books on the counter and watched Graff bag them. When he got to the last book, *One,* he stopped.

"What?" I asked.

He shook his head, putting it in the bag. "Only book in this store I haven't read yet," he said. "I'll get around to it eventually."

"You haven't read it?" My mouth dropped open. "How did it manage to get on the shelf, then? Thought you only stock this place with books you've read."

"Normally, I do, but a guy came in here the other day." Graff scratched at his beard. The sleeves of his blazer dropped. "Handsome fella. He rented a couple of things. Bought a few trinkets. When he was leaving, we got to chatting, and he mentioned a novel, saying it was his favorite, and asked if I read it. Me being as well-read as I am, assumed I'd read it. But when he told me the name, I honestly hadn't a clue. He stumped me. He told me he had an extra copy on him that I could have. And voilà."

My eyes shot open now. "And you *still* haven't read it yet?" I shouted. "I can't believe you've let this sit this long. I can take a bit of time to read a book or two, but *you?*"

Graff's eyes narrowed. "I, unlike some people finish books I start before I move on to the next," he said. He crossed his arms.

I opened my mouth, then closed it. Checkmate. "Just ring me up for the rentals," I responded, smiling.

Graff shook his head. "Just bring them back so you can pick up some more." He passed me the bag. "Don't take so long this time."

"Graff, I..." I couldn't form sentences. Then I settled a bit, and simply said, "Thank you."

He walked back into his office. "Go now, you shouldn't be spending your weekend with an old man."

I grabbed the bag, heading back into the morning dew. I climbed back in the Jetta and pulled out of the parking lot, heading toward my house. I'm sure if it came down to it, Nyx could find me, but I doubted he was having a fun time not knowing where I was at. Then I remembered one thing I couldn't forget and took the next left.

I found myself at the nearest pet store, down an aisle I had no business in. There was more cat food than I was ready for. Dry food, wet food, and I swear, there was even some kind of in-betweener. A petite store worker in a red t-shirt walked up to me. She smiled, asking, "Can I help you find anything?"

I wanted to tell her no and struggle to find whatever I needed, but I was in a foreign territory and there was no way I'd know what to get. Who was I kidding? "Yeah," I said. "Actually... I sort of got a cat yesterday. I guess you could call it an impulse decision."

"Ah, say no more," she said. The young lady grinned from cheek to cheek, and I knew I made a mistake. I wasn't sure if she was more excited about all the commission she was about to get or the fact that I was a new cat owner.

"How old?" she asked.

"Twenty-five," I said. The store clerk looked at me as if she wasn't sure if I was telling a joke or not. Then I felt firsthand embarrassment when I realized what I had done. "Sorry... He's..." I thought for a bit.

"Well, we have kitten, junior, and adult." The clerk used her pointer finger to count off the different ages.

"Adult," I said. I thought of the way Nyx spoke to me yesterday and laughed to myself. "Yeah, he has to be an adult."

She grabbed a large bag of food off the shelf behind me. Along with the dry food, she also placed a small pallet of wet food in the cart. The employee took me toward the back of the store. "How many times were you planning on changing the litter? Daily?" she asked.

I blinked at her. None was the obvious answer, but I didn't think that was an option. "I honestly hadn't thought about it."

"This should do the trick, then." She grabbed a large square box the size of the shopping cart itself and placed it on the bottom. "This one is automatic. Cleans the litter for you. That way you won't have to think about it. Just replace the litter every couple of weeks. I actually have this one myself, works wonders." She finished showing me everything else the store had to offer (and I didn't care about) before she took me back to the front. She made sure to tell me how much I was going to love having a cat before she disappeared somewhere in the store.

The cashier went through the cart full of items. With each scan, I saw the total amount jumping, up and up and up. After the fourth or fifth time, I forced myself to stop watching. This was going to hurt—bad. When the last item was scanned, the cashier looked at me and asked, "Would you like to get a toy today, too? We have these great ones on sale." She dangled a multicolored ball with a feather coming out of it like it was some yoyo.

I glowered at the total, then back to her. "Sure, why not?" I said. It wasn't like it'd make a difference now.

"He's going to love it," she said, cheering to herself. "Thank you for shopping with us, hope to see you again soon."

I stuffed my car with the cat starter kit. Hopefully, I had bought everything I needed. The pet store was worse than Lix as far as I was concerned. The trunk was packed full of a bunch of things I still hadn't thrown out, so I opted to use the backseat. Once I was home, I made my room cat-friendly. The litter box advertised itself as odorless, so I hoped it kept to its word. My room was the only place it would be out of the way. The food and water went to the other side of my bed, closest to the bathroom.

Nyx entered the room, sniffing around. The demon glared at me with muddled eyes. "What are you doing?" he asked.

I kneeled and scooped some food into the kitty bowl. "If you're going to be living here, I figure you might eventually get hungry and thirsty." I put the bag of food away, then went to my work desk near the window. "Litterbox is set up, too."

Silence.

Nyx crept forward. His tail swiped left and right in a rhythmic, slow manner—left, right—left, right. I watched him stare at the bowls. Nyx took another step, then sat. It was faint, but I could feel a sudden feeling of pleasure and confusion. The emotion wasn't so much happiness, but a liking—or feeling of respect. Nyx didn't eat anything, though he drank a little water.

"You didn't have to do that," Nyx said. He leaped on the bed, letting the light that had found its way through the window shine on him. Nyx glared at me; his expression was that of more concern than what he'd shown me so far. "I tried looking for you."

"What are you talking about?" I questioned.

"For years, I searched this realm trying to see if the bond would grow stronger. But no matter where I went, nothing happened. Until recently, at least."

I sighed. "And that means what exactly?" I asked. "Sorry, sort of new at this whole Otherworld thing."

DEMONOLOGY

"Our bond was severed, and I don't know when or for what reason." Nyx's face scrunched a little as he thought. "The only thing I know for certain is it was done so I wouldn't be able to find my way to you."

"Do you know how long ago that was?" I asked.

Nyx thought it over. "I can't say for certain. Time in the Otherworld doesn't respond the same as it does here. Therefore, I won't age the same as you would. So even though I've only lived in your world, I can't be certain how long it's been exactly. But if I was guessing, I'd say anywhere from twenty to thirty years."

"Probably for the best," I said, trying to process everything. I couldn't imagine having to deal with the Otherworld as a child. I couldn't help but think of Quin. Was that why she didn't speak to anyone? I couldn't imagine what things she had seen at such a young age. And I could probably guess how any parent would react if their child started talking about demons and the Otherworld one day.

I rested my chin on top of my hands. Life was difficult enough to try to figure out how to survive on my own. Sure, my father managed to fund a steady roof over my head and food in the fridge—but that was all. Don't get the wrong idea. His care was only monetary. My father died before I was old enough to remember his face. Apparently, he committed suicide after my birth. It was for the best. Growing up alone made me tough and resilient, unlike my coward of a father. Better alone than living with someone who took their life to get away from my mother and me.

I leaned back and looked over to Nyx. "Just because I believe what everyone is saying doesn't mean I'm going to get up and start fighting crime." I shook my head, thinking of Tara's deadline. "I still have a life to live, you know. I can't put that on the back burner."

Nyx brought his paw to his mouth and licked it. "I could care less what you do with those Hybrids. My only concern is your safety."

"Of course, so you'll be able to use my body for whatever you want, right?" My words came across much harsher than I intended. But the point was made, nevertheless.

Something changed in Nyx's demeanor. Nyx was angered, but then his emotions dulled to the neutral state he normally carried. It all happened so fast that I could have easily missed it. "There is something I must do," he said. "Until that goal is complete, I'll be watching over you, making sure nothing happens." Nyx paused. "After my mission is complete, you're free to live whatever life you choose."

Maybe I was a bit on edge, but I found myself fighting back rage at every turn. "That's it? You find me and completely change my life, and then what? You use me until you complete this 'goal' then leave me, too? You're a fucking joke." I took a deep breath as I tried to stop shaking. A part of me was embarrassed. Mainly because I wasn't exactly sure why I got so heated.

Nyx's frustration grew, then subsided. "Somehow our bond was damaged. That was done deliberately for a reason, but one I was not sure of yet. But now that it is back, it's growing. This won't go unnoticed for long." Nyx pressed his body against the bed and stared at me. His eyes never wavered. "At least let me tell you a bit about my world so you don't get yourself killed."

Whether I wanted to hear it or not didn't matter. Nyx was right. Without knowing anything about the Otherworld I was on a highway leading straight to death. I needed as much information as I could get. My laptop stared at me like some type of ornament that had gone so long without any use it had become staging furniture. It watched me disregard my responsibilities. I imagined telling Tara how I didn't have anything to submit because I was talking to a demon that I found out I shared a body with. There was no way she would believe me. I would be surprised if I still had a chance after she heard that.

I pressed a few keys on my laptop, unlocking it. "Talk while I type," I told Nyx. Maybe this way, I'd be able to submit something to Alekka *and* avoid getting killed.

13

Within the first thirty minutes, I had already written a few hundred words, deleted them, and then decided I should start with the title. Random words came to mind; ones I deemed "cool" if I was to see them on a book cover. *Resurrection*, no, wait —*Revival*, horrible. It would have to do. But then I stared at the word, "revival." What could I possibly do with that? Nothing was backing it. I grunted and deleted the title.

Nyx made himself comfortable on one of my pillows. He watched me struggle, enjoying it. I glowered at him. "There are tiers of demons—Seeds, Germs, and Synths," Nyx started. "You've only encountered Seed demons thus far."

"Both of those were Seeds?"

"Yes. There are many variants to Synth demons, though. Much like how humans have different ethnicities and such, just many more variations. When Seeds feed and become stronger, they germinate and become Germs: stronger... and hungrier."

"And you're what, a Synth, right?" I asked.

"When a demon becomes a Synth, they develop speech and thought."

"Makes sense," I said. I glared at the computer in thought. Maybe I could write a story about… about… *blank*. I turned back to Nyx. "What happens after that? They gain thought, then what?"

"They fight," Nyx said. His voice was flat, yet strong, like a sheet of metal.

"Fight? Who?"

Nyx opened his mouth slightly; his fangs crept out like daggers. "That is where you humans and us demons are alike. You give us thought and we think we are the best, who should rule who, who deserves to be on the throne. A hierarchy was created, much like yours. Power is the nectar that fuels our demon blood."

I never thought of the Otherworld as a place that had a ruler. I sort of assumed it was a place where all these things gathered and lived their version of a life of leisure. Was it even possible to rule over demons? And for them to have a hierarchy… "Who sits on the throne now?"

"Nobody," he said. Nyx saw the confusion in my gaze. "The last king died before I was born. Now if anyone dares to take the throne, they're killed before they can stake their claim. The throne has remained vacant for years now." Nyx sighed, putting his chin on his paws. "Anyways, if you want to stay alive, at all costs, avoid Germ and Synth demons. In your current state, and our current bond, we won't be able to handle them."

Something was weighing on me, begging me to ask. Yet up until this point, I was starting to think that I was going crazy, so I put it off. "When did we become connected?" I asked. I recalled Gyle telling me the moment he became a Hybrid. There wasn't that moment for me. "When did we become *one*?"

"I can't say for certain. The bond wasn't strong enough for me to find you, but I've been able to feel it for as long as I can remember." Nyx shook his head disapprovingly. "Someone must have bonded us together, but who—and why?"

Minutes passed, me staring at my laptop, the Lenovo staring back at me. "First person or third?" I rasped my fingers against the keyboard.

Nyx tilted his head to the side. "Depends," he said. "On how close the author wants you with their character." He glared at me for a moment. "But I've taken a liking to your human novels as of late. They… amuse me." Nyx rose and moved toward the edge of the bed. "For now, just avoid letting your emotions get away from you. If you stay under control, your voltage won't be strong enough to draw any demons to you. And even if, I'll be around."

"So that's it?" I asked. "No big speech or anything else?"

Nyx jumped from the bed and walked through the door. "You're my companion, but you have your own decisions to make. I have my goal, but you have your own goals as well. I can't force you into anything. The bond grows as we grow."

I leaned my chair as far back as it allowed and stared at the ceiling. White. Plain. Dull. There was nothing to it, yet so much. I sat back up and peered at the computer screen. The same whiteness watched me, only now a blank page on an empty screen. I was going to make a good draft if it killed me. Time wasn't on my side, but when had it ever seemed to be?

I scrapped the idea of a title. It wouldn't do any good if I didn't have a story to go along with it, anyway. A part of me wanted to create something new—fresh. The story was there. I felt it festering, waiting to be told. Too bad now wasn't the time for any Frankenstein creations.

In simpler terms, I had already fucked up. I would never make the deadline, not at this pace.

I searched over my desktop and glowered at all my monsters of failures. I wasn't anywhere close to finishing any of them. Feeble attempts. I developed a bad habit of starting new projects for a few years. Hence why I had a stockpile of novels with the first seven to twelve chapters. Guess I was a bad finisher, but who wasn't? Starting, for the most part, was easy. That excitement of a new story would keep anyone going for the first ten thousand words or so. It was after that when the marathon began.

But I was determined to get something completed. This might be my one chance at my dream. I couldn't mess this up.

I went to the last story I worked on. It had potential, don't get me wrong, but I was bogged down with graduate school and trying to find a job, and made excuses to not write. That turned into a shelved idea that never fully got fleshed out. I opened the document and frowned at the fifteen-thousand-word count. It was doable.

Day turned to night before I realized it. My stomach pains forced me to take a break. I made a quick trip to Lix and bought enough food to last me until payday. Once home, I ate a bowl of ramen and then rushed back to my computer. The nighttime bugs echoed out their songs in the distance. I listened to every tune as I buried my fingers into the keys.

Nyx came into the room and bounded to the bed. "Still at work?" he asked.

I didn't answer. I wasn't trying to be rude, but I was in a zone I hadn't been in for a while now. I couldn't risk it being disrupted. My fingers flowed across the keyboard for several minutes, then stopped. Done. Holy shit. It was done. It was well past midnight, and I was beyond exhausted with only a few hours to spare before work—but I finished. It wasn't my best work by any means, but I wouldn't be embarrassed for Tara to read it. It would have to do. At least, I would have something to put on Tara's desk in the morning. I printed the pages downstairs. Call me archaic, but I liked my manuscripts to be physical. Nothing like the feeling of turning the page. I headed to the fridge and filled a cup with cold water while I waited. Sheet after sheet printed. I even changed the ink cartridge halfway through. This whole weekend proved to be more expensive than I thought it would be.

I put the manuscript in my bag for the morning. There was no way I was going to risk forgetting it. As I walked back to my bed, it dawned on me that I had forgotten one thing at the pet store. "I forgot to get you a bed," I said.

Nyx turned his head from me and held it proud. "You act as if such things are necessary."

"Well, until I get you one, you can sleep on the bed with me. Much comfier than the couch downstairs."

Nyx picked a spot at the corner edge of the bed by my feet. "If you insist," he said.

I followed suit and tried to find my comfort zone. "Nyx," I said.

"Hmm," he purred.

"I can see you, and other demons, as clear as day now. But it wasn't like that until recently." I pulled my blanket over my body until I felt snug and secure. "What happens when normal people see you?"

"Most humans can't see us at all," he said. "You must believe and have enough voltage yourself to see us. I'm sure those who do see us likely write us off as paranormal activity and move on with their lives."

That made more sense to me than anything I've heard thus far. Alekka's words still bothered me, though. She didn't seem the type to let the little things trouble her, but something was different—she seemed on high alert. I turned on my side and pulled a pillow close. Maybe I could get enough sleep to last me through the day.

Before the first bit of light finally found its way through my window, I had already been awake for an hour at least—maybe longer. I could have only slept three or four hours, but I felt good. Not my peak energy levels by any means, but well enough to start my day without hating my life. Teeth, clothes, food, water, car, what could I say—I had perfected the art of getting out of the house in the morning.

When I came outside, my next door neighbor, Ann, was securing her sleeping daughter into her car seat. She yawned, turning to me with a tired smile. Her short brown hair bounced around as she rolled her shoulders. "Early morning?" she asked.

"Yeah, I didn't get much sleep," I said.

She closed the car door. "I know a few things about that." She laughed a little. "I better get this one to daycare before traffic gets too bad. Have a good day." She still managed to seem somewhat peppy even though I could see the exhaustion in her eyes. As I watched Ann pull out of the driveway, a sudden rush of sadness took over.

Seeing Ann and her daughter immediately brought thoughts of my failed relationship and the child we lost. Sometimes, I managed a day or so without thinking about it. But other days it ate me alive, devouring my every thought. I ignored the feeling and got in my car. Nyx sat in the passenger seat and stared out the window while I drove. There was no need for music, words, or even sound. My emotions reached Nyx and he understood.

When I parked, Nyx hopped on the dash of the car and looked up. "This your job?" Nyx asked.

I pulled into a parking space at the side of the building. "Yup. Welcome to The Bar. Where you lift shit and get strong." I sighed. "Or something like that."

Nyx hopped on the dashboard and looked up at the building. A man in a dental floss stringer and a gallon water jug shaped like a dumbbell walked by the car. Nyx glanced over at me and then back to the gymgoer. "I don't see the point in wearing that top if it's going to show everything," Nyx said in a confused tone.

"Neither does he, trust me," I replied. "If he didn't have to wear it, he wouldn't." I exited the car and went inside. I didn't make it two steps when I felt Dave's eyes focused on me, though he was with a client, so he didn't move—yet. My phone buzzed as I settled in. I had one message from Alekka telling me she was going to call me. I wondered what it could be about.

Nyx hopped on the desk next to the phone and looked toward the entrance. A young woman approached, giving me her phone number to sign her in. I nearly had a heart attack when she looked at Nyx, though she didn't respond in any particular way. Instead, she continued walking as if Nyx wasn't there at all.

Dave came to the desk a few minutes later and leaned against it; only a few inches from Nyx. Before he spoke, I interjected. "Look, Dave, I'm sorry," I said. "I got caught up the other day. Sorry."

I must have looked as bad as I felt because Dave asked me if I was okay.

Okay? Of course, I wasn't okay. I shouldn't even be alive. My heart quickened to a drum. I closed my eyes, inhaling. When I opened my eyes, I cracked a smile and exhaled. "Yeah, Dave, I'm good. Just been dealing with some stuff but should be all good now."

Dave rasped his fingers against the desk. Thankfully, he didn't pry. "Don't make a habit of it," he said. "I never liked the front desk. I need to walk around and stretch my legs."

"I won't," I said. My phone rang. I fumbled in my pocket to see Alekka calling. When I answered, she was already talking.

"So I don't know what I'm supposed to do, you know?" she said.

I had no idea what she said, and I wasn't about to sit around and try and guess. "No, I don't know. I don't even know what you're talking about, Alekka," I said.

Alekka took a second then spoke again. "Hometown Press HQ decided it would be a great idea to send the head branch editor of the Florida division on a press tour. You know, visit all their branches so they can show us they care and all that shit. I hope they know I can feel *all* their love."

I nodded while waving at someone who signed-in and walked by. "Cool, I got the back story." I paused. "I don't want to be rude, but what does that have to do with me? Or did you need someone to vent to, because then I'm all ears."

Alekka laughed. "Get here as soon as you're off work," she said. I didn't say anything. "Please," Alekka added.

"Wait, what's going on?" I glanced at Nyx, who was lying across the table now.

"Shit, I have to go," Alekka said. "See you soon." She hung up.

I thought about the million things that Alekka could possibly need me for. With the HQ editor there, I would think that was even more reason to lay low. I ended up settling on the fact that Alekka needed me to come to make an excuse to leave. She would probably make an excuse about who I was so she could get out of the corporate shenanigans.

Dave bit into an apple that I never saw him grab in the first place. He smiled and walked back to his desk. "Sounds like a world of fun," Dave said.

"Yeah, it's definitely something," I said. "Just not sure what yet."

"Ahh, to be young again," Dave said. He shot around when the next person walked through the door and showed them to his desk. His chipper voice carried through the building even with the music in the background. Top 40 hits every day, rain, hail, sleet, or snow.

Nyx turned his head around to me. "What do you think the woman wants?" he asked.

I put my phone back in my pocket and returned to the computer. "I'm not sure," I said. "But it can't be anything good."

I returned to Hometown Press after my shift at The Bar. It was only a few blocks from my office, which made the drive short and sweet at this time of day. When I pulled into the parking lot there were significantly more cars than there had been the first time I came. That only made me more anxious. I never was the type for crowds—and don't even get me started on group projects. The moral of the story, me and numbers don't add up very well. I left the car and went inside the building, Nyx right behind me.

When I entered, the last person in a group of people entered the elevator. I decided to use the stairs and made my way to the third floor. More voices in the distance, a few laughs here and there. Before I could make it halfway to the office, Alekka rushed out to meet me.

"Perfect timing," she said. "We were just coming back from a late lunch." Alekka leaned down to Nyx. "And how are you doing this morning, Nyx?"

Nyx glared at Eira, then up at Alekka. "Fine," he said.

"Perfect timing for what, exactly?" I interjected. At this point, I felt like she loved keeping me on edge. "I actually needed to see you." I grabbed the manuscript from my bag. "Got something for ya."

"Great!" Alekka stared at the paper as if she was a child staring at cake. She swiped the papers from me and beckoned me to follow her to her desk. Alekka put the pages on top of her keyboard and then turned back to me.

"First things first." Alekka glanced over my shoulder to where the noise was coming from. "I guess you could call it networking," she said. She led me past the receptionist and toward an office in the back next to a printer.

A woman with a freckled nose speed walked down the hall toward us. She carried an aura about her that demanded respect, whether you wanted to give it or not. The woman wore a messy bun and a gray blazer. If it wasn't for her nose and eyebrow piercing, I would have pinned her for the stereotypical corporate type.

"Both of you, in my office," she said. Then she stopped and turned back to me. "Sorry. Where are my manners? I'm Tara." Tara shook my hand. "Now, in my office."

I laughed a little. I wasn't sure if I was supposed to or not. "Nexus," I said.

She stared at me for a second, then pointed at Alekka. "Get the notes from earlier to me when you have a chance," Tara said as she went into what I presumed was her office.

"Of course," Alekka responded. She waited for the door to close and then grunted. "I swear, if it isn't one thing, it's another. She doesn't stop." I felt her frustration.

Eira appeared. The leopard stalked ahead, her form disappearing and reappearing in the frosted area surrounding her. Eira moved with pride, holding her head high, The bandana she wore around her neck swung subtly. She phased through the door and continued inside.

"That's my cue," Alekka said. "Text me if you need me."

I rubbed my hands together, breathing into them as I cupped them around my mouth. At least the temperature debacle was solved. With Eira always at Alekka's side, it's no wonder she was always in a hoodie. It was probably the only way she could stay warm.

There was more laughter coming from Tara's office—it made me cringe. I couldn't imagine myself in a room full of people that I either respected enough to kiss their asses or only kissed their asses because I possibly needed a favor from them in the future. Maybe I'll understand it one day. But that was why they sat in their seats, and I sat in mine. My fake laugh came a long way. The facial expressions that went with it, not so much—little steps.

"Wait, what is going on?" I asked again, growing more frustrated.

Alekka stopped and looked me over, patting my shoulders. "Look, just go with the basics, be yourself, say no if you don't want to do something, and smile." Alekka held her fingers out, nodding to herself with approval. "Oh, and make sure you play along. Now get out there, champ!"

"Wait, wait, wait, what am I ev—" Before I could finish my sentence, Alekka tossed me into the deep end without a life vest.

14

Being in a room full of branch employees from Hometown Press headquarters brought a level of tension and paranoia that I wasn't ready for. It felt like being stranded in the wrong neighborhood and leaving your car overnight. You expected to come back the next day to nothing but the shell of your car, if that. Now take that and multiply it. That was what it was like having Nyx and Eira sitting in the room, as well as everyone continuing their conversations. Nyx was right. Each person in the room was none the wiser. Nyx could have pounced on one of their laps and I doubted anyone would have flinched.

Alekka came into the room and shut the door behind her. She walked around me and stood by the wall to the left of me.

"You must be Nexus," a man said. My eyes shifted to the man sitting in the seat to my right wearing a velvet-colored suit. He was middle-aged, probably in his early forties. "Heard you're going to be sending us some work soon. I'm Charles." Charles was average height, but he was as wide as he was tall. In his defense, it did seem like he was more muscle than fat. His head was shaved which said a lot. Some men understand it is gone and embrace the baldness—most hang on for dear life and have to go through the awkward breakup. I respected his choice.

We stared at each other for a second. "We met the other day, actually.

Well, not formally," I said. "In the lobby." I tried to keep calm. What the hell had Alekka gotten me into?

His eyes widened. "Oh, yes!" He snapped his fingers. "I remember now." He rubbed a hand to his bald head. "Wait until you start aging a bit, it isn't as easy to remember everything." Everyone laughed except for me. I could tell Alekka's was forced.

To his left, a woman who was as tall as Charles waved at me. "Susan," she said. Susan wore thick glasses; ones that weren't fashionable years ago but have become high fashion now. Though something told me she didn't buy them because of her fashion prowess. Her hair was also tied in a messy bun, comfortable but professional. She had a sense of importance that took over the room, and I made sure to take note of it.

"Where you from?" Charles asked me.

I looked at Alekka, as if she was my parent and I was hoping for the right answer. What the hell had she gotten me into, and what was I supposed to be "playing along" with? I turned back to Charles. "I'm from Union City," I answered. "Born and raised."

"The literary community here is growing," he said. "Though it's still a long way off if it wants to compete." He pointed at Alekka. "That's where people like you come in, hopefully." He clenched his fist. "We have those who keep the lights on and things moving. Now we must find those who will take the press to different heights. Fresh voices."

Susan wagged a finger. "Don't mind him. He gets excited when he gets around other writers. What he means to say is thank you for escorting Alekka to the Halloween party. She told us you were in the area, and I told her to have you stop by. I hope I didn't inconvenience you."

My eyes darted for Alekka. Halloween party? This was the first I heard of it.

"Oh, no worries," I said. "It was no problem at all. Are you throwing the party?" I had no idea what they were talking about. But at this point, this would get me to the answer quicker than waiting to find out.

Susan's phone rang. She checked it, then put a finger up. "I have to take this. It'll be just a moment." She answered the phone while walking out of the office.

Charles pulled up the chair next to him. "Take a seat. Nexus, was it?"

he asked. "Interesting name, first person I've ever met with it. Who gave it to you?"

I hesitated, the question catching me off guard. I still wasn't used to the name yet. "It's a family name," I replied.

Charles nodded. He turned to Tara. She glowered at him as she tapped her pen against her keyboard. "We should probably cut to the chase. Boss lady's getting upset."

"If you keep talking, you might actually make me mad," Tara said, smiling.

Charles leaned over to me. "Is she always this scary?" he asked.

I didn't respond. How would I know? This was my first time meeting her. I shrugged my shoulder, figuring if I ignored him, he'd stop and move to the next thing. Corporate talk wasn't one of my strong suits, and I wasn't about to start working on it now.

Tara cleared her throat—Charles went silent. The door opened and Susan entered, chiming in as if not missing a beat. "Each year, Hometown Press's head branch throws a Halloween party and I'm heading up this year's."

"Halloween party?" I questioned. "Are work Halloween parties a thing?"

She shrugged. "Of course, they are," Susan said in a shocked tone. "If you know, you know. And now you know. It's nothing crazy, but it is a great networking opportunity."

I didn't have words. On one hand, I didn't think I wanted to be anywhere near a Halloween party... or any party, for that matter. But this was an opportunity I'd jump out of a moving plane to be at.

"But why me?" I asked, forgetting to play along.

Susan looked at Alekka, then back to me. "I was going to escort Alekka but with managing the event, I'm going to have my hands full. And when Charles offered to take her, she let us know she had asked you about it."

"Oh, yeah, sorry," I said, clearing my throat. "She didn't tell me it was a Halloween party. Forgot it was already Halloween. This year's flying by." Shit. Shit. Shit. What was I supposed to do? It wasn't that I didn't want to escort Alekka. I mean, who wouldn't jump at that opportunity? There didn't seem to be many negatives with this request. Except for the fact I wasn't good with the whole party thing. And ever since the breakup, I've steered clear of them at all costs. I doubted someone who barely went anywhere but work and home was the best choice for an escort. Sure, Alekka and I got drinks the other day, but that was no pressure—my first time out in over a year. A Halloween party, as far as zones are concerned, was an entirely different time and space.

But what could a simple networking function kill? It was an opportunity—one I was sure Alekka wanted to attend as badly as I did. And even if I didn't want to do it, I couldn't leave Alekka on an island by herself. The least I could do was throw her a raft for having my back lately... and saving it—literally.

"There's nothing like a good Halloween party," Susan said.

"Better wear a good costume," Alekka added when she decided to speak.

Halloween had always been a sort of fly-over holiday for me. I had never been into it. So it was typical of me to forget about wearing a costume. Me picking a good costume out—unlikely. I let out an awkward laugh and said, "Trust me, I got this." The only thing I *had* was a big mouth that didn't know when the hell to shut up.

Alekka raised a brow. "Is that right? Good. That makes this easy, then. I assumed I was going to have to help you pick something out."

"I sort of missed the part where that was an option," I said. Everyone laughed. I didn't, on account of it not being a joke. I would have loved to choose that option. But I let them have their moment.

"Then it's settled," Susan stated. She clasped her hands together, grinning behind her spectacles.

"When's the party?" I asked. "Friday or Saturday?"

"Wednesday." Susan waved her hand in the air as if my words brought her disgust. "It's a Halloween party, Nexus, it must be held on Halloooooween!" Susan pointed at Alekka. "You, along with the rest of the attendees, will be off the rest of the week. That gives you plenty of time for recovery."

The rest of the week? Just who was this woman? It was killing me to know. I saw Tara out of the corner of my eyes, looking far more stressed than a person who just got an early vacation should.

Susan took a few steps and sat on the edge of Tara's desk. "Don't worry. If I'm not at work, none of the branches in Florida publish. Nothing prints without landing on my desk first. Just think of it as a

Halloween miracle." Susan touched Tara on the hand. "You can make a Halloween miracle happen, right, Tara?"

"You're the boss," Tara said. She leaned back in her chair. The sun's rays touched her eyes from the window behind her.

Charles grumbled. He clasped his knees and jumped up. "Perfect," he said. "Now that the looming danger is quelled, should we get some work done?"

The rest of the group agreed. Tara's fingers glided across her keyboard. In a span of a minute, she might have sent out four or five emails. She was efficient, if nothing else.

I felt uneasy as if there was work I had forgotten about. It was always best for me to follow my gut feelings. "I should get going," I said, making my way to the door.

Susan waved and smiled. "I'll get your number from Alekka," she said. "Be on the lookout for the address."

I took out my phone. "Should I just grab it now?"

Susan wagged a finger at me. "Can't build up suspense like that, now, can we? Don't worry, I'll be in contact."

I didn't press. By now I was already in way too deep. Pushing further would do more harm than good. Alekka opened the door and left the office with me. When the door shut, she slammed her back against the wall and sighed. "I don't know how much more of this shit I can take," Alekka said. "How do they do it all day?"

"So you're going to hop over the whole you signing me up for a party without my permission? Where do they even do that at?" I half-laughed.

"Sorry." Alekka pointed toward the door with her thumb. "I was afraid if I didn't tell them I had a date, they were going to have Charles escort me. And I'd rather not, ya feel me?"

I nodded. "Is this normal life for you?" I asked genuinely. For a long time, this was the life I envisioned for myself, so it was interesting to know someone on the inside.

"I don't get it," Alekka said. "One second, it's a meeting, then it's a meeting about a meeting, then it's lunch about the meetings. By the time you have time to do work, the day's over and you're exhausted…" Alekka flipped through the pages of her notepad. "But no, life has become much more difficult since I started shadowing Tara."

"That sounds draining," I replied.

Alekka screamed into her notepad, so the sound was muffled. When she rose, she patted her blazer top. "But I'll make it through. Besides, Tara's easily doubling the workload I'm pulling. I couldn't tell you when she gets sleep."

I shoved my hands into my pockets. "When will they leave?" I asked.

Alekka shrugged. "Hopefully after the party. Then I can get my normal life back."

Normal... What does normal even mean anymore? "Yeah."

"You ever find time to get from behind the desk and work out yourself?" Alekka asked.

Rule #1, never work out where you work if you happen to work at a gym. I narrowed my eyes at Alekka. "Yeah. I go to Union Gym." I was all about functionality. If I could be quicker than most—and lift a good amount, I would be fine. Although as of late, I have missed more days than I normally would like to. With all the added stress it was the first thing that dropped off.

"You want to hit the gym later? A few more hours of this and I'm going to need to blow off some steam."

I let out a short laugh. "At least you don't have a novel to finish in the next few days."

Alekka smiled. "Yeah, I'd hate to be that person." Her eyes flashed from their normal hazel to a snowy white. "I'll meet you at Union Gym after work." Alekka opened the door. Before the door closed, Eira jumped atop Alekka's shoulder.

I followed behind her. No point in me overstaying my welcome. Besides, I didn't have as much time left to kill now that I was working out tonight. I rubbed my neck; it was stiff with all the new stress. Alekka was right, maybe the gym was exactly what I needed.

15

Union Gym wasn't one of your typical run-of-the-mill gyms. It provided much more than any fifteen-dollar-a-month franchise gym knew it needed to offer. From the outside, Union Gym didn't look like anything special. It shared a parking lot with a U-Haul dealership and a mixed martial arts gym. If someone wasn't looking for it, they could miss it. Inside told a different story.

Two clerks at the front desk had their faces buried in their phones when I entered. I scanned in, greeted the clerks (they didn't respond, obviously), then continued in.

Pictures of celebrities who had worked out at the gym lined the walls. Then came the signed memorabilia and the side room where I was told they had one of those bodyfat pods. I never took the time to check it out. As I made my way, the familiar blare of music from a variety of overhead speakers touched my ears. It was one of the main reasons I went to this gym. Usually, I had my headphones on, but it was nice to feel the rumble of the gym as I lifted. For me, the atmosphere was everything. If the energy was off, there was no way I'd have a good workout. So not having the Top 40 hits shoved down my throat paid for the gym itself.

Several stair machines lined the wall to the right as soon as I emerged from the hall. On the second floor, people ran on treadmills and rode bikes. Before me was one of the turfed areas that resembled a football field, where a woman was pushing a sled back and forth every thirty or so yards.

I avoided awkward eye contact with anyone as I turned and went to the locker room. A man jumped up from the bicep machine to my right and then started stretching. Another person cut me off to get to the water fountain next to the locker room. Oh, how I loved the gym.

Too bright lights flooded the gray and brown room as I entered. I picked out the same locker I always chose, locker number six. It had always been my lucky number. I also happened to be born on the sixth, which always drew me closer to it whether in sports or picking out a locker in the gym. I tossed my things inside and headed toward the back of the gym where things are a bit more secluded. The back room was empty, but that likely wouldn't last long at this hour. Much like the area up front, there was turf going down the center. Along with it came lifting areas for Olympic lifts and squat racks.

The clatter of metal echoed through the building. A grunt here and there followed weights bouncing off the ground. It all came together to make the perfect symphony. I forced my eyes shut and breathed, listening to the music.

Nyx groaned. I opened one of my eyes and saw the demon cat pacing, trying to get comfortable. He found a spot next to me, void of any weights, and plopped himself down. "I don't know how you listen to this vile music," he said.

"I didn't ask you to come," I replied.

"A true statement," he admitted.

I glowered at Nyx. "How long have you been here? You know, like, in my world?"

Nyx returned my gaze as if confused. He thought for some time, probably figuring out a way to tell me what I wanted to know while omitting what he didn't think I would understand. It was only natural; Nyx was as wary of me as I was of him. "I've been here since I can remember. I have no recollection of anything else. I've never been to my home world as far as I know." Nyx didn't move. I could feel a faint blip of sadness. "Traveling to the Otherworld takes a large amount of voltage —voltage I wouldn't have without our bond growing."

"Why don't you go back now?" I asked. "I've seen you in action. I'm sure you have more than enough power to cross over now." I watched as a man walked by to grab two kettlebells behind me. As he went back, I almost called for Nyx to move out of the way. Nyx simply moved to the side, letting the man pass.

"I've already told you. Synth demons have one goal, to kill each other. What you've seen is nothing in terms of power. I'd be signing a death warrant if I went back as I am."

That blip grew, if only ever so slightly. I reached for my toes, stretching out my hamstrings. My body was in knots. I pressed my head as close to my knees as possible. "Do you want to go home? Like to the Otherworld?"

The gym went silent as the song changed, then returned to a cacophony of noise. Nyx gave me a look halfway between sadness and anger. "It doesn't matter. I have no home, neither here, nor there." I watched Nyx. His emptiness reached me, no matter how hard he tried to smother it. It was familiar. I had been consumed by that same emptiness my entire life. Whether he was a demon or not, these emotions were the same. I couldn't fathom being born in a foreign land, unable to return to where I belonged—and being alone.

"Sorry," I said. It felt right, though I knew it wouldn't change anything.

A sudden chill took over the gym. I turned to see Alekka walking toward me, Eira at her side. "Heya," Alekka said. Her eyes went from me to Nyx. Within seconds, she analyzed the room and came up with her own assessment of the situation. "Am I interrupting something?"

"No, you're fine," I said. Looking at Alekka, I instantly realized this was the first time I had ever seen her in the gym without her signature oversized hoodie. She was more of the stand out or don't stand at all type of person. Today she wore a black sports bra, one of the ones with the back cut out. Fashionable, but not everyone could pull it off. Her leggings were pink, with black leopard print down the side. They were flashy, but Alekka made it look casual as if this were any other day. She pulled her socks up, so they covered her leggings, then laced her Chuck Taylors tight, and finished it off with a hat pointed forward.

I'm no slouch, but in comparison to Alekka, it looked like I wasn't even trying. I've always been a fan of black. Don't get me wrong. I enjoyed colors, but black was always a good choice. Black joggers and a black shirt cut so I felt free enough to enjoy my workout were my go-to. It seemed the right choice earlier. But now I'm wondering if I've made the wrong decision. There I went, analyzing everything to the smallest molecules again.

"What are you working out today?" Alekka asked. She adjusted her ponytail, pulling it through her hat.

"Leg day," I said.

"Are you serious, or are you trying to impress me?"

"Trust me, it's not for the reason you think," I joked. "I figure might as well get the worst out of the way. Plus trying to get anything chest or back-related today is out of the question."

Alekka laughed. "Touché." She showed her palms to me. "After you."

I didn't have a plan, so I went to one of my golden workouts—ones to kill the legs and make you feel like you've earned your gym time. Rubber weights hung on the squat rack. I loaded one side while Alekka did the other.

I wasn't weak by any means, but I also wouldn't be mistaken for the strongest guy in the gym. The last time I did front squats, I probably lifted a hundred and thirty-five pounds. Out of habit, I put a few twenty-five-pound plates on and went to warm up. I placed my body under the weight and slammed my feet into the ground. Nothing. The weight could have been ornaments at this point. I could barely feel them. I squatted the weight, ten times, then fifteen, then enough times to lose count. When I placed the weight back on the bar, Alekka took the plates off and added the forty-five-pound plates.

"First day back to the gym since becoming a Hybrid, huh?" Alekka asked. She got under the weight and started squatting with my max weight as if she was lifting a broomstick. There was no way this could be right. Was this all because of Alekka's bond with Eira? Sure, the Hybrid concept had credence, but this wasn't real. I watched as Alekka re-racked the weight. This whole time there have been people with these abilities living amongst me. And now I was one of them.

I smiled genuinely. Everything had become such a whirlwind of the unknown of late—my body included. At least if things were changing, they sometimes worked in my favor. Maybe *other* parts of my life would benefit me. One could only hope. If this was what it meant to be a Hybrid, I might be able to get used to it—heavy on the *might*.

Alekka took a seat on the turf while I tried a new personal best. "Sorry for getting you roped into the Halloween party," she said. She took a sip from her water bottle. "I sort of panicked when Susan asked me. I could see Charles getting ready to volunteer himself as tribute."

"And here I was thinking I was invited because of my literary prowess." I laughed. "It's fine, It will be a good opportunity to 'network.' If I'm ever going to be a writer, I need to start putting myself out there." I shook my head, sighing.

Alekka unloaded the weight after I finished my set—she didn't raise her weight this time, but I had a feeling it was because others would start asking questions when she started front squatting at the gym. "When are you going to tell me what you're wearing?" she asked.

"When I pick you up for the party, I think."

Alekka laughed and nodded. "I respect a man of his word," she said. "I shall wait and see."

I started setting up the next workout as she stretched near the turf. "Can I ask you something?"

"Shoot," she responded.

"If Hybrids are stronger than others naturally, what's the point of coming to the gym?" I asked. I felt ashamed after asking. "Not that I was planning on never coming again."

Alekka laughed. "Uh-huh, suureee. But muscle control is muscle control. You need to be able to control your body and your voltage as one." Alekka paused. "You know about voltage, right?"

"Yeah, a little bit. Not enough to mean much of anything."

Alekka frowned. "One day at a time, right?" I watched Eira who stayed close to Alekka the entire workout. For a lack of words, she was Alekka's shadow. Whichever way I twisted it, she was as fond of Alekka as Alekka was of her.

"When did you and Eira become bonded?" I questioned suddenly. I barely remembered saying it. "You're both really close."

Eira pressed her body against Alekka's leg, purring. "I was ten, maybe eleven. I forget sometimes. Though my situation was a bit different than most." Alekka continued working out while she talked, maintaining her breathing. She told me of the day she saw Eira sprawled out on the ground on her way home from school. Eira was being attacked by another demon and escaped to our world.

Alekka continued. "At the time, I would have been easy prey for Eira. But I did something that puzzled Eira at the time. I could see the demon, yet instead of running in fear, I came to Eira's aid. I grabbed her and rushed her as far from danger as I thought possible. Eira told me to leave her, but I decided to stay."

"And you still don't listen," Eira interjected softly.

"I'm sorry. I'm trying to do better." Alekka put her hands together, apologizing.

"Anyways, Eira didn't want me to die for making a poor decision." Alekka went on. It was clear how much she loved Eira. Her face glowed any time she spoke of her. Alekka told me how Eira wouldn't allow a demon to rip Alekka apart. A child that could see Eira, yet didn't fear her. And a child who came to her aid out of pure reaction. Eira, at that moment, named that girl Alekka and created the bond so she would have a chance at escaping their enemy and surviving.

"And this little lady has been with me ever since," Alekka said. Eira rolled over as Alekka nudged her with her foot.

I let out a tired huff as I finished the exercise. Alekka leaned her back on the machine behind her. "You holding up?" she asked. "I know it can be a lot at first. I've been able to see demons for as long as I can remember, so I wasn't as surprised when it happened to me. I can only imagine how you must feel tapping into your voltage this late."

I inhaled, filling my lungs. "That's just it," I said. "Believing isn't my problem anymore. I've seen it firsthand; I know it's real. But I don't have a story. Nothing. I don't know how Nyx and I became bonded." I scratched my hair in frustration. "Ironic, a writer with no story."

Alekka touched her chin and nodded. "The amount Hybrids retain after their incident varies. Your mind might be foggy still. The puzzle pieces must not be fully lined up yet. Do you remember anything?"

"All I remember is you saying my name funny the other day. And then even I started to forget my name." I hated the way that name sounded coming off my tongue. Nexus. Who names somebody that? It sounded like a character out of some anime.

Eira turned her chin up at Nyx. "Maybe the bond wasn't formed properly. Forming the bond incorrectly can have dire effects on both the host and the demon. An amateur could have easily made a mistake." She sat, licking her paw.

Nyx's mouth opened like a water gate ready to let in the flood. "I'd watch that tongue of yours if I were you." His words struck true, but I felt something else in them. She turned the gears of Nyx's mind. He was thinking.

"Nyx, stop." I sighed. "Not now." I stood between the two demons. Nyx huffed, mouthing something, then stalked away.

Alekka tapped Eira on the head with a finger. "I'm sorry, she isn't normally this bratty." I watched both. The way they interacted with each other was pure, natural. It was clear how much they enjoyed each other. In a sense, I was jealous. I thought about getting a pet once, but that thought was removed when I realized caring for myself in these times was already difficult enough. Besides, I would have only gotten one for selfish reasons. I promised myself if I got a pet, it would be because I really wanted one, not because I was lonely at the time.

Then there was Nyx. I wanted to laugh. If I could have chosen a pet, he would've been the last animal I would have selected. Don't get me wrong. In his normal form, he was cute, but cats weren't my thing. Not even in the top three of things. I doubted we would ever be all cute and adorable like Alekka and Eira. We were more like fire and wind. It was only a matter of time before something burned to the ground.

After we finished most of my workout, Alekka rested her hands on her knees, breathing heavily. "Who would have thought you'd have me out of breath," she said. "I normally run through these things."

I shrugged. "Guess I'm full of surprises."

She snapped her finger as if coming up with a bright idea. "Mind letting me take over for a minute?"

This could be dangerous for me—but what did I have to lose? Alekka did my workout so far. It was only right. "Why not?" I said.

Alekka grinned. "Great. Follow me."

We went upstairs to an area of the gym that housed some more cardio equipment, and a set of the rings gymnasts use, next to the monkey bars. Along the wall were more mirrors, and underneath them mats for core work. Alekka grabbed the cleaner and wiped off both mats for us.

"Pick your poison," she said.

I lay on the mat, dreading what was to come. Core wasn't my strong suit. And by that, I meant I rarely worked core any longer. I've been lucky enough to be blessed with a lanky frame. With that frame came a decent core if I maintained a healthy enough diet and workout.

"I would tell you what we're doing, but you'll hate me," she said. "Just follow what I do."

I regretted agreeing to the activity before I even knew what it was. Alekka took her phone out, clicking away on some application. She put the phone on the ground in between us, taking a deep breath. I followed suit. The last thing I wanted was to be winded before we even began.

A bell chimed, and Alekka eased into toe touches. I shadowed her movements. At first, I kept pace, even feeling a little better about myself, but then the seconds seemed long and I wondered if the bell was ever going to sound again. I tried to clear my mind of thoughts that sounded similar to defeat. We continued, grueling second after second until the sound of bliss pricked my ears.

"Break," Alekka huffed. She rested her hands against her midsection.

"I guess that wasn't so bad," I said. "Maybe I—"

The bell chimed again. Alekka flipped over and held a plank. I reluctantly did the same.

Alekka turned her head to me. "Maintaining your voltage alone feels like going through a circuit. You're trying to catch your breath, all while your core is screaming with fire. And that's just maintaining a constant amount of it. Trying to weaponize your volt is a whole other battle."

The bell dinged. We both lowered our bodies to the mat. When the break was over and the bell sounded, Alekka did Russian twists and I followed.

"And to make things more difficult..." Alekka did a few more, controlling her breathing. "The relationship you hold with your partner depicts how well you're able to control and manifest your volt. You can't only focus on the physical. The mental game is as important."

I was dying, but my mind was racing. "So my relationship with Nyx can have positive and negative consequences even with control?" I asked.

"Not can. Does," she replied. "Without a good relationship, trying to manifest volt can feel like treading water in the ocean with no sign of help coming. No matter how much you try, it takes all your effort to stay afloat, but hell if you're going anywhere."

Another break, finally. We continued this, jumping from workout to workout, while taking rest breaks in between. Somehow, we managed to keep our conversation going.

"When I've fought, Nyx... I felt everything he did." I looked at Eira. "When Nyx fought, he turned his tail into a blade. Is that like what you and Eira do?"

"Sort of, sort of not," she said. "Some demons can change their bodies, but it takes a considerable amount of volts and skill." She paused, thinking, then continued working out. "In your case, it'd probably be the best way to fight since you are fresh to manifesting volts. It won't happen overnight. Learning to properly control your voltage, and then learning to weave it together to fight with your partner, can take years. It's an art. I've been working on it for what feels like forever now, and I still feel like a novice."

"That's because we are novices," Eira purred, though I could tell she didn't mean it with any negativity.

If Alekka was a novice, what did that make me? Lucky, of course. Lucky to be alive. And lucky to have Alekka and Gyle. Waking up felt like a blessing more and more each day.

"How do I know how large my voltage reserve is?" I asked, frowning. "I guess, how do I know when too much is too much?"

Alekka grunted through the exercise. "Not sure, to be honest. Is trial and error a bad answer? With ever-growing bonds, your reserve will also grow. Of course, there's eventually a limit to what each person's body can handle. Just make sure you never tap out your voltage reserve."

I didn't have to ask the follow-up question of what would happen if I depleted my voltage reserve. It was laid out plain and simple. Play within your limits and you will be fine. Though facing what the Otherworld had to offer might require living in a state outside those limits. My first encounter took more out of me than I ever expected. One false step or estimation could easily issue my death. A chill caught my neck—or maybe it was the sweat doing its job.

The bell chimed one last time before Alekka touched her phone. We both sat there for a second and caught our breath. I lay back, my arms sprawled out to the side, staring at the giant fan spinning overhead. "Not going to lie, it's kinda cool you're an editor," I said.

Alekka rubbed her hand against Eira's side. Eira's white-blue eyes adored her partner as she sat next to her. "Thanks for that," Alekka responded. "Sometimes I think so, too. Other times... I'm not so sure."

"Are you happy? You know, like, are you happy with the work?"

Alekka scrunched her mouth, then nodded. "Yeah, I'm happy. It's hard as hell. But I know I'm doing my part in getting authors's voices out there."

"That's your answer, then." My breathing started to slow. Much faster than I thought it would take, I noted. "As long as you're happy, then keep pushing. Something in it is bringing you that happiness."

Alekka rose. "Geez, one day in the gym and you're already giving me advice. I didn't know we were that close of friends already." She laughed as she helped me up.

We headed down the stairs to our respective locker rooms to grab our things. I checked behind me to see Nyx in tow—though he trailed far behind to distance himself from Eira. We went out the entrance, waving goodbye to the new staff on the way out. I stared at the muted sunset as I walked Alekka to her vehicle. One glance at Alekka's car reminded me that I hadn't taken the Jetta for a wash in months. Her blue Jeep looked like it got a wash and the works weekly. She checked her phone, huffed, then opened the door. "Looks like I have a new fire to put out while I grab dinner," she said.

"Hey, let me know if there's anything I can help with," I responded.

"Get home and get some rest, It's getting late." Alekka's Jeep engine roared. "My legs are tight already. Thanks for the great workout."

I waved bye to her, then went to the Jetta. Alekka was right. My legs felt like a rolled-up wet towel. That's what I got for setting a personal best on every workout. I was going to need to set new boundaries. Luckily, Union Gym wasn't far from the house—I needed a long shower and food.

I turned right, then merged into the far left lane. Nyx remained silent in the passenger seat. As I neared the neighborhood entrance, Nyx spoke, his head never turning in my direction. "Keep driving," he said.

"You like car rides or something?" I replied, laughing. "I learn something new every day."

Nyx didn't laugh. "We're being followed." Nyx's eyes tracked to the rearview mirror. I followed his gaze. There were only a few cars behind me, all happening to be driving at a similar speed. I took a left at the next intersection and continued. Only one car from before followed now. My tailer. My paranoia rose.

"How long have they been following us?" I asked.

"Can't be certain," Nyx said. "I felt something when we were at the gym, but I couldn't be sure until we left."

My breathing was unsteady. "Do you know what it is?" Nyx glowered at me, silent. "Right, probably would have told me if you did."

"All I can say is it's not a Seed demon," Nyx said.

I thought back to what Nyx told me previously. He made it clear that if anything besides Seed demons came after me, I was to hightail it out of there. The dark sedan behind me gained a few inches. Whoever was driving was going to make me as uncomfortable as possible until I pulled over or crashed. And I doubted the Jetta could drag out enough speed without ending up on the side of the highway with the caution lights on.

There weren't many options, and the highway was coming up. If I didn't decide soon, something told me I might never have the chance to regret not making a better choice. The sedan was damn near bumper-to-bumper with me now. Fuck. There wasn't time to come up with some elaborate plan to get me out of this. I would have to do with what the world gave me. I hoped it was something good.

16

I drove down a side route that led behind North Florida University. To most, it was a road that served no purpose. It was the type of area you'd get lost in quickly if you didn't know where you were going. I'd lost my way plenty of times when I was an undergrad. After the third or fourth time, I just opted to always use my GPS, or took the highway and went around. It was quicker, anyway. I knew the roads well enough now to get out if I needed to; I hoped the driver behind me didn't.

I gained a few feet on my pursuer. The constant winding road forced them to slam on their brakes multiple times, whereas I rolled along at a constant speed. In a bit, the blinding lights behind me disappeared, though I didn't dare slow. After a minute, I saw my destination in the distance and sped up.

"Where the hell are you taking us?" Nyx asked.

"I have a plan... Well, sort of." Nyx didn't respond. He turned back, staring out the car window. After the next stop sign, I pulled into the large parking lot next to the main campus. "Follow me." I jumped from the car and sprinted down the road toward the student union building. Halfway there, I began to regret doing leg day more and more. I almost tripped as I rounded the corner and crossed the street to where the three flags waved overhead.

Just a bit more.

The main walkway of NFU was the only open space I could think of on campus once you got past the student union. The only other open area on campus was the field in front of the art building. I ran from where the ground was made of granite to the grassy field before the man-made pond. The fountain billowed in the background, the water making a rhythmic sigh as it splashed upon itself.

I've never watched horror films. I respected the art—just wasn't my thing. But what I saw approaching me had to be straight out of a slasher film. A figure about average height trudged towards me. The person was fully shielded in a black cloak. It stopped and glared at me with glowing, dark blue eyes. The world felt small, almost like I was in a vacuum. All I could focus on were its eyes, the blue crystals staring into me. The air around me thickened, making it hard to breathe.

"H-hunt," the creature uttered. The voice came out in a low, screeching tone. Nyx took a step in the figure's direction, his head pointed toward it.

"What did it say?" I asked. "Wait, is this a demon?" Speech? My eyes went back to the azure eyes that consumed me. "Speech means a Synth, right?"

Nyx's eyes narrowed. "In most cases, yes," he said.

"What about this case?"

"This one isn't a Synth—not yet. Someone sent it here after us."

That made me a bit more optimistic that we might survive this. The figure in the cloak took a few steps in our direction, its movement unnatural.

"How long do you think you can hold up?"

"Not sure. A minute, maybe two." He huffed in frustration. "If our bond was fully reconnected, he'd pose no threat."

The nighttime lights on the corners of the school buildings were all illuminated. Blue-white light flooded the campus, showing small droplets of water on the blades of grass. The demon pulled the sleeves of its cloak back. Its arms changed from a tan complexion to a dark blue. It looked as if all their life had been drained from them. It pointed one of its blue hands at me. Like a lasso, the hand extended and curved around my body in a long motion. The arm whipped around me before it bulleted directly at me.

It all happened in a second. I barely noticed when Nyx changed. He came to my side, pressing his weight against my body. Everything was silent for a moment. Nothing moved, no one breathed, utter silence.

"Nexus," Nyx purred. My body was engulfed in a healing warmth. Any soreness from the gym I had felt vanished. I felt every muscle in my body readily fueling itself with rage.

Nyx flicked his tail and the world filled with sound again. His tail sliced clean through the demon's arm, cutting bone, cartilage, and muscle alike. It plopped on the ground, drawing a horrific, deafening scream from the demon. I flicked my head around. Only the light from the walkway gave any visibility.

Soon. Soon. It had to be soon.

Nyx was fully engaged with the demon now. He swiped his tail in ferocious strokes as if a painter in disgust with their canvas. The demon hardened its arm into some metal-like substance to defend against Nyx's bladed tail. I wasn't even sure if it could still be called skin. Sparks flew as Nyx's tail met the demon's hardened skin. There was nowhere to move, nowhere to insert myself. Not without fear of making things worse.

For a moment, Nyx seemed to be making way. The demon was on defense. Nyx refused to give it an opening. I waited and watched. Nyx said "a minute, maybe two." There had to be something I was missing, something I was not aware of. At my feet, the arm that was severed moved and then dissipated into the ground. My eyes traveled to what was left of the demon's arm.

If things couldn't get any weirder, what was left of the arm began to writhe—then piece-by-piece it began stitching itself back together. In seconds, a new arm replaced the old, and the demon was back to full strength.

Can't I catch a break?

The arm flew at me again. It didn't even make it a foot before Nyx chopped it off again. I hopped aside as I avoided being grabbed. The least I could do was stay out of the way and try to not be a liability. More sparks flew overhead. Another arm slithered for me going in all sorts of sporadic directions. Nyx jumped back while he sliced another arm to the ground. Every few seconds, the demon's arm grew back and took a different approach to get at me. If anything, it was adapting quickly.

A minute passed now. Another minute was beginning to feel like an eternity away.

Nyx gazed at me from his peripheral vision. "Here," he said. "Make yourself useful." Nyx slammed his paw into the ground. I couldn't quite explain the sensation that took over my body. It was like the first sip of tea after a day in the cold. Nyx licked his lips, his body emitting a golden glow. When the light disappeared, a short sword lay before me in the grass. The blade was black and curving. Its hilt and handle were covered in the finest gold. The metal of the sword matched Nyx's coat, a void of darkness ready to engulf the world. I wished there was a beginner's manual to all of this. What was I supposed to do? What were we even doing? How was I supposed to make myself useful?

The demon shrieked loud enough to cause Nyx to flinch. It then took the opportunity to attack. For a moment, I believed the arm-demon was after me. Every time its arms weaved themselves back together, it came for me. Again and again. Over and over. But then, it became clear what it was doing. With each attempt, it gained a few inches—gained a bit more distance—and drew Nyx's attention from attacking that much more. The battle sped up, the demon pushing his attack as Nyx tried to keep up.

It felt as if I had been dropped onto an old battlefield. The clamor of the weapons as they chimed off one another, over and over again, buried itself in my ears. It was hard to breathe, to keep myself standing. Shit, Of course. I was scared. Who wouldn't be? But I had to stay focused.

I took a glance behind me at the fountain that shot water into the sky. We were running out of room to work with. One arm got through Nyx's defense, and it came for me. I twisted my body out of the way, but only in time for it to clip my shoulder with its fist.

Nyx sprinted to my side and chopped the demon down again. When the arm remade itself, instead of coming for me it simply lay at the demon's side, twitching. As I lay on my back hearing the sound of splashing water, I had an inkling, one that called me like an irritating gnat. It was setting Nyx up—but when was it going to strike? They proceeded, blow after blow. I couldn't be sure I was right; I had no experience or knowledge to draw from. Hopefully, my gut wasn't leading me wrong. Nyx continued his onslaught, only now he expertly evaded incoming attacks as they came. The demon let out another deafening scream. Nyx hesitated, surprised by the screech. That was it, the moment the demon was waiting for. But it was also my opening.

I saw it clearly. In an instant, he drew Nyx away, and his right arm swiveled around, circling Nyx. I reached down, already in a dead sprint, and lifted the sword from the ground. The demon's arm tightened as if it was some sort of zip tie. Nyx jumped back but was met by the left arm of the cloaked being. If there was ever a time to run, that would have been it. Yet I found myself headed toward what I knew might be the end for me. Maybe it was because my body was still burning with an ardent flame, or maybe it was because I watched Nyx put his life on the line for this long, trying to buy my plan time. Sure, if I died, Nyx did as well. But that didn't mean he had to stick around and suffer through it. In this moment, he trusted me and that was enough. And I was sick of sitting around letting everyone tell me what the hell I should and shouldn't do. It was time I took back control.

Union City would sink under sea level before I ran away again.

I propelled my shoulder into the demon's forearm—or what would have been a normal person's forearm. The arm moved off-axis, giving Nyx enough space to dodge the attack. I had thrown my weight so hard that I nearly toppled over. From my downward position, I ripped the sword up in a sweeping motion.

While watching Nyx fight, I noticed something. The demon, whenever it blocked, always tried using the lower area of its arm near the hands. It could have been a coincidence—or the demon had a preference. But I was hoping that wasn't the case. My theory was that the demon could harden parts of its skin, but not all of it at once. If its lower arm area hardened, then its shoulder area wouldn't have enough voltage to have the same strength. Hopefully, my theory was right. I threw all my power into my strike and aimed for the demon's armpit.

It connected, and I felt every muscle in my body explode as I twisted into the attack. To be fair, it didn't slice completely through. That was possibly on account of its body still being harder than most—or it was because of my horrible strike. Note to self: practice swordsmanship.

The sword embedded itself in the bone of the arm-demon. I grunted, pushing with all the force I could gather. The sword shook, and then the blade slipped through. Bluish-black blood oozed from the wound. I wished the demon had given me time to enjoy my victory. Instead, it ruined it by swiping my feet from beneath me and then driving its leg into my stomach. My abdomen burned like a furnace as I flew back, my body tumbling and rolling several times.

My vision blurred and my ears rang. To the right, I heard the ripple of the water crashing. Fuck. This wasn't going as planned. The pain in my gut died down. I guessed that was another perk of the whole Hybrid ordeal—faster healing. Though the extent of that healing, I wasn't too sure of. I knew better than to test it.

I rose, inhaling. It had been almost two minutes by now, right? Soon—soon. Nyx stood between our enemy and me. His breathing was heavy, yet he still maintained a strong posture.

"That plan you were talking about, how long?" Nyx asked. His voice came out heavy and slow.

I was getting nervous. What if I was wrong? My decision could get us both killed. I rose to a knee. There was no right or wrong in this. I had to be right. It was the only option if we were going to make it out of here alive. "Any second now," I assured him.

Our enemy pulled the sleeves of its cloak back. Another arm wove itself where the last had been. Both its arms turned the type of blue you only saw in the deepest ocean—nearly black.

"Death," the demon uttered. It raised both its hands toward us. I clenched the sword's hilt. I didn't know if I would be able to do anything with it, but it gave me a sense of false security.

Then it lowered its arms, scanning the area like a bloodhound. For a moment, it stayed in a silent, still mode, contemplating the options it had. I grinned. The patter of shoes clacking against the walkway echoed off the pond. All the night classes I had taken had finally paid off. Classes had just ended. And if there is one thing I knew, the science building next to the Student Union always had at least one or two night labs. And something told me the creepy crawlies of the night weren't much for crowds.

Voices—emphasis on the plural—approached from the east, coming from the art building, and others from the other buildings to the west. At least two dozen students approached, chatting away. They shared a few laughs while a couple here and there grumbled about how much they hated night classes. Their steps grew louder. Our demon friend seemed to struggle between its natural desire and better judgment. That terrified me. A demon set on bloodlust who didn't care about how much blood they spilled. They would have a field day with this. Shit.

"Get ready," I told Nyx. He nodded. But I knew he had little left. In truth, he also probably could not care less what happened to anyone other than me in the situation. But Nyx could feel my emotions. He knew I wouldn't allow that.

I shook my head of any ill thoughts. I had to trust my judgment. What did this arm-demon gain from killing more than me? It chased me all the way here, which meant it had a purpose. Which meant it had something to lose—I hoped.

It straightened its back and then lowered the sleeves on its cloak. I watched the lonely flames of its eyes as they danced around. Then the cloaked demon walked back toward the Student Union Building and the gym. Before long, it was gone, but I still felt like it was breathing over my shoulder.

I dropped the sword and sprawled my body against the grass, gasping for air. God, I wished I had a cold Gatorade right now, preferably Cool Blue or Orange. I was a beggar, but sometimes you had to be a chooser, too. Nyx came to my side, turning into his house cat form. Beside him, the blade fizzled into a dust-like substance until it was nothing more than another speck in the night.

"What the hell was that?" I asked between breaths.

Nyx was panting, though he held it together. He sure as hell did a better job at maintaining than I did. "I'm not sure," he said. I believed him. "It was a Germ. I know that much. A Synth would have disposed of us in seconds." Nyx lowered his body into the ground, flattening out into a smush-ball of fur. "But it moved with purpose—and spoke."

I sat up, placing my head between my legs, my elbows tented on my knees. Already, something came for us. Nobody could call this happenstance any longer. How much time had it been since the bond reformed enough for Nyx and me to notice, and already there were things out there coming after our lives? I brought my head up. "They were targeting us. That much is certain." I laughed. I was so deep in shit, all I could do was laugh.

"And they're being controlled to do it," Nyx said. "No Synth would be able to chase us down and attack us like that. Someone has an agenda." The doors to the business center opened as more students appeared. "Before any of that, we need to get home." Nyx began walking toward the car. "I need rest, and there's something I need to show you."

"Music to my ears," I said. I got to my feet as quickly as possible—as slowly as ever. There was more enthusiasm in my walk than I expected. Home was the only place I wanted to be right now.

When I made it to the Jetta, my eyes traced the windshield to the orange slip in my wiper—classy. I swiped the paper, crushed it, and then jumped into the car. Nyx chose to phase through the door this time. I began to feel stupid for opening the car door for him earlier.

Nyx placed his head next to the AC vent, letting the air pat his whiskers. I tossed the ticket in the back seat—that's a problem for future Nexus to handle—and pulled out of the parking lot, happy to be alive.

17

I wasn't sure if I would ever match the utter excitement I felt when I pulled into the driveway. And the dread that followed directly after. I left the car, fumbled in my pocket until I found my keys, and then opened the door in one smooth motion. I closed the door, slamming my back into it as it sealed. My body slid to the floor. There was nothing to say, nothing to do. I was angry, but at who—at what? I was almost murdered and there was nothing I could do about it. I hit my forehead lightly with the palm of my hand and grunted my frustrations out.

"I hate this," I said.

"Hate what?" Nyx asked.

"This. Not knowing. How am I supposed to be okay with what the hell just happened?"

Nyx turned to me and sat. "You humans think so small." He shook his head. "Who said accepting meant that you're 'okay' with anything? Accepting only means you understand the reality of the situation. What you do with it is ultimately your decision."

I wanted to curse to the sky until my throat was sore, but what would that do? Nyx was right. I've always had control of everything in my life, like a puppet master weaving his strings. I wasn't a huge fan of change. Recently, I had been losing track of strings faster than I could find them. But I had to take the good with the bad. I survived. A chill went through my body as I thought of how easily it could have been the end. I had to be glad that the cards played the way they did. And for Nyx. I looked over to the demon cat walking to the living room. Without him, I would have been gone in a second.

My stomach growled. There were a few things I needed to do, but none were more important than what was inside the refrigerator. I put together my best attempt at a meal—ending up with a sandwich, some Doritos, and a glass of water. It would have to work for now. A mix of turkey, cheese, and bologna always went down nicely. Add in the mustard and mayo, and you can't go wrong.

I finished half of my water before I sat on the living room couch. It was an old sectional, dark gray, with enough character to fill any room. Lumpy in all the right areas and gave way in the perfect places. It has been with me since my early college years, and with any luck, it wouldn't be going anywhere anytime soon. I pulled my phone from my pocket and went through my messages.

Nyx jumped onto the couch next to me. "What're you doing?" he asked.

My eyes never left my phone. "Deciding if I should call Gyle or not," I said. I pulled at one of my curls, pondering. "We can both agree I'm way over my head at this point, especially now that things are coming after us. Seems like this work is right up his alley."

Nyx took a second to respond. "But you hesitate."

I sat still, hunched over, staring at my phone. "What if what Alekka was worried about is true? Telling Gyle means letting Voss in on things. And I still don't know anything about him. But who am I kidding, what would that change? I could have all the information in the world and still would be hopeless."

Nyx didn't respond at first, but he didn't seem nearly as worried about it as I was. "You might be right," he said finally. "But we should be safe here, relatively speaking."

"Safe? We were just chased down by a literal villain and almost killed. You call that safe?"

Nyx jumped from the couch to the glass table, then sat and stared at me. "First, I need you to calm down so I can talk to you," he said.

My left eye twitched... Maybe Nyx was right. Calm. Calm. "Sorry," I said. "You were saying."

Nyx nodded. "Otherworld beings are tied to rules when they come to your world. We can't just do as we please."

I took another bite of my sandwich. "Give me the SparkNotes."

"SparkNotes?"

"Cut the fluff. Just give me the important parts," I said.

Nyx sighed with displeasure. He thought for a bit. It was clear he was rearranging words, omitting things he probably would have said otherwise, and pulling out the important pieces. "Homes are a natural repellent against Otherworld beings. People naturally feel protected in their homes, thus creating a natural ward against outside beings. That will keep most Seeds from causing you any issues. It takes voltage to go where you're unwanted."

"What about the Germs and Synths?" I asked.

"We put up a ward," Nyx responded. "With your help, I can put up a ward that will keep out any Seeds and Germs, for the most part." Nyx didn't take his eyes off me.

"But?" I asked. "There has to be a *but*."

"But... I'll be honest. Our bond still has a long way to go before it is fully repaired. The ward will take a lot of voltage while activated."

I finished my food, sighing. "So while it's up, if anything happens, we're shit out of luck?"

"Essentially," Nyx said. "At least, until I can bring the ward down and rest a bit."

None of my options were appealing. On one hand, I could let Nyx stay at full strength, but then risk something coming in and trying to catch us off guard. On the other hand, Nyx would ward off as much as he could but if something bigger and stronger came around—it spelled death for both of us. I grunted, then slapped my face twice. If something that big and bad found its way to us now, it would be death, either way.

"How do we put this ward up?" I asked. Nyx had trusted me earlier. That gesture, though small, meant a lot to me. In return, it was my turn to put some trust in him. Whether I liked it or not, we were connected. Death for me meant death for him. Talk about a fucked up situation.

Nyx took his time answering, probably dumbing it down to a level I could comprehend. I appreciated the gesture. It was better than staring at him with the what-the-fuck face. "Certain demons can manifest objects to come to their aid," he began. "Similar to how I created that sword for you earlier. The ward is essentially the same. Manifest the voltage, give it direction and purpose, then the rest is all imagination."

I blinked at him a few times. "It's that easy?" I asked. "So all Synths can just manifest objects?"

Nyx blinked back at me. "Well, I've never been around other demons, but I would assume so."

I nodded. "Imagination. Got it."

Nyx scoffed, but then cracked a feline smile. "If you say so. I'll conjure the voltage; you handle the imagination part." Nyx closed his golden eyes. I followed his command. At first, nothing happened. All I heard was the subtle hum of the house. In the distance, the refrigerator's water filter circulated. The electrical circuits in the wall flickered every so often. It was a quietness I hadn't experienced in some time. My breathing slowed—relaxation crept in. But then something tugged at my being.

In the darkness, I saw Nyx clearly, though my eyes were still shut. A dim gold light covered his body. "Come," he said. He sat in the center, a golden figure, waiting patiently for me to join.

I stepped into the darkness until I was a few inches from Nyx. I sat, placing my hands in front of me with my palms toward the ground, breathing. My body took control. A golden spiritual veil loosely coated my hands. Fleeting thoughts swarmed my mind. I fought against them and focused on the task at hand—Nyx's emotions reaching me. As he gathered voltage, he first thought of protection. Protecting the home, then me... He never thought of himself even once. My body was filled with a warming energy.

Nyx then focused his volts on repelling anything that didn't belong. He thought of warding off anything that would cause me harm. It was at that moment the truth struck—Nyx cared more about my well-being than his own. Whether he'd officially been to the Otherworld or not, he was used to dealing with their beings. He could protect himself, or at least avoid trouble before it got to him. I, on the other hand, was a baby deer, hoping I lived long enough to learn to fend for myself. God, I was pathetic.

"Control your emotions," Nyx uttered. "It will affect the ward."

"Sorry," I answered. I exhaled all my negative thoughts and then continued. I could feel our volts rising, pouring into the space we inhabited, the gold within the darkness. It was evident, the difference in conjuring volts when we were stationary with no distractions, versus when we were in the middle of battle. I took note of this—the feeling of peace. Once Nyx collected enough volts, I knew it was my turn.

I kept my hands open and thought—imagining something that would keep the nightcrawlers at bay yet warn us if it couldn't. Think. Think.

"Now," Nyx said.

A blinding light occupied the space, engulfing the darkness, and then I was back in my living room. It felt like an eternity and a blink all at once. I wasn't sure how much time passed while my eyes were closed. Nyx sat across from me. His head went down to the glass coffee table.

In between us, bouncing around in a tiny circle as if performing some dance routine, was a bird—if I could even call it that. On the surface, it appeared to be a raven. The little bird's head swiveled almost to the point where it was uncomfortable for me to watch. Its eyes were small golden peas, though the rest of its body was coal. The form of the bird was solid in some places, yet a type of miasma in others. It rotated its head, nibbling at its wing, then turned to me—its head bobbing.

Nyx glared at me, his mouth open. Several seconds passed with the bird circling back and forth. He shook his head finally. "You sure do have an imagination," he said. I only wished I would have chosen something more... threatening. I lowered my head. Out of all the things to think of.

The raven jumped and took a practice flight around the lower level of the house. I watched as the bird zigzagged through the kitchen, then traveled upstairs to do more reconnaissance before finally coming back to the living room. The bird finally settled and hovered before me. "It's doable," the bird squawked.

"What's doable?" I asked. I guessed a talking bird was the only thing that made sense. I barely batted an eye.

"This home. You called for its protection. I can grant it."

No matter how harmless this bird looked, when I glared into its golden eyes, I knew without a doubt it was a demon. A demon weapon I had created with Nyx. I threw my hands in the air and laid back on the sofa. "Protection is what we want. Protection is what we get. Simple. I like it," I said. I turned so I could see the bird. "So what's your name?"

The tiny bird spun in a circle. "I have no name," he answered.

Nyx jumped from the table, starting for the kitchen. "A weapon need not be named," he said.

I thought it over for a second, then chuckled a bit. "Why not?" I watched the bird's movements as he floated around the living room. He was protecting us, like our very own flying watchdog. Then it came to me. Years of reading and gaming finally paid off. "Amon," I uttered.

"Amon?" the bird asked.

"It's from a game. *Shadow Hearts*." I grinned. "You're going to be watching over us and living here. That basically makes us friends now, right?" Nyx grumbled something under his breath before going up the stairs. I looked back to Amon. "Make yourself at home."

"Got it, boss," Amon said. He threw his wing up in a military salute and flew off to sit atop the refrigerator.

My phone chimed with a text message. A message from Alekka with a picture, though all I could see was blue and a lot of it—and a text saying: *If you're going to have a Halloween party, you gotta do it right.* There was no way she would show up to the party as an Avatar, or a Smurf... Would she? That thought stressed me out more than it should have.

Panic found a home within me. My Halloween costume was the last thing on my mind. Where the hell did Alekka find the time to fit getting her costume into her schedule? I always had my backup costume I wore a couple few years back if I couldn't find a better solution. There were multiple times I thought about throwing it away. It was the last Halloween I bothered to participate in. And it was also the worst Halloween. My ex and I broke up a few months after that day. It wasn't the costume's fault, of course. But I've always been a bit superstitious. Maybe it was time to wear it again and get the negative juju off it.

Maybe.

I texted back: *I still have a day to get myself together, don't worry.* I put my hands over my face. After everything I've dealt with, exhaustion was taking over. The world didn't feel the same anymore. But who was I to complain? Alekka was dealing with the same things, and who knew what else.

The costume could wait. I needed sleep. "'Night, Amon," I said, waving wearily.

"'Night, boss," he replied.

"Just call me Nexus."

"Sure thing, boss." Amon rolled his head to the side. I shrugged. The little bird tweeted a song of passion to an invisible tune. A small golden orb of light emitted from his broad little chest. The sphere grew and grew and grew, until it began engulfing objects in the home. I watched the aura pass over me, popping like a bubble. It pushed against the walls, pressing against the surface, and popped onto the outside of the house. I couldn't help but open the door to touch the energy and feel the way it pricked against my skin. The aura coated itself over the home in a fluorescent golden glow.

I nodded a sign of approval. The security guard drove his golf cart by the house, waving at me. I returned the greeting. At least now I knew I would have some sort of *security* through the night.

18

I dragged myself through a shower and then got dressed the following morning. Nyx chomped down some kitty kibble, then spent a few minutes sharpening his claws against the cat tree. I made what resembled a breakfast downstairs and filled a glass with orange juice. "Morning," I said, passing Amon who was perched on the windowsill staring outside.

"Morning to ya, boss," he squawked. "Clear night. Nothing significant to report." He threw a sharp salute.

I returned it; I didn't want to feel like a grade-A asshole for leaving him hanging. I yawned. My phone rang while I was mid-bite into my eggs. "Hello?" I answered the call. In all honesty, my voice probably came out as a garbled mess, but I'm sure whoever it was got the point.

"I need to meet with you today," Gyle said.

I rubbed the bridge of my nose between my eyes. "No can do," I replied. "Gotta work the gym today."

"I don't need you long. I'll bring lunch." He hung up before I had a chance to tell him no... again. It wasn't like he was giving me much choice, anyway. I called upstairs to Nyx when I finished my breakfast. At least I knew Gyle was bringing food later. Nothing was better than free food. It would be a consolation prize for all the stress I'd taken on.

I went to the gym and was greeted by Dave and his morning apple.

My face must have shown how tired I was because he didn't come over and speak to me like normal. It was for the best. I was in autopilot mode for the foreseeable future. After last night, work was the last place I wanted to be. Hell, if the gym gave PTO or sick days, I would have taken one. I leaned over the front desk and looked at nothing in particular. There was no way I could keep this up, my body wouldn't allow it. I needed rest. Fighting the creatures of the night took a toll on the body. I wasn't sure how Batman kept it up so long.

I went through the motions, checking members in as they came. Even with the ward up, I couldn't truly feel safe. Maybe that came with time and experience. As of now, I trusted what I could quantify—and maybe that was my problem.

Nyx yawned as he stretched his back and sat up. "I swear, no matter how many naps I take, I always want one more," he said. He walked over to a spot where a pool of sunlight hit the tile floor.

"I'm glad one of us is feeling good." I rubbed at the back of my neck where stress gathered. "I can't seem to catch a break." I thought about the manuscript I had submitted to Alekka and wondered if it was the right choice. Since I'd submitted it, I had this lingering feeling that I was missing something. Only I had no clue what. I felt like I was falling from a cliff with no means to an end. I would keep falling, thinking I would eventually hit the ground, only for it to never happen.

A state of constant anxiety I would never escape.

"So this is your place of business. Not what I expected." Gyle said. He placed his hand on my shoulder, nearly scaring me to death. "For some reason, you didn't strike me as the gym type." Somehow, I didn't notice him enter the gym... nor did I notice him come behind the front desk to stand directly behind me.

"That's because I'm not any *type*." I turned so I was facing Gyle.

"So, what, you just sit here and daydream all day and talk with Apple Guy over there?" Gyle pointed at Dave.

"You sure have the mysteriously popping up thing down." I leaned against the desk. "And the apple guy's name is Dave."

Gyle placed an Italian sub from Lix on my desk.

I scanned the gym, then waved at Dave. "I'm going to take lunch," I said.

"Yeah, yeah, sure thing," Dave replied. "Don't take all day this time."

I stood and beckoned Gyle to follow. Further back in the gym and around the corner was a small break room. It wasn't anything fancy, just one round table with a couple of chairs and a loveseat. There was a fridge where people fought over whose food was whose, and a water cooler where no talking was done. I sat on the loveseat and unwrapped my sub. Nothing like a Lix sub to make my afternoon. They're famous and the lines for them wrap around the store on a good beach day.

Gyle sat at one of the chairs at the table before tossing me a water bottle. At the rate I was eating, I would choke without something to wash the food down with.

"What'd you need to see me about?" I asked.

"I might need some help," he said. Gyle looked pensive as if he was hesitant to tell me everything. "Voss came back with some information. Isn't looking too hot."

Nyx raised his head. "Explain," he ordered.

"Please," I added. Nyx might have been ready for what came with his harsh tone, but I wasn't. Not that I feared Gyle, but I didn't want Nyx writing checks that my ass couldn't cash.

Symon appeared from inside of Gyle's jacket. The ferret sniffed around, then laid upon Gyle's shoulder. "Halloween always attracts those that roam the night." He scoffed. "Demons, ghouls, all that type of shit. It's one of the days the Otherworld and your worlds are the closest."

"Closest?" I had to make sure I followed correctly.

"The more people believe, the easier it becomes to bridge a gap between worlds," Gyle said. "Opening a door between worlds won't take much effort on Halloween."

"I see," I said, nodding. I took another bite of my sandwich, which I admitted tasted better than anything I've had recently. "Meaning if anyone wants to stir something up, Halloween would be the day to do it?"

"Exactly," Gyle said. "And we won't be able to pinpoint exactly where it's coming from since there won't be as large of an amount of voltage gathered." For a moment, Gyle didn't speak. Then he sighed. "I have a bad feeling about tomorrow. I told Voss I'd patrol the city with him, but there's only so much we can do."

"And you want me to help?" I asked.

"Hell, no!" he shouted, much too quickly for my liking—I almost felt bad. "You'd get yourself killed out there. No offense." Offense taken. "You're still a noob. I need you to lay low tomorrow. Stay at our place where we know you'll be safe."

I shook my head. "Believe me when I say I would. But I kind of have plans."

"Plans? You?" Again… his surprise was alarming.

"Yeah." I shrugged. "I got this Halloween party that Alekka's publishing company is throwing. I'm Alekka's plus one. I can't miss this opportunity."

Gyle went silent. Then he burst out laughing. "Wait, so you're taking *her* to the party, too!? Oh, cruel world, however do you smite me." He nodded, patted himself down, then focused back on me. "How'd you manage that one? I couldn't even get her to look my way." He put his hand over his face. "You try to make sense of things and you end up more turned around than ever."

"I didn't know you took drama classes," I said. "Way to make it sound like the end of the world." I waved my hand. "Besides, it isn't like that. I sort of won by default."

"Still can't believe you two know each other. What are the odds?" Gyle said, drinking more water. "Small world, huh?"

"What's with the whole water thing?" I asked. I took another delicious bite of my sub. "I know staying hydrated is important… But I've never seen you without a bottle in your hand."

Gyle stretched his neck, his scar showing more. Gyle started laughing. "All Hybrids are affected differently by their change—as well as a couple of similarities," he said. "Since bonding with these two, I can't put away enough water. Go figure, dehydration was my side effect. Sucks having two water bills a month—but I manage."

Of course there would be side effects. "When did your side effect first kick in?" I asked.

"I remember learning early I couldn't go to sleep without water next to my bed." Gyle shrugged. "It's been so long now." He grinned at me. "It'll come to you soon enough. Just hope yours isn't too bad."

I drank more water. I did feel a bit thirsty, but that was because my mouth was watering from the taste of the sub—right? I slouched onto the couch and inhaled. Nyx rolled his eyes at me. Maybe I was being a bit dramatic. There was no point in worrying over something that hadn't happened yet. That stress would kill me quicker than any side effect could.

"You have any Halloween plans?" I asked, changing the subject. Gyle glowered at me like I already knew the answer to my own question. He was right, I did. Instead, I followed up by saying, "Where you heading?"

"A couple of my friends want to hit the beach bars," he said. "I swear, I'm getting too old for this. Never thought I'd say this, but I thought about skipping the holiday all together. The lack of sleep takes a toll on the body."

"Ahh, the beach bars. I haven't had the entire bar hopping experience in a while now."

"Trust me when I say, I'd much rather be in your shoes."

I narrowed my eyes. Union City was the largest city land mass-wise, but it was also very small. All friend groups knew each other to a certain degree. If Gyle was the type to frequent the beach bars, I was surprised I hadn't seen him before.

"How old are you?" I asked.

Gyle finished his sub. "What is this, 21 Questions?"

I blinked at him. "Seeing that you're a Hybrid, you could be my age, or who knows, you might be eighty."

Gyle nodded, scrunching his bottom lip. "You have a point," he agreed. "Twenty-five. And you?"

"Twenty-five," I responded. Just who was Gyle? And why had I never seen or heard of him before? He was someone who people would want to know and associate with. I could only ask one more question without risking looking like I was probing for information. If I was going to ask, I needed to make it good. Something that would get me further than the normal brick wall.

I came up with nothing good and instead went with something easy, hoping for the best. "Are you from here?"

Gyle tossed his sub wrapper in the trash. He used the hand sanitizer on the desk. "Georgia. My parents moved here from the islands. I moved to Union City for high school." He stopped talking, grinning. "Bet you wish you knew where I went to school now."

He read me like a book. I admitted to it, nodding. "Caught me," I said.

"Can't give you everything," he replied. He wagged his finger back and forth. "How do you think I maintain my image? I gotta keep the mystery about me. Always have them wanting more. Rule number one in marketing." He reached into his pocket and tossed me a bullet. It was golden with purple etching spiraling around it. I studied the item as I rotated it in my hand. The bullet hummed subtly. I've never held a bullet, but it was clear this wasn't man-made. "If you're with Alekka, you should be fine. But if you run into any issues on Halloween, pour some voltage into that. No matter where you're at, Claudy and Symon will be able to track you."

I examined the bullet, touching its edges and feeling its weight. "This woulda been helpful last night."

"Whatchu mean?"

I sighed as I put the bullet in my pocket. "Where do I even start?" I shook my head trying to recount the night.

"We were targeted by a demon," Nyx interjected. "It had a motive, a purpose." He glared at us, his attitude stoic. Then he said, "I'm sure it won't stop until it completes its mission."

My eyes widened. Somehow, I thought yesterday was a one-off incident. It didn't occur to me that I was being hunted by a demon. I wanted to say something, but my throat was tight with fear. But then I felt a sense of confidence emitting from Nyx that drew me back, though I remained silent.

Gyle checked his phone. "Fuck. Luck really isn't on our side, is it?" He stared at me for a while. His eyes shifted from purple back to brown. "If I was giving my opinion, I'd vote for you staying in," he said. "But you're a grown boy. You can make your own decisions."

"Man," I said.

"Huh?" Gyle looked at me with a perplexed expression.

"A grown man," I replied.

Gyle chuckled while nodding. "Yeah, *man*, I got you," he said. "You're okay with me, Nex."

"Nex?" I raised a brow.

"Yeah, like short, for Nexus," he responded. He nodded with approval. "I have a habit of giving everyone nicknames. As long as it comes naturally."

I stared at Gyle. I never had a nickname growing up. To be honest, I didn't have many friends, period, so getting a nickname was out of the question. So, to say the least, I was speechless. I didn't know whether to thank Gyle or get mad. I wasn't even sure if I liked the name.

"He will be fine," Nyx said before I could think myself into oblivion. "I won't allow harm to come his way."

Gyle frowned, then nodded. "I'll leave it to you, then."

"Yeah." I sighed. "I have to rub elbows with the right people if I want to get anywhere in life."

Gyle downed the rest of his water. "Trust me, I know. Gotta do what you gotta do. Be careful." He clasped his hand against my shoulder. "If you're in any trouble, holla, 'kay?" He snapped his finger.

There was an uneasy air about this conversation that I hated. It bothered me that Gyle was showing this much concern. He knew more about the Otherworld and what it carried than I did by far, which meant he also knew the threat and the severity of it. Was I still holding onto some ignorance, being oblivious to the real situation? Networking wouldn't matter if I was dead.

"I'll be in trouble if I can't figure out what costume to wear to this party tomorrow," I said. I needed something to take my mind off of... you know, the demons consuming me.

"Take it from me, be yourself." He shrugged. "Apparently it works, believe it or not." He flipped his wrist in a dismissing fashion.

"I told you, it isn't like that," I said. When I turned, Gyle was gone. Creepy. He really should stop doing that. I took the bullet from my pocket and held it between my thumb and pointer finger. At least I had a lifeline. Even if I was in a dire situation, I doubt I'd have enough time to wait for Gyle to arrive. I placed the bullet back into my pocket, then slapped my thighs twice lightly. Time to be social. My favorite.

My first stop was the nearest party store once I left The Bar. Of course, it was a waste of time—the store was clean, not a costume in sight. Shelves as white as hockey rinks watched me speed walk by as I searched. I mulled over my options. There was a moment when I thought about texting Gyle and seeing if he had something I could borrow. But I dropped that thought as quickly as I thought it up. First off, I barely knew the guy. And even if he did help, I felt it would come with a healthy amount of shit-talking. And he would want to talk about the party. After returning home, I sat on the floor in my closet, feeling out of options.

The last Halloween I decided to participate in happened to be my very last social gathering. Going to the bars and being in crowded areas while pretending to have a fun time wasn't appealing anymore. Plus, I'd lost most of my friends in the breakup. Friends always had to choose a side—it just so happened they didn't choose mine. I thought it worked out for the best. It was better for me to go cold turkey from the situation entirely.

Not like I wanted them to stay. I would have driven them away, anyway.

It was always difficult for me even when I did go out. I was not the cool guy in the group. Sure, I could get a good laugh out of everyone. I guess that would have made me the funny guy. Now I wasn't sure if I knew how to act at a party. Who knew if I could hold my own? Nyx came into the closet and glanced around. "What're you doing?" he asked.

"Sitting," I said. Hmm. I still had it, right? There's no way I could lose my wit. Or maybe I was delusional to have thought of myself as quite the comedian. "I'm trying to find my Halloween costume. I'm going to have to use an old one for tomorrow. And for some reason instead of finding the outfit, I'm procrastinating because…" I didn't need to continue. Nyx felt the emotion that came with the memories. I took a deep breath, then exhaled slowly.

"I don't know why your people dress up as ghouls and demons as if they wouldn't piss themselves if they saw one in person." Nyx sniffed around the closet. "Demons would never dress as humans and parade ourselves about."

My mouth opened, then closed again. "Touché," I said. I couldn't argue that fact. Even though, they did come to my world, take human bodies, and parade themselves about. But they didn't plan a whole day around it. "Congratulations. I would say we're close to two sides of the same fucked up coin."

I rose, opening a small plastic drawer I kept below with some of my lounging clothes. I combed through the drawers until I found what I was searching for: poufy white pants with the accompanying patch, a purple vest, and a small hat to finish it off. All in all, it wasn't a bad costume—I would just rather avoid wearing something that brought back so many bad memories. I should've thrown it away, along with the rest of the relationship, yet it remained a constant reminder of the past. It was also a reminder of why we didn't work.

That Halloween I wanted to go as Aladdin, and she wanted to go as Miss Bellum from The Powerpuff Girls. She told me I looked stupid. I told her a few things I'd rather not repeat. In hindsight, I would have loved the costume for obvious reasons. Though it furthered the thought that we weren't on the same "page." I couldn't remember the exact phrase. Long story short, the night didn't end well. Sometimes I wondered what would have happened if I had dressed in the costume she wanted me to. But I tried to keep that to a minimum.

It was getting late, and I already knew tomorrow would be a long day. I prayed the damn outfit still fit. My weight wasn't all bad. I went through my revenge body phase and put on a good amount of muscle. But that didn't mean a few extra pounds weren't added as well. I brought the costume with me and placed it on top of my work bag. Halloween wasn't my favorite holiday. I had my doubts that would change anytime soon.

19

I received the address for the party the next morning, along with a note from Susan telling me to bring the fun. I read the address over a few times, while I tried to figure out which side of town the party was on. Queens Harbor Blvd.... There was no way. I pulled my phone out and put the address into the GPS. Holy shit. How much did a head editor make? Susan owned a home in The Harbor, the wealthiest neighborhood on the south side of Union City, pre-intercoastal.

It was the neighborhood where all the local NFL players and other wealthy individuals congregated. The people there never had to leave. The community had its own shopping center, for Christ's sake. Groceries, appliances, electronics—anything they wanted was in stock there. When I was younger, I went there to hang out with a teammate before one of our basketball games. I never thought in my adulthood I would know anyone who lived there.

At least the light was starting to look bright at the end of the tunnel.

The party started at six. I stood above my bed with my Aladdin costume laid out in front of me. Don't get me wrong. I liked my costume. Aladdin was my favorite Disney movie. Who knew how many times I'd seen it? I've always had this absurd idea that one day I would find my Princess Jasmine. Cheesy, I know. As was evident, that was just a fairytale. I picked up the vest, glowering at it. Maybe it was time for Aladdin to see how everybody else had been living.

"You're more nervous than I anticipated," Nyx purred. He found his way onto the bed after eating.

I dragged myself to the bathroom. "I hate these types of things," I said, grabbing my toothbrush. "Too much pressure." I paused. A thought had sprung to my mind. "Question."

"Speak."

"Symon turned into guns when Gyle fought. Eira, if I'm correct, turned into that glaive thing." I powered on my toothbrush and brushed. "What's your thing?" I turned on the faucet, spitting. The wheels spun as I thought about manifesting Amon and using the weapon Nyx made for me. I'm sure Gyle was strong on his own, as were Claudy and Symon. But when they turned into weapons that he used, it was like they were in perfect sync. I was willing to bet it made them twice as strong. As I sat next to Nyx I could feel our bond—loose still but growing stronger by the day. "If I'm correct, a Hybrid must combine with their demon to use their full strength, yes?"

Nyx turned from me and scoffed. "I don't know," he said, then added, "and I don't want to find out." He laid his head somewhat off the bed with his paws beneath him. "To let anyone use them like some tool. It's... deplorable."

Malice trailed from Nyx's tone—though he wasn't directing it at me. Humans. Nyx hated humans for whatever reason, and who could blame him? Hell, I was one of them, and I lost faith in us more and more every day. I couldn't imagine the things Nyx had seen while living here. He looked free, yet he had been shackled all this time in a world full of humans that he detested. But it wasn't only humans. The other half of the hate was focused on demons. Nyx felt as much contempt for them as he did us—maybe more. It made me sick to my stomach thinking of it. My problems were minuscule in comparison.

I grabbed the plastic bag that sat next to my work shoes. Although I didn't find a costume at the store earlier—I had made a purchase. But I wasn't sure how it would go over, and the more I thought about it, the longer I put off showing it. "If you want, I got you something," I said, reaching for the bag. I pulled out a small pet bandana. It was orange and black with pumpkin patterns that covered the entirety. Being that it was

Halloween, there wasn't anything less... obnoxious lying around. "I know you won't be dressing up," I said. "But I figured, since you'll be at the party, you might want to be festive."

Nyx glared at me. "You're serious, aren't you?"

I rotated the bandana in my hand and looked at it. "Well, yeah," I said. "You don't have to if you don't want to."

Nyx glanced at the bandana. I wasn't sure if he hated it or didn't understand it—or maybe it was both. He sighed, then said, "Make it quick." Nyx extended his neck for me, enough to make him look vulnerable—though I knew he could easily turn back into his true malicious form. I knelt, tying the bandana around his neck, then adjusted it so it didn't curl upon itself.

"Done," I said. Nyx rose, hopped off the bed, and jumped on the bathroom sink. He stared in the mirror for much longer than I thought necessary. I was getting anxious watching him. By minute two, I was close to taking the bandana off and throwing it away.

Before my anxiety reached its peak, Nyx said, "It'll suffice."

"Wait, really?"

Nyx rolled his shoulders in what I thought was a shrug. "A gift is a gift. I appreciate the gesture." He turned his small body on the sink to me and glared at me with eyes that scared me. "But after the night, this thing comes off of me."

"Deal," I said. Now that Nyx looked as dapper as any demon attending a Halloween party could, it was time to get myself together. I didn't want to keep Alekka waiting or make her late. Knowing her, she would take over the party the second she walked inside.

After I got dressed, I checked the mirror to see if I could still play the part. It would have to do. Get a couple of drinks in me and I might break out in song. "Come on," I said. "I have to pick Alekka up."

"A night of dealing with that unbearable woman," Nyx said.

"Alekka isn't that bad." I waved to Amon as we left the house.

"I am speaking of that winter creature," Nyx said as I hopped into the Jetta.

I almost burst into laughter. Nyx's natural enemy, Eira. A part of me felt bad for wanting to be around them and forcing him into it. If anything, Alekka and Eira were strong. They had seen more battles and Otherworld activity than I was ready for. Being close to them was the safest place I could be to get through this and still make a good appearance. Killing two birds with one stone. I only hoped I didn't *need* to be close to them. I would appreciate one night void of Otherworldly commotion.

I waited for Alekka to send me her address before setting out on my way. She lived thirty-five minutes away, central to one of the shopping districts on the south side of the city.

Alekka stayed in an apartment complex behind a string of restaurants, and what I assumed to be the production of another. Construction projects have been going on throughout this part of the city for as long as I can remember. Once one project was completed, another started, and the cycle continued. It wasn't all bad. If I'm around long enough, I will finally get some use out of some new overpasses and ideas the district had. I drove over the entrance speed bump, circled the roundabout, and headed toward the back of the apartment complex. A group of children ran past my car on the sidewalk. They were all dressed in matching wizard robes with wands. It was good to see children out playing. I was beginning to think the days of kids being kids and going outside were extinct.

I drove to the last building and checked my text to verify the apartment number. I never heard of this complex, probably because I couldn't afford anything over here back when I had searched for homes. Everything was modern. The roofs were square, and even the stairs seemed as if the tenants hadn't brutally beaten them over the years. New studio apartments. Somehow they got people to pay more for less and to feel good about doing it.

I parked and climbed to the second floor and found Alekka's unit. Outside was a plastic pumpkin packed to the brim with candy. I picked up one of the Reese's cups and devoured it—there was nothing like that perfect peanut butter chocolate blend. At my feet was a welcome mat that read: *Spooky Season.* I couldn't help but think of my home, void of any holiday cheer. Maybe I would decorate it for Christmas and get more festive. I didn't want my neighbors to think I was some grouch.

I found myself gazing at Alekka's door, though not moving. Nyx walked between my legs and turned his head to look at me. "What now?" he asked.

I shook my head. "Nothing," I said. Either way, I'm here now. No point in bringing up things that I couldn't change.

"Let's get this over with," he said. He was right, there was no point prolonging the inevitable. Whether I crashed and burned at this party, it would happen one way or the other.

"Agreed." I knocked twice. From the other side of the door, I heard Alekka shout, "Come in!" Music graced my ears first as I stepped inside. I didn't recognize the song, but it had a downtempo, and the woman had the voice of a goddess. The delectable fragrance that filled the home (and I mean that literally) struck me next. It smelled of sage and cinnamon, which brought a welcoming warmth. There were several paintings on the wall to the left once entering, and one large one over her couch. These weren't the average paintings you could buy at a superstore, either. They were all fresh, done by hand, possibly by Alekka herself.

Plants lined the living room, though it didn't feel overbearing or suffocating. Sometimes people could get a bit plant crazy. In this case, it seemed that Alekka picked and placed every flower for the need and ambiance she was going for. A large TV was mounted to the wall and a sectional couch was pressed against the opposite wall. Two candles sat on the coffee table with a couple of books staged beside them. Though, I wouldn't be surprised if Alekka had indeed read them.

"Sorry, I'm finishing up!" Alekka yelled from the bedroom. "There's drinks in the fridge. Help yourself."

I hugged my body tight as I went to the kitchen. That warm feeling was only in appearance. The home was freezing and not your average cold from the air conditioning. Being around Eira in only a vest might be an issue. It wouldn't be long before I would regret my outfit choice. Inside the fridge were more hard seltzers and beers than I could count. The entire drawer normally reserved for salad and cold cuts, now held a liver's worst nightmare. On top of the fridge was enough liquor to supply the whole apartment complex. I grabbed the first beer I saw and then sat at the kitchen table.

I sat around for another ten minutes or so before Alekka made her appearance. I'd always thought Alekka was beautiful and I would have been a fool not to. But seeing her now made the previous thought meek. She was stunning.

"How do I look?" she asked, twirling once. Maybe the world was playing tricks on me. It must be. There was no other explanation for what I was seeing. Alekka was dressed as Princess Jasmine. This wasn't the type of costume where you could vaguely tell who they were, either, like mine. Instead, it was as if Alekka embodied Jasmine entirely—all she needed to do was turn Eira into Raja and it would be a complete match. She even found the time to braid her hair for the event. She was wearing the signature blue blouse with blue pants. Even the circlet she wore around her hair was perfect.

"Y-you look great," I said. I paused, staring. "And who would have thought Aladdin and Jasmine? Fitting."

"Wait... You like Aladdin, too?" She jumped up excitedly. "I figured you'd go as something more... practical. I'm so glad, though! This works better."

I lowered my beer. "Wait, why can't I like Aladdin?"

Alekka waved her hand. "Oh, of course you can," she said. "I just honestly thought you might be one of those superhero guys. Don't get me wrong. Great movies. Just not *Aladdin*."

"You know what, Alekka? You might not be so bad after all." I grinned.

"So I was bad before?"

Luckily, Eira came from the hall, wrapping herself around Alekka and saving me from myself. When she saw Nyx, she paused—then shook her head in disgust. "I see someone is being festive," she said.

Nyx's lips parted, showing his fangs.

"Quiet, Eira," Alekka said. "What did we talk about?" Alekka went to the kitchen. "Besides, I happen to think it looks great." She grabbed a hard seltzer, cracking it open.

I knew things would only get worse the longer we stuck around. Leaving things up to Nyx and Eira, they'd be at each other's throats in no time. "Ready?" I asked.

Alekka grinned, and I knew she had something up her sleeve. "We can leave once you get another drink in your hand. The Uber will be here in fifteen minutes, so hurry." She opened the fridge and tossed me a hard seltzer. I stared at the can. If I left the Jetta at Alekka's house, I wouldn't have an excuse not to drink. She had me there.

"You know, I'm starting to think you're a bad influence on me." I laughed, then started on the drink.

"I think this is exactly what you need. Loosen you up a little."

"You calling me tight?"

Alekka sipped from her can. "When's the last time you went to a party? Or even a club or a night out? I've known you for how long, and you just now finally decided you'd be okay saying more than 'hello' or 'goodbye.' And I'd probably guess you don't have many friends outside of work, either. Face it, Nexus, you're stiffer than a dive bar rum and soda."

Talk about reading a person. There was nothing I could say and denying it wouldn't take away the fact that it was the truth. I'd isolated myself from the world—crawling into a shell. The only reason my life had become a constant circle of home and work was because I had let it. My previous relationship did more damage than I thought. And by the time I'd realized it—I was already too far down the spiral to find my way out. It wasn't that I didn't want to crawl back to the top and quit this plunge for good, but I found comfort in the cycle. It was safe with no ups or downs—only a constant level of monotonous emotions that I obtained bliss in.

I peered into the mouth of the bottle. "I used to have a pretty decent-sized friend group, you know," I said. "We'd go out to the bars. Hit Trivia Night. Go bowling. In this boring city, we always found shit to do. I really thought they'd be my lifelong friends. I would have done anything for them. Then, 'poof.'" I snapped my fingers. "It's like we never even knew each other."

"What happened to them?" Alekka asked. She rested her body against the wall, studying me.

"When me and Nya split, everyone chose her. She brought more fun to the group and knew them longer. It only made sense." I tapped my hand on the table. "Sometimes I thought about going out and meeting new people. But then I think about seeing one of them or her out there —and think it wasn't worth it." I kept rambling. My mouth moved on its own, weaving a story together, word upon word, all crossing until I said too much all too quick.

Alekka nodded, taking it all in. Now, I honestly didn't care if she listened. Since things derailed, I had never talked to anyone other than myself about what happened—even if it was only about surface-level issues. I didn't care if anyone chose my side—it wasn't about that. There had just been a weight tugging me down for so long, tainting my soul and making me feel worthless. Some days I couldn't muster the strength to get out of bed, let alone try to force myself out of my comfort zone.

"It really broke you, huh?" Alekka said, her voice somber. I turned my head toward her as I came out of my trance. She finished her drink and checked her phone. "Uber's here." Before she left the kitchen, she glared at me with melancholy eyes. "Can you tell me one thing?"

"What is it?" I downed the rest of my drink, feeling it light my insides ablaze.

"I don't want to pry. But what happened?"

I knew the question was coming but it wasn't easy to hear. Thinking about it meant reliving the pain, and God knew I didn't want to do that. "If you don't want to pry, then don't," I said. It wasn't until I finished saying it that I realized I sounded like an ass. Alekka had listened to me vent without so much as a word. The least I could do was tell her what she wanted to know. Hell, I'd want to know if I was her, too. I placed my hand on the door before opening it, then turned back to Alekka.

"We were expecting," I began. "When we lost the baby, I took it rough. I wasn't around. Honestly, I don't remember much of the days… I wouldn't speak to anyone. She had to go through it alone. It broke us both. I know I should have been there—I just didn't know how."

No one in the apartment moved. I felt all of their eyes against my back. Before the tension completely killed the night, I did all I could to cut it. "Party time," I said, letting the door shut behind me.

20

We got lucky with our Uber driver. He wasn't one of the usual ones trying to force a conversation down our throats, which helped the initial silence that clouded the car. We couldn't talk through the tension after I had killed the mood. Instead, we listened to the radio play in the background until enough time passed and Alekka brightened the ride. "Where's your costume?" she asked the driver.

The driver was an aged man who was rounder than he was tall. He had a scruffy beard that needed a trim. But who was I to talk? My facial hair had only recently decided it was time to grow in—and even now, it still wouldn't grow in fully. The driver tipped the brim of his cap. "I'm a taxi driver," he said.

I didn't know if I laughed because it was so ironic, or if it was actually funny. The driver grinned before asking, "Going to a party in The Harbor? That's big time."

"It's for a work function," Alekka said. She rubbed behind Eira's ear as she purred with delight.

"Must be nice," the driver replied. "My old work friends have parties in one-bedroom apartments. And seeing that my new work friends are this old chip bag and water bottle, I'm not going to parties much anymore outside of this car." He snorted a bit.

"Get it?" I joked, elbowing Alekka. Jesus, was I getting old? That type of joke should have never landed. Alekka rolled her eyes but laughed with me.

We drove for a few more minutes before turning at the light that led to The Harbor. The Uber brought us down a long, straight road, which reminded me of a dragstrip. How much money did this neighborhood spend on landscaping each month? Their HOA fees had to be insane. It was a tad on the outrageous side. The trees were all perfectly spaced out with branches clipped to the same lengths and leaves all trimmed to match one another. It was as if it was taken out of a home décor magazine and recreated here. I could only hope I had a yard that green when I owned a home one day. Even the raft of ducklings that waddled along seemed happier than most. Some plopped around in the man-made pond, while the mother and some of the others sat at the edge deciding whether to join in. Everyone was living a life of luxury. It had to be nice.

We stopped at the gate and waited for a guard to approach. A short woman arrived and asked, "Where you heading?" The Uber driver gave her the address and waited while she stepped inside her workspace. She returned and did a quick check of the vehicle, presumably getting the plate number. She came to the driver's side window and handed the Uber driver a slip of paper, then let us know we were free to go. And I thought my neighborhood had decent security. The Harbor's setup made my neighborhood guard look like a Sesame Street character.

At least a mile passed before we reached the first home on the left—if you could even call it that. I could fit at least four of my townhomes in the lot supporting the mansion. It was a cottage style home that stretched far beyond my vision. That much space scared me. Besides cleaning, I wouldn't know what to do with all of it. The next home was a Georgian Colonial followed by a mid-century modern home. It was like I was on HGTV getting the tour of Union City's most luxurious homes.

We took a right turn, then another right, and finally, a left. By now, we were so deep in the neighborhood, I had no chance of getting out on my own. At the end of the street were three contemporary modern homes (nice places, trust me on this). On the left, cars piled into a circular driveway and drained onto the street. The Uber pulled in. His neck was pushed forward as he stared at the home, whistling. "Looks like your work friends know how to throw a party," he said. A person in one of those T-Rex suits waddled by as their costume brushed the car lightly.

"Thanks for the ride," I said. The moment I opened the door, a man, whom I assumed was a caveman, pushed by.

He spun around as he hit my shoulder. "My bad, bro," he said. He was higher than the clouds on a spring afternoon. A few seconds passed while he stared at me. "Aladdin. Nice." Then he turned, rushing up the driveway as if he had forgotten something important.

"He's right," Alekka agreed. She shrugged. "Whaaat? It is a nice outfit."

I smiled as I tugged at my vest a bit. "You think so?"

"I do," she replied. She placed her hand on her face as she pondered. "So much that I think my plans have changed. I was hoping I'd have a chance to win the costume contest alone. But us as a duo, I don't see how we could lose."

I raised my brow. "Costume contest? They have one of those?"

Alekka grabbed my forearm, dragging me with her. "What's a Halloween party without a costume contest?" she continued, refusing to look back at me. She knew I would be against it, and I would vehemently tell her no the first chance I had. I stopped and gazed into the blood-colored sky. The clouds crept along. They all seemed gray on the painted background of the coming night.

Alekka tried tugging me toward the house, but I didn't move. "What is it?" she asked. "Don't start spacing out on me now."

If I knew what I was feeling I would have told her. It was like the world was in a constant loop, playing the same second over and over again. The night was here, and I knew it would bring nothing positive. Something was out there, watching—I felt it. It didn't feel like the eyes were on me. There was something else. A sensation that draped over my being. It was as if I was in a bubble, trying to escape—and before the bubble finally struck a wall to pop, it shifted back in the opposite direction to start again.

Then it dissipated, though there was still a lingering sense of it. Whatever it was, it didn't want me to find it—not yet. As I peered at the open field of grass, a protective nature swept through me. Don't get me wrong. It wasn't protection for those in the home or the house specifically. Not that I didn't care about them, but this was different—this was personal. This party, as senseless and stupid as it was, could be the very thing that opened avenues for me. Susan wasn't just someone else who worked at Hometown Press. She was a lead editor at one of the head branches. She directly worked for the founder of the company. If I made a good impression on her, it could change my career. And I would be damned if some demon ruined that for me.

I raised my thumb to the sky. Alekka scanned the area. "Yo, you good?"

I nodded. "Yeah, better than ever," I said. Maybe it was the fact that I vented a bit, but I meant it. I felt... in control, for the first time in as long as I could remember. Tonight, I was going to have fun—for me. It was time I hopped back in the driver seat, even if I was going at a tortoise's pace.

Alekka's eyes flashed a cool, frozen white, then back to hazel. "Don't worry," she said. "Nothing will get close to us without me or Eira sensing it first. Tonight, we drink!"

It should be easy to agree with Alekka on this matter. I should have been able to simply nod and follow in her footsteps. Her skill and knowledge in this area were far superior to mine. But tonight, I was certain I was right. We had to watch each other's backs. I glanced at Nyx from the corner of my eye. He returned the gaze, and I could tell he was suspicious. "Lead the way," I said.

As we entered the house a soft guitar strum emitted from the overhead speakers. The beat dropped, and a woman started singing in a tone so high it rivaled a bird tweeting. The home was dark with pink lights that exuded ambiance. The strong odor of marijuana and hookah smoke wafted through the entrance. If this was a normal editing function, then I really missed out on not landing an editing job.

"Aladdin...You made it in," the caveman from earlier said. His hair covered most of his face. "Follow me. Drinks are over here." He moved in a commanding fashion, pushing a few aside. For some reason, he seemed set on us following and I doubted he'd take no for an answer.

"Uh—sure." I shrugged. I blinked at Alekka a few times. "I guess we're going this way."

We opened a door that led outside into a grassy area with a hammock and several lounge chairs that were as long as trucks and, of course, a pool. Across the way was a tiki bar with an enclosure that circled a standing fireplace. Maybe I was a little off in my assumption earlier. Being head editor paid well, but it was clear Susan had high standards and I doubted she lived this lifestyle with editing money alone. Either way, color me jealous.

Caveman entered another wing of the house and continued until we were in a kitchen. "Help yourself," he said. "Fully stocked with everything you need. Ice is in the fridge." He pointed to a stainless-steel fridge in the center of the kitchen.

"Thanks," I said.

Alekka grabbed a plastic cup and filled it. I grabbed a beer. "Sorry, I'm Nexus, and this is Alekka. What's your name?" I reached my hand out.

"Christian," he said, shaking my hand. "Who are you guys here with?"

"Susan," Alekka answered. "I work for her... Well, technically. And Nexus here is my date for the evening."

"Ahh, Susan." Christian nodded.

"You know her?" I asked. "You work for Hometown Press, too?"

Christian methodically searched the room before finally settling and crouching down. When he rose, he held a large plastic club that finished his costume. "Sorry, I lost my club earlier. And no... I wouldn't be caught working for my sister. That would have to be a conflict of interest or something, right?"

Alekka nearly spit her drink out. "Susan's your sister?"

Christian sighed. "Sure is. Susan and Christian Keaton."

Keaton wasn't an uncommon last name. But then again, it wasn't a common one, either. And the chance that they would also have the funds to afford this home made me even more suspicious. Only one person came to mind when I heard that name. "Oh, like Sylvia Keaton, the actress."

"Exactly like her." Christian poured himself a plastic cup of vodka and Sprite. He held his finger up to us and drank the cup until satisfied.

It wasn't until he filled his cup back to the brim that he spoke. "Don't get me wrong. Mom's great—but she's going to work herself to death. What sixty-year-old woman spends all day on a movie set?" Christian drank more, then sighed, staring into the core of his cup.

Holy shit. Sylvia and Robert Keaton were two of the most decorated method actors of our time. They became known for their earlier roles in several dramas. Robert even tried his hand at a few noir films—one that was a hit. Sylvia, on the other hand, had decided she wanted to go the indie route and had found much success. Now that I could see past his hair, I couldn't help but see the obvious resemblance. He had the same staggering brown eyes and high cheekbones. Honestly, he did hold a likeness to a modern-day Tarzan, who his father acted as in numerous showings onstage for a few years.

"Ahh, now you can't unsee it, can you?" Christian said. "People tell me I look just like my dad." He shrugged. "Me, on the other hand… Well, I don't see it."

He one hundred percent looked like a copied image of his father.

"Drinks up," Christian said as he raised his cup in the air. We all drank. After we finished our first cup we talked for a little before we filled another. "Follow me. The party's just starting. Nexus, right?"

"Yeah," I said.

Christian pointed his club ahead as he opened the door. I glanced at Alekka. I already felt a slight buzz. Alekka grinned.

"Come on, it sounds like fun," Alekka said. She held her drink out ahead of her as she followed Christian.

Taking the night by the horns was moving along in a perfect, tipsy fashion. And by perfect, I meant I wasn't completely hating life, and enjoying myself a bit. Christian brought us to a section of the home that was laid out like a common area with a pool table. There were chairs near the outside of the room, and the two halls led to other parts of the maze that was Susan's home. Much like the other rooms, the overhead ceiling lights were off with only the fluorescent glow of the light strips that found their way around.

Alekka dragged me to an open section of the room and broke into dance. The liquor had to have gotten to me because I danced with her. Fun fact: I loved dancing and was better than most at it. It probably had something to do with my Jamaican blood. The only reason I never danced was because I didn't go out anymore. All that to say, I hit a couple of moves to see if I still had it. It wasn't my best, but it also wasn't my worst. I could work with it.

Alekka shook her head, approving. "You surprise me every day, Nexus," she said. She kept dancing and managed to be a good dancer, too. I assumed she was the type of person who could pick anything up. It must have been the same with dancing. I didn't worry about keeping up. I was in my own world, absorbing the music and enjoying the atmosphere.

Every so often, Alekka scanned the room to see if she noticed Susan or Tara. I understood it. I would feel uneasy having my boss and my boss's boss see me in this state. I wasn't plastered, but I was still vulnerable. Not fully in control. Again, that uneasy feeling. Did I really have that much of a control issue?

Nyx and Eira stayed on opposite sides of the dance floor, but both at a similar distance from us. I watched a person walk past Nyx to head toward the bathroom. I didn't know if I'd ever get used to people not seeing Nyx. I had to stop myself from blurting out 'Watch out!' at every corner. Nyx waited a couple of minutes, then came to my side and pressed his body into me enough to get my attention. His expression said, *Get your shit together*, and he was right. I needed to remain alert. There was no telling when something would happen, or even if. The last thing I wanted was to die before I had the chance to know it.

Alekka pulled me aside until we were far enough from the music to hear our thoughts again. She gazed behind my shoulder toward the small gaggle of people drinking where we were dancing. "Having fun yet?" she asked.

"Cynicism aside, yeah," I said, smiling, then adding, "More fun than I've had in a long time."

"Progress and a smile, all things I like," Alekka said.

I pondered. How stupid was I? In all my pessimism and self-doubt, I completely thought Alekka brought me here because she needed someone near her age to party with. After the week she had, I doubted she wanted to spend a night drinking and dancing with Tara and Susan (although something told me Susan might be more fun than anyone was ready for). It'd never occurred to me that more than herself—Alekka was doing this for me. Forcing me to grab drinks at Fernando's and working out with me at the gym—it was all for my well-being. This change... Alekka had been through it with Eira. She had been watching me, making sure I wasn't losing my mind through this whole process. I owed her more than I even realized.

"When you first got your name, how'd you handle the change?" I asked.

Alekka thought about what I said and beckoned me as she walked back outside. The wind blew a lonely whistle as Alekka twirled in a small circle on the stone walkway. She drank some more then reached her hand down so Eira could nudge it with her nose. "I was lonely. Lonely as shit. For the longest time, it was just Eira and me. I thought I was crazy. There were plenty of moments I questioned if Eira really existed—or if my mind had been playing tricks on me. It was a lot to handle at such a young age. Parents didn't help, either. They sent me to doctor after doctor. If it was up to them, I would be locked up in some doctor's office now. My mom would be crying to my dad that *I was seeing that thing again.*"

I turned to the sky. The moon was now full, illuminating the night. That loneliness. It was clear Alekka didn't want me to suffer through that same sadness. A part of me knew I would never have to. I'd been alone my whole life—no parents to lean on, no friends' shoulders to cry on, nothing. But nobody had time to dwell on those days. I worked better alone. I could handle alone. It was the subtle changes that terrified me, like losing my name. I tried to think back, yet nothing came. The changes to my body. It was all so sudden.

And for what?

"To be honest..." I hesitated. Or better yet, my body stopped, like it always did when thoughts of my father came to mind. There was a piece of me that hated what came next. "I just want to know what the hell my father was thinking." The mention of him made me want to vomit.

Alekka frowned. "What do you mean?"

I stared into the empty red Solo cup. Small liquor droplets pooled at the bottom. My father was a subject I steered clear of at all costs. It was my coping mechanism for masking my hate for him. Now he was peeling that mask off, making me face him for the first time since he took his own life. God, I had done more soul searching this week than I had done my whole life. I wasn't fond of it.

"From what I've gathered, no matter how much I hated him, my father was an intelligent man. Cunning. He planned everything down to the most minute detail. Everything he did had a purpose." When I was a child, day after day, I would spend hours seeking information on my parents. I'd organized all their traits and habits in different folders so that I wouldn't forget. Apparently, my father was well-organized and meticulous about things, at least from what I was told by someone who knew him. I pursed my lips and shook my head.

I grunted, and then I turned to Alekka. "But I can't figure out why he bonded Nyx and me together. None of it makes sense."

Alekka came close to me, placing her hand on my shoulder. "None of it has to make sense," she said. "If you want it to all make sense, you'll go crazy."

The door behind us swung open, flooding the night with music. "Turn that shit down!" Christian yelled back into the house. He leaned over awkwardly. I'm not sure how he was even standing in that contortion. Drunk people are superheroes, I swear. "Come with me. It's time for the costume contest. You two are entering. I got my money on you."

"Money?" I asked.

"Call it a friendly wager between siblings." Christian smiled. "For charity, of course. Now move it." He went back toward the front of the house.

Alcohol had a way of making you think you could do things you know you have no business attempting. I fixed the cap on my head and followed behind Christian. "Fuck it. Let's go," I said, grinning at Alekka.

"After you," she said, smiling.

21

We went inside and made it to what might have been a living room. Most of the furniture had been removed and a small stage was in the front of the room. The budget for this party was insane. I scanned the room. There were more people than I'd ever seen in one room packed in like they were on the city bus. Susan stood at the top of the stage, dressed as Cammy from *Street Fighter*, which I had to say she pulled off well. With military attire, she wore her hair in a long braid and a red beret atop. Next to her was who I assumed to be Charles wearing a bad werewolf costume. And I mean bad. I didn't know where he got his facial hair from, but he needed to give it back. It was horrible. Personally, I would have bought a mask to cover my face instead of looking like a shag rug, but who was I to judge?

"Finally made it, you two?" Tara asked as she approached us. She looked like she was hating every moment of dressing up. Tara was dressed as Belle, which made Charles's costume make some sense. But then again, it also made Charles's outfit look that much worse. *Beauty and the Beast* is never an easy option. If you wanted to pull it off, you had to throw the monetary backing behind it.

"Yeah," I replied. "We've been in the other sections of the house. This place is a maze."

KADEEM LOCKE

Tara looked over the two of us. "You both look great," she said. "And to match, on such short notice. I'm impressed." She had a drink in her hand, but I doubted if she'd even take more than a sip the entire party. It was more for show than anything.

Alekka leaned in closer to Tara. "I hope you two weren't planning on winning the contest," she said. "Charles could easily be mistaken for Teen Wolf over the Beast."

Tara had to stop herself from bursting into laughter. She waved her hand. "It's better off that way. It gives me an excuse not to enter. If he'd come up with a better costume, Susan wouldn't have taken no for an answer."

Charles came over to us as Tara mentioned him. "Looks like the gang's all here," he said. He opened his hands, presenting his costume. "As you can see, I don't only wear great suits." I laughed, more because I felt I had to than anything. His eyes trailed off for a moment, then locked in on me. "Glad you made it." He shook my hand. "Let me grab you a beer."

I put my thumbs through my vest. "Thanks," I said. I glanced at Alekka, confused. I never understood how people could act so forward with people they didn't know. But I followed Charles to the corner of the room where a cooler sat.

He grabbed himself a drink and passed me the other. "Having fun?" He touched the glass to his lips.

I nodded. "Yeah. Honestly, it isn't as bad as I thought it would be. It's a lot… cooler than I would have expected."

Charles laughed. "Get a bunch of art majors in a room and see what happens. Everyone here is from Hometown Press or one of the neighboring agencies."

"I work at The Bar, the gym downtown," I said. "You probably haven't heard of it."

"I actually haven't," he replied. I don't think he got my humor. When we walked back to the group, Charles gripped my shoulder a bit too tight for my liking. He must have been tipsy already. "Connect with me on LinkedIn when you get a chance. Make sure you have fun. Nights like these are ones to remember."

Glad he reminded me that my LinkedIn needed a major update. Being antisocial in the social world was becoming increasingly difficult.

It was then that Susan saw us in the crowd. She grabbed a microphone from the stool on the stage and addressed the room. "Settle down, everyone." Susan cleared her throat. "Now, I know everyone's been patiently waiting for this year's costume contest."

The flock erupted in a roar of claps. Who knew a costume contest could draw such a crowd? And who knew that Susan had been throwing this party annually? Oh, to be one of the chosen few. As Susan continued her speech, someone placed their arm around my shoulder.

"Nice costume," a voice said. It was deep, smooth, as if telling everyone, "I'm too good for this shit." I checked to see a man who could easily be confused with a model standing next to me. He had dark skin with tattoos all over—the kind of tattoos done by a good artist--each line seemed to hold meaning—and teeth so white he had to have bleached them. And of course, he was roughly the same height as me. His life must consist of win after win. He was wearing an Aladdin costume as well, though he was doing a way better job at the whole Disney prince thing than I was. My vest didn't feel as tight suddenly.

"You, too," I replied after some time. "Great minds, I guess."

"I'm King," he said, offering me his hand.

I hesitated, then shook his hand. "Nexus," I said. "And this is Alekka."

Alekka stepped aside and waved. "Hey, nice to meet you."

King came closer. "May I say, you, my friend, are a lucky man." He shook Alekka's hand, his smile lighting the room. "And you make a beautiful Jasmine."

Alekka smiled. "Thank you. And you make a fine Aladdin as well."

He glanced at the stage. "Who are you guys here with?"

I nudged my head toward Susan. "Alekka works with Hometown Press, Union City branch. I work at The Bar, downtown location."

King chuckled. "I'm with Aria Press," he said. "Guess that means you hate me, huh?" he added, looking at Alekka.

Alekka rolled her eyes, then looked at me. "Tara makes sure to leave Aria out of any discussion. Their name's taboo in the office. The few times I have heard her mention them was never anything good," she began. "Tara's always complaining about them going behind our backs to grab clients we had hoped to publish. Apparently, there was a few years stretch where every client Tara went after, Aria Press's head editor came right behind and snaked them right from under her. At this point, it's basically a football rivalry."

I whistled. "Surprised to see you here, then," I said. "Shouldn't this be against the rules?"

King shrugged. "I might work for Aria Press, but I'm not dumb. I wouldn't burn any bridges because I work for one company."

I zipped my lips shut. "Secret's safe with me." Plus, who was I going to tell, Dave?

"Everyone entering the contest, please come to the stage." Susan's voice echoed through the room from her microphone. Christian pointed to Alekka and I.

"Guess that's our cue," Alekka said.

"Oh, you two are in the contest." King took a sip of his beer. "Well, you two have my vote." He smiled at me and waved. "Good luck, twin."

"Thanks, I'm going to need it," I said.

Christian took the mike from Susan and grinned. "Now, everyone, we need you to be objective here." He held up three fingers. "We have three contestants, all sponsored by a different member of the party committee." Christian turned to Susan. "What you got?"

Susan swiped the mike from her brother. "Always the loudmouth. You never seem as energetic when you lose. I think that's the only time you're quiet." Susan licked her lips. "I doubt anyone will be able to compete with my selection. If you will." Susan waved her hand toward the group of us gaggled together. Two people brushed us as they took center stage.

The two partygoers chose the DC-comic route. They both wore great outfits, don't get me wrong, but I didn't think they were doing anything special. Those costumes were popular right now. There was no going to a party without having a handful of superheroes or villains loitering. The man was wearing an Aquaman costume. His hair was bright blond and gelled back, and his wetsuit was covered in scales. He held a golden trident, which honestly took dedication. It looked like an exact replica. I couldn't imagine lugging that thing around all night. His partner in crime was dressed as Wonder Woman. She posed for the crowd, adjusting the crown on her head. The bangles on her wrist shined golden when hit by the spotlight. By the sound of Susan's extra commentary, this must be who her money was on.

DEMONOLOGY

The crowd was making noise and cheering, but not as much as I might have thought. Maybe Alekka and I did stand a chance.

Christian called Alekka and I to the stage next. I wasn't much for the show, but the liquor took care of that. Alekka clearly hadn't heard of the word shy. She strutted across the stage, posing on either side so the crowd could see all the necessary angles. I did what I could to draw in excitement. I made a move here and there, drawing cheers, but who did I think I was? It had to be the liquid courage. By now, everyone was well past inebriation. Applause and cheers erupted much more than the first group, I noted.

I was beginning to think we might have a decent chance of winning. That was, until I saw the last pair walking up. The crowd's excitement started before the two even fully stepped onto the stage. People whistled, while others clapped. I found myself joining in the fun. Good was good. I had to respect it. The two came across the stage as Jessie and James, the villainous duo from Team Rocket. And they managed to bring along their cat to play Meowth. That's right. There was no way anyone would compete with a cat. I watched as the cat's eyes moved to Nyx who was next to me. The cat's eyes eclipsed as it stared at Nyx. Luckily the woman dressed as Jessie petted the cat and turned its view from Nyx.

"Looks like we know who the winner is," Susan said as she clapped.

Christian lowered his head in defeat. "Shit, guess I lost." He motioned to Susan. "At least I didn't lose to you, though."

Tara joined the rest of the lot on stage. "A loser is still a loser," she said. "My charity appreciates both of your charitable donations."

Alekka brushed up next to Tara, grinning. "Wow, Tara, I want to be like you when I grow up."

"Keep working and we'll get you there, don't worry," Tara said.

Alekka blinked at Tara with excitement. She mouthed a few words, but nothing came out. After she pulled herself together, she said, "Thank you. I'll do my best, boss."

Who knew the party wouldn't be bad? I might even go as far as to say it was a good time. But as all things come, they must also go. While everyone around me talked and enjoyed their conversations, a feeling began to take over. It felt like I was trying to cross a road made of black ice. Or it could be my street smarts that told me to wake the hell up. Either way, it focused my thoughts, my gaze. I scanned the room—nothing. Nyx closed in on my position, gazing around the room, his body tense. Alekka and Eira followed suit.

"Something's here," Alekka whispered. She had a brief conversation with the people on stage, laughing like she was having the time of her life. Then she turned in my direction and called for me to grab a drink with her.

"I'm going to take Nexus with me to get a drink," Alekka said. "Does anyone want anything?"

"No, we should be good," Susan said.

Alekka moved her cup in a circle. "Okay, we'll be back, I need a refill." Before I could react, Alekka grabbed my wrist and dragged me away from the main party area. We snaked through the crowd; every second having to bob and weave through drinkers lounging about. When we got to the kitchen, Alekka counted the number of people in the vicinity.

"We have to get everyone out of here," she said.

My heart raced. The sensation from earlier, the one waiting for me outside the mansion, crawled back. A chill of malice found me and tried to hold me captive. It was close, I felt it next to me, watching—waiting for the right moment to strike. I shook the feeling. I had to remain focused.

I've been in contact with Otherworld beings a few times now, and none of them have been pleasant. This party would turn into a massacre if we couldn't do something—fast. I searched through the drawers until I found something of some use. "I have a plan," I said. "Start clearing everyone out once you get the signal."

Alekka paused, confused, then nodded, and went to the back section of the mansion.

I turned to Nyx. "Can you find the area with the least amount of people?"

"Of course," he replied. "Don't belittle my strength." Nyx moved along with caution. We took an adjacent hall that went much further than I anticipated. But what else should I have expected at this point? At the very end of the hall, I opened the door to the bathroom and closed it behind me.

Since it was a half bathroom, it was the only room that seemed a reasonable size to me in the entire home. I climbed the massive toilet, stood on its polished top, and pulled the lighter I took from the kitchen out of my pocket. I flicked the light and hovered it directly below the smoke detector. I waved it back and forth and evenly spread the heat across the face of the detector. After a few seconds, the alarm in the bathroom started blaring. I kept the flame lit and continued fanning it as the alarm screamed at me. Shortly after, other alarms in the home went off until the mansion became a cacophony of wailing sounds.

I hopped from the toilet. My body was still a bit wobbly from the liquor, but I kept focus. Nyx looked back at me, licking his lips. "Don't worry, already on it," he said. Nyx moved with purpose, bringing me to a jog to keep up. People drank while they made their way to the entrance like herded cattle. In the distance, Alekka yelled.

I waved my hand at the gathering of partyers ahead of me. "We gotta get moving. No telling where that thing is coming from." The one wearing a *Mortal Kombat* costume took a sip from his cup and stared at me. Finally, after more awkward seconds than I needed, he nodded and began walking. The crowd slowly began funneling from all parts of the mansion, and out the entrance.

Susan came into my vision as we caught eyes, and maneuvered her way over to me. "Come, come," she beckoned. "I'm on the phone with the authorities now. They'll handle whatever the issue is." She turned to a person who casually walked along. "Move it!" she shouted. "This is my house, and I am responsible for everyone... Clear—out!" If anyone was moving slowly before, they were coasting along now.

"I'm going to grab Alekka and get her out," I said. "Don't want to leave her alone with all this commotion."

"Good idea," Susan said. "Hurry, now." Susan didn't say anymore, but her eyes spoke for her. If I didn't hurry, I would pay for it.

I nodded, rushing to the back of the house where Alekka waved the remaining people out. "All clear," she said.

"Susan left with everyone else," I said. "She's on the phone with the authorities now to get someone out here."

Before Alekka responded, a gruff voice interjected, "Is everyone out of here?" We both turned to see Charles in his horrible Beast costume. He half-jogged to us, breathing heavily.

"Yeah, we were heading out, too," I said.

"I wonder who set the alarm off?" Charles asked.

"Not sure," Alekka responded. "We should all get out of here, though. No telling where it's coming from."

"Lead the way," Charles said.

I put my hand up. Whatever previous voice that told me to run, was screaming at me now. "Why so eager for us to lead?" I asked. "That ready for us to turn our backs on you?"

Charles rubbed his bald head. He stared at us in a confused manner. "What are you getting at?"

"I'm just wondering what made you say that something *set* the alarm off, rather than think there's a fire like any rational person would," I said. The feeling grew, the room becoming muggy and clammy. Above all, there was a stench that filled the room. It was strong, pungent, and foul. "What the hell's that smell?"

Alekka narrowed her eyes, clearly not smelling what I was. "I have no idea what you're talking about," Alekka said. She turned her head to either side as she scanned the room.

Nyx appeared. His body faced the side, though his head turned to Charles. "Your senses are sharp," he said. Nyx licked his lips. His golden eyes never moved from Charles. "There's no point in trying to remain hidden. You reek of a demon."

Charles flashed a wolfish smile. "Doing this the easy way suits me better, anyway. I was never the one for trickery. And I'm not much for crowds." One of Charles's hands went for Alekka's throat, while the other clamped my vest. His arms shifted to a dark blue color as if they were rotten and void of any kind of blood flow. Charles grabbed my vest and tossed me across the room. Charles lifted Alekka from the ground, squeezing.

My side panged with constant shots of pain. I hit the table hard, and at a horrible angle, and collapsed on the floor. The stuff in my pockets fell out. It happened all in a second. Even having the advantage meant nothing if I couldn't move quickly enough to react. I glanced over to see Alekka rising. Shit. I couldn't fall behind. As I grabbed my things, I saw the bullet Gyle gave to me, remembering his instructions. I willed my voltage into the bullet as I stuffed everything back into my pockets.

Nyx glowered at me. "Reason fast. React faster," Nyx said.

Nyx was right. I better get my shit together, I doubted there were going to be many more "learning opportunities" thrown my way.

"I'm tired of playing these childish games," Charles screamed. "I'm tired of waiting and waiting for the right opportunity... I'm going to finish the job."

"Wait, you fought this thing before?" Alekka asked.

"Yeah, at the NFU. Long story." I pushed over a group of Solo cups and what I hoped was liquor. *React. React. I got this.* I grabbed the rest of my things and shoved them into my pocket, groaning as I rose to my feet.

As I looked up, Eira was in full pursuit. The snow leopard jumped with utter grace. She whipped her body as she reached out her paw, slicing Charles's arm enough to cause him to draw back.

Alekka ripped the arm away enough to slip out. "G-glad you saved us the trouble of having to track you down," she said, coughing. "You'd have done better to stay hidden."

Charles retracted his arms. He placed his hand on his head and laughed. "Stay hidden? As if I was hiding. You half-bloods stand no chance at harming me."

I beheld my ruined costume, dabbing my liquor-soaked pants. "Honestly, I have no idea what you're talking about, and I couldn't care less." I kicked a stack of cups out of the way. "One time... The one time I decide to get out and do something for me, the one freaking time." My rage rose. "And you ruined my outfit. I wasn't much of a fan of you before, but you aren't doing a great job of turning my opinion around."

"Your words mean nothing to me," Charles said, his voice echoing. Charles's eyes burned bright blue. I took a step further.

The emotions—rage, anger, hate, they all flowed out of me. This wasn't like last time, or any of the other times I had encountered a demon. Before I was on my heels trying to run at every corner. Nyx pulled one way while I pulled another. Whether I wanted a fight or not, it was happening. Going through Charles was the only way to get through tonight alive. Now I had something to direct all this anger at.

My emotions reached Nyx, fueling him with voltage. His golden eyes shone bright. Nyx flicked his tail once and cut through Charles's arm.

The arm gushed a dark blue ooze as it fell to the ground. Charles looked with cold, still eyes as if he didn't register the pain.

"Eira!" Alekka yelled. Eira stepped elegantly across the floor, her feet barely touching the ground. She moved gracefully; no step was wasted. The demon leopard pressed her body into Alekka. Alekka rubbed behind Eira's ear and said, "Thank you." White-blue light filled the room. When the light died, Alekka wielded a long glaive. The blade vibrated with a calming, white aura. Near the neck of the weapon was a fang hanging from the shaft. The entire weapon was a snowfield of white with fur and spots akin to Eira's normal appearance. Alekka spun the glaive around effortlessly as if it were her own arm while she tested the weight.

A cool mist encircled Alekka as her eyes followed Charles. Alekka gripped her weapon. She crouched, then lunged at Charles. She embedded the blade in Charles's torso. A blood-like substance spilled from his body. "You picked the wrong princess to fuck with," Alekka said.

A fresh arm jutted from where Nyx severed the last. Charles grabbed the blade of Alekka's glaive. "Let me show you the difference between you half-bloods and a true demon." He ripped the blade from his body and threw both it and Alekka across the room straight into the stage. Charles moved until he was standing over Alekka.

I sprinted ahead. Nyx felt my thoughts as he conjured voltage. Willing my voltage into him and my thoughts, I saw the same blade Nyx created for me at NFU—its gold etching, its curved blade. Nyx roared. A golden light shined. I grabbed the black blade before it had a chance to hit the ground and flipped it in my hand. That drew Charles's attention.

The demon spun around, slapping me with a way-too-long arm. I put my sword between his arm and me, though it only did well to defend me against the full brunt of his attack. My body was thrown across the room again, only this time, I pissed Charles off in the process, cutting into one of his ever-regrowing arms. Nyx went ahead without me but drew on our energy.

The black jaguar jumped, spinning his body like a high-powered wheel. Charles threw his arms up in a cross-guard but flinched and chose to jump clear of Nyx instead. Nyx landed on the ground a few paces from him and slid to a halt. His bladed tail flicked from side to side. Alekka slashed her glaive vertically across Charles's body. I followed suit, rushing in a low sprint, slashing upward at the other side of his body. Charles shouted, throwing his arms to either side. Sparks flew as our blades met his steeled arms.

"Seriously," Alekka grunted. "What can't his arms do?"

"Probably should have warned you about that," I said.

We continued our onslaught, no one gaining anything. But it was in those moments of idle battle that I noticed a slight difference in the way Charles defended our attacks. It was subtle, but enough that it drew my attention. Charles wasn't faster than Alekka by any means and he knew it. Adding in my unorthodox (novice) fighting style didn't make things any better off for him. With only a moment's notice to react, Charles opted to deflect our blows with his arms. It wasn't until Nyx attempted a blow that he dodged completely. I narrowed down the conclusions to the most logical. Charles could regenerate, but it depended on the surface area of damage he was restoring. My sword and Alekka's glaive, though possible to get through his arms, likely would not deal enough damage to kill him in one fell swoop. The same could not be said for Nyx.

Charles feared Nyx.

I stepped into my attack, slashing my sword at Charles's body. Charles defended, letting my blade slice into his arm, but only enough for it to cut halfway through. The demon then strengthened the skin surrounding the blade, lodging it inside. He retracted his arm, then extended it again into my stomach. Excruciating pain jolted through my body. My nerves were thrown into panic mode. My stomach was set ablaze, so much so that I didn't know where to feel pain. It was as if my body was surrounded by a swarm of bees, all stinging me. He must've hardened his fist before he punched me. I fell to my knees but not before Charles grabbed me by my vest and pitched me into Alekka. My body tumbled over as we went down like hurricane rubble.

"All right. Baldy over there is really pissing me off," Alekka grunted.

"Aaa-gr-eed," I think I said. I rolled myself from Alekka's body. "Can you get him up in the air?"

"Can I get him up in the air?" Alekka hissed through her teeth. "Of course I can."

"I can live without the sarcasm right now," I said, rolling my eyes. "Get him in the air. We'll handle the rest."

She smiled. "Got it. Stand back for a sec, would ya?" Alekka's eyes turned a deeper, white mist-like color.

Alekka flipped her glaive between her hands. She twirled it around her back, up towards her neck, then caught it back in front of her. She fought alone, and in that moment, I received a glimpse at how large the gap between Alekka and I was. Those years of experience she had meant more than I could have ever imagined. Alekka shifted her fighting style. She went closer, inch by inch, chopping Charles's arms down as quickly as they could grow back. Whenever the demon hardened his skin against her relentless strikes, she maneuvered, focusing her attacks on his body.

Charles stepped back, deflecting Alekka's glaive. The blade screeched as it skidded across the demon's arm. Lowering herself to the ground, Alekka slammed her weapon down and kicked Charles upward. The demon jumped back, realizing it had made a mistake. Alekka licked her lips in feral satisfaction and grabbed Eira. She twisted in a shot put motion and launched her glaive at Charles.

The blade whispered through the room as the glaive sliced through air and sound alike. The blade struck true in Charles's chest, carrying him back and nailing him into the wall. "High enough?" Alekka asked, her breathing heavy.

I took a moment to stop fanboying over Alekka, before I said, "Perfect."

Nyx pressed his front paws into the ground. I felt Nyx's emotion, his hate, his want to kill. I had to maintain my composure to not let his emotions consume my own. Charles flailed, unable to move. His leg kicked, and his arms tried to grip the glaive, but the hairs on the shaft of the blade pierced through his hand. In his vulnerable state, he began to look... human again. His eyes still glowed with a demonic aura, but he looked human. How different was he from us?

"Get it together, Nexus!" Nyx yelled. He readied himself. His body now glowed in a dim, golden hue. I exhaled. Whoever he might have been before was dead now, and the demon had full control over his body. *Charles* was just a shell for this demon to use as it blended with society. Only now, the demon had reason to do otherwise. Letting this demon survive would only spell death for everyone outside. I thought of Susan. I thought of Tara. And everyone else at the Halloween party here who tried to have a good time and maybe even make career-changing friends. I couldn't let this demon destroy it.

I focused my volts on Nyx, fueling him. I felt the tank filling, bit by bit, until it reached its peak. Again, Nyx rushed forward, then he leaped ahead. He spun his body at Charles like an electric saw. A moment passed. Eira morphed from her glaive form back into a snow leopard, landing on the ground with light steps. In that instant, Nyx's body spun and sliced Charles into two halves. Blood spurted as Charles's body slumped to the ground in two lumps of meaty flesh. The body still moved though it was clear that Charles was dead.

I wasn't sure if it was from the gut-shattering punch from earlier, or if what I had seen was too much, but I threw up. It wasn't a proud moment, and Alekka ignored it, saving me the embarrassment. Eira met Alekka. I sat, grimacing, trying to find an angle that didn't make me feel like I was dying.

"You mean to tell me you fought that thing already, by yourself?" Alekka asked.

"After we went to the gym," I said as I moved to my side. "Not really fight, though. We ran."

She glanced over at the body. "That's one of the strongest ones I've ever seen," she said. "Glad you made it out of there."

"Me, too. Can you give me a hand? We need to get out of here before the firefighters arrive and realize one of the alarms was set off." I glowered at Charles's lifeless form. "Wonder what they'll make of this whole mess."

Alekka lowered herself as she helped lift me. "Don't worry. Demon blood dissolves after some time for the most part. It's no different than rain. The body is much the same. It's soil to the earth. People end up seeing what they want, so they'll think all the blood is spilled liquor. Idiots."

As I stared at the corpse, I realized how right Gyle was. There were not many choices. No one would believe this... and anyone who did had to be crazy. But there was no denying what was so blatantly striking me in the face. The demons were real. They were active. And if we didn't find out why soon, things were going to get bad. Alekka led me from the room, and my body hated each step. When we reached the door, something came over me—a dark feeling, or maybe an instinct that screamed at me to move. I pushed Alekka from me and crashed to the floor. My body was going to kill in the morning.

The door where we'd been standing was ripped off the hinges, leaving a crumbling frame. Behind us, with palms pointing up toward us, stood Charles with his body intact. "Now you've pissed me off." He huffed.

22

"Nyx!" I shouted.

"Already on it," he replied. He zigzagged across the room, drawing Charles's gaze.

Nyx's blade collided with Charles's hardened arms. I glanced at Alekka. She gathered herself from the fall. Eira shifted back into her weapon form as she prepared for battle. "You think you could back me up?" Alekka asked. She turned to me, a smile now on her face. In this dire situation, she seemed as if she knew something I didn't. As if she had answers up her sleeve that I couldn't even fathom at this point. Was her confidence that high, or was she doing it to make sure I remained calm?

Maybe my eyes told a larger picture, because she followed up, asking, "Do you trust me?"

I paused as I stared at her. There was no way—it couldn't be. I nodded to her. "Yes," I replied. Alekka, more than anyone, knew how I felt. My lungs were cold, my body heavy. Between Nyx and I, we had gone through more voltage than ever before. I wasn't sure how far I could keep pushing. Alekka knew her limits whereas I had no clue when I couldn't push any further. I had to rely on listening to my body when it spoke to me. And I knew my tank was nearly empty. Nyx understood the change. He was doing the bare minimum now, deflecting Charles's arms when they gained.

Alekka stepped past Nyx. "I'll take offense, you grab defense, okay?"

"Do what you please," Nyx said.

Alekka grinned. "As I will," she said. She paused. "Thank you." Nyx didn't turn her way, but I felt the tiny, sudden ping of gratitude.

The temperature in the room plummeted. Within seconds, my breath was visible. Alekka glided along the floor, her body became like snow, elusive, with no true form—each piece a different being. In each place she stepped the ground turned to ice. In a sense, she mirrored the movement of Eira. It was as if as they fought, they became one being.

Alekka threw safety aside, turning to the offensive. She left defense to Nyx and me—though it was a struggle for me to keep pace. Nyx batted down Charles's arms as they slithered at Alekka. The demon hardened each of his arms fully, striking with devastating force. Charles's eyes were brighter now than ever.

"There," I said, pointing to the left.

Charles yelled; his hardened arm jetted at us. Nyx sliced down Charles once more. I rose. Alekka had a plan, and if she trusted me enough to go on an all-offensive attack, I better make sure Charles kept his slimy hands to himself. I focused on maintaining my volts. Nyx drew steady from our reservoir; I knew I wouldn't last much longer like this. But this was the best way. Nyx knew how to conjure and control voltage—I was a novice at it, if that. As I looked at the intent in Alekka's pale white eyes, I knew it would be enough.

All the sound in the room escaped—complete stillness fell. Alekka's steps echoed against the ice beneath her. A thick frozen mist filled the space, making it difficult to pick out any figure. Alekka crouched into what looked like a sprinter's stance with her head lowered. "Lend me your strength, Eira," she whispered.

Nyx jumped, using his tail to rip one of Charles's arms from his body. Charles came around with his other arm, grabbing Nyx. He slammed Nyx into the ground, then smashed a fist into him. Nyx cried out.

My legs moved before I had time to process my actions. Demons didn't play fair, and Nyx was his target. There was no way he would give up an opportunity to deal the final blow. I rushed ahead with everything

I had and threw my body into Charles's incoming arm. Excruciating pain shot through my frame, nearly knocking me unconscious. I stood, my body between Charles and Nyx.

Charles grinned, showing ghoulish fangs that hadn't been there prior.

Time froze.

Alekka exhaled, her breath escaping like a train horn. She propelled ahead, ripping her glaive across Charles's torso as she sailed by him. Sound returned, popping my ears. Charles turned his head to his waist, to see a gouge of his flesh taken out. At first, he didn't seem to be concerned, but then, from the gouge, ice began to populate. Each crystal formed as it took over his body. Charles slammed his fist down, shattering the ice. Alekka fell to one knee.

"Try as much as you like. As long as there's ice on you, it'll keep growing until you're smothered," Alekka said, gasping. "Shit… I haven't had much time to practice that."

Charles fell, his leg now half-frozen. He cried out, trying to crawl away through the open door leading to the pool area.

"My king," he shouted. "It… isn't enough…"

Thunder cracked, though there was no rain or lightning following it. The world ripped open in the grass of the backyard. The darkness held, and small red and gold sparks flashed every couple of seconds. Hands of char grabbed out from the void. Emerald eyes stared at me from the darkness. A demon wrenched itself through. Its body burnt black, resembling an adult-size man. It was the limbs and head that freaked me out. The thing's head was that of a snake. Its scales were thick and glistening with a blood red glow. While one of its arms looked human, its other had a pincer where its hand should be.

Along with Snake-Face, a woman, or what appeared to be a woman, stepped out from the void wearing a long black nightgown that sagged off her body. She peered around, her hair cut in a buzz. I could feel it, stronger than anything I've felt thus far— she was dangerous. Her eyes met mine from afar. Just being in her presence made me feel small— weak.

"More souls to devour?" she asked in an ardent voice. She turned to Alekka. She appeared to be young, though in her eyes there was a loss that only someone who'd lived centuries could have. "I'm going to enjoy killing you."

Snake-Face went to Charles. "Was help sent for me?" Charles asked. "I promise, I'll consume more power and kill these bastards. I can still be of use to the king. Please. I only need a little more…"

Some things stay with you forever. Charles's words went nowhere. The snake demon stared through Charles with emerald eyes. Its head swayed left, right, left…right—then it struck. The snake's jaw divided. It began with Charles's head, then continued until it slapped its mouth around his body—and finally legs. I watched what used to be Charles travel down the snake's throat and disappear. I thought they were Charles's backup, but now, I wasn't sure what their purpose was—though I knew they didn't have positive intentions.

"I hate lamb," Snake-Face said. "They have no taste." It roared, rolling its shoulders forward. Snake-Face turned to us. "Now, which one of you lambs are first?"

I couldn't move, no matter how bad I wanted to. My body wouldn't react. I fell to my side, watching the demons in the distance. Alekka was in a similar state. That last attack was supposed to finish the job and it likely depleted most of Alekka's volts. She wasn't thinking of saving her volts for another battle.

I had to do something. There was no other option. Pain was no longer the issue; I'd gotten used to the constant stabs and coldness in my lungs. My form simply rejected the notion of moving. The woman opened her hands. Her fingers turned to claws.

"Let me devour their souls," the woman said. "That boy has a strong will… I want it."

Snake-Face watched me for what seemed to be an eternity. "It's him," the demon said. "The jaguar." As the words left the demon's mouth it was upon me. I hesitated. I fucking hesitated. *No. I can't give up.*

I rose as much as I could and shouted, "Stop!" It was all I could manage; my body was tapped. Maybe my actions surprised the demon, making it take a second to think. Or it could have been fearful of abilities I didn't yet have or know how to use. Either way, it stopped, even if it was only for a second, it was enough.

When Snake-Face glared at me with confusion, I grinned.

"Alekka, I need you to trust me," I said, my body shaking. Alekka had put herself in harm's way trying to protect me. She refused to bat an eye. I hadn't so much as heard a complaint or seen her look at me as if I was a burden. I'd seen those sorts of eyes; I knew them well. It was time for me to return the favor—even if only a little. I straightened my body and stood tall. "I always have a plan. Do me a favor. Go to Tara and Susan. Keep them busy until I finish in here."

"You're insane if you think I'm leaving you here alone." She stumbled ahead. "Give me a second—I'll figure something out, I'm sure." She was barely standing.

"I'm not alone," I said. "I got Nyx with me. And just in case, I called some backup in."

Alekka paused. Then her eyes widened. "You're being serious, aren't you?"

I stared at the demons. Time was up, and they were going to attack any second. "Deathly," I said, swallowing. "You have enough volts to manage?"

She nodded as she rose. "I swear, if you're trying to play hero, you can pick an easier scene. If something happens to you, I'll revive you and kill you myself."

"Noted," I said. "Figure you might not want to be here for our guest."

Alekka raised a brow, then sighed, palming her forehead. "Yeah, yeah, yeah," Alekka said. "Don't do anything stupid, Aladdin." She glared at the two demons, then back at me. "Give them hell."

I waited until Alekka left the room with Eira at her feet, before glaring back at the snake.

"What happens when the lamb calls in backup?" I asked, grinning, standing face-to-face with the bastard.

23

"You question my strength?" Snake-Face asked as if it was blasphemous to even suggest it.

I shrugged. "Not me," I said, pointing behind the demon. "Him."

A flash of purple zipped by and pierced Snake-Face through the head. The demon moaned as chunks of its flesh slapped the ground. It stumbled. Two more shots. The first to the left knee, downing the foe, the second to the wrist of the demon's pincer hand. The third, and final shot, scattered the demon's brain tissue and gray matter across the ground. In seconds, the demon's body was nothing of what it once was. Something so strong, so frightening, in seconds it was nothing... Like everything else. The thought both scared me and made me feel small, but now wasn't the time to get emotional over it.

I inhaled, watching what was happening before me. Did I have it in me to be so true with my decisions? Sure, I had fought, but it was more to defend myself. Could I kill someone... or *something*?

Gyle turned to me, waving. "You call?" he asked, tapping Symon, in his pistol form against his shoulder. I had never been happier to see someone in my life. Seeing Gyle demolish the demon that made Charles look like a toddler, once again enforced how far I had to go just to be on par with those around me.

The demon-woman didn't seem to care that Snake-Face was brutalized next to her. Instead, she watched me from afar. Gyle pointed his pistol at her. "How about you do me a favor and die like your pal?" He pulled the trigger, but the demon woman slapped the bullet away as if it was a gnat. Gyle started circling around the woman. He continued firing, but no matter what he did, the demon-woman swatted the shot away with what seemed to be no effort at all.

She held out her finger, wagging it. "You're weak. But your voltage is worth devouring." She dodged, deflecting Gyle's bullets as they came. Her long claws emerged, closing in on Gyle's face. He fell backward and rolled away.

"Go!" Gyle tossed Claudy at the demon. The demon swiped at itself, cutting its own skin. Claudy traveled up the demon's body. The ferret dug its small fangs into the woman's thigh, then jumped off and scampered back to Gyle.

Claudy spat on the ground in disgust. She sat on Gyle's shoulder, her eyes glowed bright purple, her tongue sticking out as if she'd tasted a rancid fruit. Then she licked her lips slowly, tasting the demon's blood. Her eyes grew wider.

"Whatcha got?" Gyle asked.

"Dead," Claudy said. The blood seeped into her small fang.

Gyle halted and wiped his brow. "Sorry, Claudy. Let's try to make this as quick as possible. I know it's going to be your bedtime soon."

Claudy huffed. "No, no, I've been meaning to get a little rust off."

"I'll make sure to get your favorite snack for both of you tomorrow."

"Ready," Claudy said as she took position on Gyle's shoulder.

Gyle's demeanor changed. It was as if his confidence, though already high, elevated further. "Get to your partner," he said as he looked over to Nyx. He seemed calm—entirely too calm. No, there was something different. He was clenching his jaw. Gyle was mad. He turned his gaze back on the robed woman. "I'll handle this."

I shook my head. "Doubt he'll be okay with that," I said. I nudged my head at Nyx. Nyx trudged toward me. If by pride and adrenaline alone, I felt a bit left in the tank. "Make the kill. I'll back you up."

Gyle shrugged. "Do as you please."

Nyx appeared at my feet. He manifested a short sword next to me. "You sure you can handle this?" he asked.

I nodded. "Thanks, Nyx." Nyx took two steps back, then planted his feet into the ground, conjuring what little voltage he could. I grabbed the sword, feeling the hilt, expecting coolness, yet surprised by its warmth. A golden aura coated my body. It was simple. If Nyx couldn't fight anymore with our lack of volts, I would do the fighting for him.

Since realizing our bond's existence, I'd already seen considerable change in how my body reacted from healing to strength. With Nyx focused on fueling me with volts, I assumed that would only advance my abilities. At least that was my hope. I could always push a bit more and give more effort, if Nyx maintained. It was the most we could manage—I only hoped it was enough.

Gyle raised a brow at me. He nodded. "Don't get yourself hurt," Gyle said. Gyle twirled Symon in his hand and moved toward the demon in the black dress. Gyle stopped, pointing the pistol at her. "Sorry for keeping you waiting. Where were we?"

The demon-woman must have been as confident in her abilities as Gyle, if not more. Instead of heeding his warning or even becoming slightly defensive, she squared her body to Gyle and went into a crouching stance. She smirked before sprinting at him.

I reacted to her attack. My legs took me faster than I knew was possible. The demon's claws caught against my blade. It took everything in me to keep her at bay. Another strike, then another. I defended against her claws, dodging when I knew defending wasn't possible. The demon lunged at me. Her claws funneled toward me. They shot out at me, barely giving me time to react.

The demon's claws shattered, as they deflected against a faint violet shield that appeared before me. "Keep going, honey!" Claudy yelled. I blinked my eyes, grateful to be alive. I faced the woman again and noticed a dark purple mark that appeared on her thigh. It was in the same place Claudy bit into earlier.

I took the demon on again, and I felt my power waning. Though it didn't seem to make a difference. I was able to keep up. Something was off. I knew I was slowing—I had to be. The demon slowed as fast as I was. We were racing to see who hit the end first.

Then it hit me. Claudy, unlike Symon, wasn't built on offense. Her power lay in other areas. One obvious area was Claudy's ability to create barriers. I imagined she had more abilities up her sleeves that I wasn't aware of. Whatever Claudy did when she bit the woman, it took effect and fast. I didn't have to be stronger or faster. I just had to outlast her. Then Gyle would have his chance to end this.

Gyle shot at her. Instead of dodging, she caught the bullet with the nails of her right hand, while still attacking me. She was toying with us like it was some sort of game. She flicked the bullet back at Gyle with speed that rivaled his gun. Claudy diverted the bullet before it arrived. Apparently, the demon wasn't aware of her slowing speed. Or was she just delusional? I traded blows with her. My body felt fatigued. I wasn't ready for the trauma my body was going to be in from continuing the battle. Breathing became harder and harder by the second—but my opportunity was near. I knew it.

The demon-woman shrieked. She threw her arms to either side as her claws extended again. She swiped her arms back, her claws surrounding my body like a ball of yarn.

Before the claws fell upon me, I slipped from my vest and tossed it where my body had been. I could see the surprise in her eyes when she mutilated the vest I had been wearing. Thanks to Charles and his long arms, I half-expected the demon's claws to have more features than just one. I stopped my motion and opened my body. The demon defended her face, the place I would go if I wanted to deal a fatal blow. Too bad for her, I was more self-aware than she knew. With my experience, I was nowhere strong enough to defeat her, let alone have the resolve to do it. My only job was to halt her movement for Gyle.

I yanked my hand up, grabbed the sword's hilt with both hands and drove the blade into her foot. The sword slipped through without resistance, planting into the earth. Before she had time to react, I scurried away from her immediate attacking range. When I was at a safe distance, I turned to Gyle. "Easy enough target for you?"

Gyle smirked. "You know... You ain't half bad for a newbie," he replied. "Though I'll have you know I could have killed her without your help." He steadied Symon, aiming the barrel at the demon-woman. Claudy muttered a few words. Violet voltage emitted from her body, transferring to Symon. "I would ask for your last word, but I honestly couldn't give a shit." Gyle fired.

This attack was stronger. A funnel of violet light emitted from the weapon, a bullet rocketing for the demon's head. The bullet struck an invisible barrier. It spiraled, digging into the shield.

Claudy snickered. "Surely you underestimate me, woman," she said. Claudy focused her volts as she fueled the bullet. The bullet sawed through the demon's last line of hope and ripped through the demon's head and the ground behind it.

The woman's gaze was distant as she blinked at each of us slowly. Her body bent backward as her legs collapsed upon themselves and she crumbled.

"Told you I'm a good shot," Gyle said, shrugging.

I tried catching my breath. Next to me, Nyx did the same. Gyle tapped me on the shoulder. "Good job out there, rook."

I had to be overwhelmed because the tears came immediately. "You came!" I cried. "You fucking came." I threw my head between my legs, trying to conceal my tears as much as possible. "It wouldn't have been enough if it was just me and Alekka. I don't think anyone here would have made it." I stopped speaking.

"But it was enough," Gyle said. "And somehow, nobody was hurt. So I'll call that a win. Sorry I couldn't get her sooner." He reached his arm out. Symon returned to his original form. "These bastards are popping up more and more these days. And they're stronger than normal. Those three had speech."

I reached into my pocket and touched the bullet. Who would have thought Charles throwing me earlier would have saved my life? If he hadn't knocked my things out of my pocket, I doubt I would have remembered to call Gyle in so quickly.

The bodies of the demons began dissolving as the door to the Otherworld closed. I gathered myself, then motioned to Nyx. He took his small cat form now; his breathing was still heavy. There was a look in his golden eyes that told me all I needed to know. I felt it, too. If I had any pride, this fight chipped away the last of it. I was out of my league. And who knew how strong these demons were in comparison to what was out there? The thought brought a nerving chill.

"How does it feel?" Gyle asked.

"What?"

"Realizing the threat." His words didn't weigh on me before the way they do now. I couldn't imagine a world that let demons do as they pleased. But then again, I couldn't imagine how most would react having seen what we fought against. There are some things you want to forget.

"Come on," Gyle said. "You need to get back with the rest of the partygoers. Everyone's probably wondering where you're at by now."

"Yeah," I grunted. "Doubt Alekka will be able to distract them much longer."

I couldn't imagine standing in a crowd right now. What just happened—it was unreal. But I was alive. My head felt like it was going to explode—my heart much of the same. Gyle was right, I needed to get back to Alekka and the others. If I was going to maintain my normal life —and a job—I had to save face. I breathed. One thing at a time. I could do this.

As I reached for Gyle's hand, I finally noticed his outfit and almost burst into laughter. Gyle stood in front of me, in a Peter Pan outfit, with all the legs I needed to see for my lifetime.

"Nice legs," I said.

He lowered his gaze at me. "You help a friend out and wouldn't believe the things they say about you." He palmed his head.

I know Nyx was reluctant to do it, but I opted to carry Nyx. Neither of us spoke.

Gyle left after guiding me most of the way to the crowd. I needed the helping shoulder. My consciousness fluttered a few times, and without Gyle's support, I doubted I would have made it. I remembered him supporting me then, like the breeze. He blended into night. I went down the driveway where Tara and Alekka rushed over to me. A part of me was surprised but also welcomed by how concerned they looked. Maybe I was looking at the glass half-empty a bit too much lately. I let out a short wave as I met with them. It was all I could manage in my state of exhaustion.

"What took you so long?" Alekka asked. I put my hand behind my head, trying to get air into my lungs casually. "And why don't you have a shirt on, creep?" she added. Alekka grinned. "Get your ass over here." She hugged me. "We were worried about you. You were taking forever." She pulled away instantly, patting my shoulders twice. "You're also very sweaty."

I didn't know where to begin. Though I knew I was going to ignore her shirt comment. Truthfully, I'd forgotten the vest, but it was time to hang the costume up. "This place is a maze. Got turned around a few times trying to get out. But everything worked out … Looks like everyone is safe?" I grimaced. "Sorry for making everyone worry."

Susan was off in the distance talking to a firefighter. Tara checked her phone. "I'm sending you a few emails I need you to follow up with me on," she said to Alekka. Alekka blinked her frustrations away. "Party time's over."

"But..." Alekka retorted.

"Next week, of course," Tara said. "But, if anything else, what have I taught you?"

"Alligator closest to the boat," Alekka huffed.

Tara smiled. "Exactly." She placed her hand on Alekka's shoulder. "I'm glad to have you representing the press. And Nexus, I look forward to reading your piece soon." She clicked around on her phone. "I guess Charles left. If any of you see him, tell him I went home. And enjoy your early weekend." Tara stretched her arms to the sky before she walked uncomfortably away in her yellow dress.

"Did you hear that?" Alekka asked, her voice rising.

"You mean the part about her asking about the demon who was swallowed whole… Or your boss saying she was glad to have you?"

Alekka glowered at me. "The latter, of course," she said. "That's the first time Tara's ever said anything so… warm. Mark. This. Day!" Alekka brought her phone out and called for an Uber. "Don't worry. The Charles situation will handle itself; they always do… The supernatural has a habit of making the things normal people don't want to believe vanish. Over time, people will forget he ever existed. Kind of sad, really."

We waited and then waited some more. By the time the Uber finally arrived, I had to be woken up to get in the car. I painfully got in, propped myself against the door, and told the driver we would make a stop at my house along the way. There was no way I could drive myself home tonight. I would call an Uber when I needed to get my car in the morning. I desperately wanted to rest and eat. A buffet, preferably. If this was the toll it took to use voltage, I wasn't going to be a fan of using it. My body wasn't going to like any of this. This fight was completely different from my other two Otherworld encounters. It was like trying to sprint a marathon—eventually, you would collapse with exhaustion. If anything, I was just glad to have Alekka with me. Without her, there was no way I would have made it out of this in one piece.

I gave the driver the code to my neighborhood when we arrived. "Fancy," Alekka said.

"Don't let the gate fool you. I'm as broke as the next guy," I said.

We pulled up to my house, and in all honesty, getting out brought more agony than I was ready for. It was as if my body was anchored to the car seat and standing shattered each bone. I thanked the driver and exited the car. Alekka reached her arms around the top of my shoulders as I shut the door. "You know, for a guy who isn't much for parties, you sure showed me a good time."

I half-smiled; half-groaned. "Thanks for forcing me out. God knows if you didn't, I would have found some excuse not to go."

Alekka walked with me to my door. Nyx jumped from my arms and made his way inside. "You know, I don't remember my human name, either," she said.

"Huh?"

Alekka tapped her head. "The name my parents gave me. I don't remember it. Even when I tried to find it in writing or hear it in a recording—it wasn't there. That part of me died when I became a Hybrid." Alekka turned to me. "But I love the name Eira gave me." She walked back to the car. "If you need me, holla." She waved as the Uber pulled away.

I opened the door to Amon greeting me. "How's it going, boss?" he squawked. Before I said anything, he flew in closer. "You look like shit. What happened?"

I placed my keys on the counter, dreading getting my car in the morning.

"I feel like it, too," I replied. I grabbed a protein bar. I needed food but was too tired to make anything right now. "I don't even know where to begin. I'm so tired."

Amon took his time placing the ward on the house. "All secure, boss," he said, saluting. "Hope you have a safe and secure rest."

I had to smile. "Thanks, Amon," I said.

I dragged myself over to the couch. There was no way I could have made it up the stairs. I take back my previous statement. I was far beyond tired.

And with that thought, my mind quickly became a blank slate, and I was fast asleep.

24

Things changed after Halloween. The world looked darker to me —bleaker. In more ways than one, my anxiety rose. But who could blame the paranoia? I called in sick the following week from work. I needed the extra time off to recover. I was sure Alekka had some idea I wasn't sick, considering her random texts checking up on me every so often. In between those texts, she sent me a meme or two telling me to "laugh with her." Half the time I couldn't bring myself to respond, but I appreciated every message.

I called an Uber to get my car the morning after, even though my body begged me not to. I didn't bother Alekka, I figured we would talk when the time was right. The last thing I wanted was to need it and not have it. I went to Lix and went grocery shopping once my ribs allowed me to walk without discomfort (which wasn't long at all). Maybe it wasn't the world that changed, but how I viewed it. Everyone had something in their eyes. Some I could look at or walk by with no issue. When I got around others, I got a sudden urge to put my guard up. Nyx maintained a steady pace at my side.

"You're starting to sense others' voltages," he said.

I parked my cart on the side of the aisle as I gathered a few things. Each person who passed me brought a new level of paranoia. I met their eyes, reading them, trying to tell a story—trying to gather anything that would give me the edge.

"How do I know who's a demon or not?" I asked.

"Hard to say. Seeds are fairly easy to tell. They can't mask their presence and won't readily be in your world unless a door to the Otherworld is open for them. Germs and Synths are another case. Like Charles, they can mask their presence and use a human vessel as a haven. But even then, if they aren't strong enough, they won't attack. Demons are aggressive, but cautious creatures."

"Then I really won't be able to tell," I said. I wasn't sure how comfortable I was, not knowing if a demon was breathing down my neck or not.

I almost jumped from my skin when someone touched my shoulder. I spun violently, readying myself. The other shopper, an older man, was probably more scared of my reaction than I ever could be of him.

He nodded at me and pointed to an item, saying, "Excuse me, son," as he went to grab it. A mix of emotions struck me. First, the feeling of embarrassment that I nearly attacked someone who wanted to grab some condiments. Second, the underlying sense that a demon could very well be in such a harmless-looking form. It was the fact that the latter was especially true. Why choose a host that would alert anyone with common sense? Rather, they would have chosen someone who played the part—someone who blended in.

That thought, of course, caused me to dive down a rabbit hole that led me to wonder how many people in power were hosts for demons. What I thought to be a normal world, where my biggest fear was making the rent while still trying to follow my dreams, could be a world littered with demons. That sure added a layer of stress to the "everyday struggle."

I moved again, going down the aisles slowly. "This 'throne...' Once a demon gets it, what happens?" I asked.

Nyx followed me, his shoulders rounding slowly with each step. "I don't know. That depends on who sits on the throne. What does anyone called 'king' do? They rule."

I shuddered, thinking of what ruling the Otherworld meant. It would go as far as the ruler's thoughts and power could travel. And I doubted letting humans live in peace would have been at the top of their minds when creating their rules. And I wasn't counting on any demons turning into saints. That brought me to one conclusion.

"We have to get stronger," I said. "Can you start teaching me how to manifest and control our volts? That last fight almost killed me." No matter which way I flipped the coin I had to get better. If only for sanity's sake. I didn't know how long I could go, knowing I was easy prey for anything walking.

I bought enough food to last me a week or two then made my way to the checkout line. The cashier smiled at me; a young boy barely old enough to work. He placed the receipt in my hand and gazed at me. And I read his eyes. They showed me fear and despair. His small glowing sapphire eyes called for help. I swallowed. I knew what he was, there was no mistaking it. Then I realized what I was witnessing. The fear, the despair. I was the cause of it—or rather, Nyx, being a Synth, was. Nyx continued, ignoring me and the cashier altogether.

I crumpled the receipt and placed it in one of the bags. "Thank you," I said.

I focused on rest and recovery for the next few days. Thanks to Nyx, sleep and food seemed like a cure-all. After a few days of good rest and eating, my ribs healed to a manageable level for the most part. And with any luck, I would get through a day without causing myself too much pain. Alekka and I didn't speak much about the events that occurred on Halloween. It wasn't that we were avoiding it or anything. We just hadn't gotten around to it yet.

I parked the Jetta in my normal spot at the gym and walked to the entrance slowly. The 5 am crew huddled around the door like it was a campfire. The appointed leader of the group made a joke about being up since three, while the rest of the small group laughed along. I unlocked the door so they could enjoy another great day at The Bar. Cold air touched my skin as I entered and took my station behind the desk.

Dave skipped into the building an hour later munching on his morning apple. "How you coming along?" he asked.

I stretched my arms out. "You know, to be honest, I'm doing great. Full of life."

Dave nodded with approval. "That's what I like to hear."

I wasn't lying. Things felt different. Lively. I went and filled my water bottle (I had one of those now). Nyx turned his head up to me.

"Why so chipper?" he asked.

I thought about his question as I went back to my desk. "I wouldn't call it chipper," I said. I grabbed my work jacket and slipped it on. "Before everything was stopped, I felt like I was standing still, you know?"

"The point being?" Nyx asked.

"Whether I like it or not, things are moving. And I don't know... I guess it isn't all that bad. That's all."

Nyx found a spot on top of the front desk and got comfortable. He tucked his head into his body, curling into himself. "I see," he said.

Alekka strolled into the gym. It was my first time seeing her since Halloween.

"Heyo," I said, giving her a short wave.

She returned the wave, or at least, that's what I assumed. All I could see were the sleeves of her sweater. "How's it going?" She yawned. "How are you feeling?"

"Hangin' in there." I rubbed my ribs. "Trying to. All this fighting takes a toll on the body. I think I can do without it."

"Tell me about it. I need to see a chiropractor. Oh, yeah, Tara wanted me to tell you sorry."

"For what?"

"Susan got held up after what happened on Halloween, with Charles 'quitting and all.' She had Tara hold off on submitting a manuscript. Tara wanted you to know we'll be reading your submission soon."

My eyes widened. This might be the opportunity I needed. "When do you think y'all will be reading?" I asked.

Alekka checked her phone. "Next week things will open back up, but Tara will be back the weekend."

"You have my manuscript?" I asked.

"Yup." Alekka stared at me with wonder in her eyes. "What are you planning?"

"I'm going to drop something off at your house later."

Alekka shrugged. "As long as I have it before I hand it off to Tara. Don't be late."

I smiled and looked at my laptop sitting on the back desk. "Don't worry, I won't be."

I buzzed the door to the warehouse where Gyle and the other Union City Hybrids live (I officially named them *Unionlings*). The door opened without anyone looking to see who was on the other side. Quin stood staring at me, with a pair of white earbuds in, and eating an ice cream cone. She gave me an expression that said, "Hurry up before I leave you out here." I hurried in. Once inside, she walked behind me, sliding the heavy metal door shut with one hand. She was young but it was clear she had more of a grasp of this Hybrid thing than I did.

"You beat *Trails of Cold Steel* yet?" I asked. She didn't react. We both stood and stared at each other in silence. Maybe she didn't hear me.

Quin placed a thumb through one overall loop as she ignored me and strolled along. She led me into the main lounge area before she grabbed a handheld device from the bar counter. I was starting to lose track of all the devices she had. Quin pulled a cellphone from her pocket and clicked around a bit. Then she disappeared from the room altogether. After a minute passed, Gyle came into the common area.

"Yo," he said, waving. "You wanted to talk?"

"Yeah..." I didn't know where to start but I knew where I wanted to end, ironically enough. We never talked about what happened. When he came and checked on me, it was to make sure I was eating and moving around fine. Now that I could move, I needed to do just that. I scratched my forehead.

"First off, thanks for saving my ass on Halloween," I said. I ran both my hands through my hair, exhaling. "Charles might have gotten away if it wasn't for you. Hell, I know Alekka and I wouldn't have been able to take out the other two as well." I clenched my hand into a fist. "I was holding her back too much." I thought back to the fatigue I felt during the fight. "I never thought sustaining voltage would be so grueling. I was on the brink of exhaustion trying to maintain it."

Gyle hopped on the barstool next to me. "You did good, man. Surprised you were able to use your volts like that, and in such sync so soon." Gyle pressed his thumb and index finger to his chin. "The only problem now is figuring out who the hell sent them. Voss's been out of town trying to gather intel on that."

Nothing made sense, but it didn't have to. I kept going back to the emotions that overcame me the night I was attacked in the alley. That fear. That anxiety. That sense of hopelessness. I couldn't imagine living through that again. I didn't want anyone living through that.

"I'm not joining the Power Rangers... But maybe I could volunteer."

Gyle blinked a few times. "Seriously?"

I nodded. "After everything I've seen, I'd be stupid not to. I won't be staying here with the rest of you, though." I stared at the bright ceiling lights surrounding the building. "I sort of like my space. This is a bit overkill."

Gyle scanned the room, then nodded. "Point taken."

I nudged my head toward Nyx. "Maybe you can help me understand more about the Otherworld and fighting these things. It'll do me some good to at least learn to protect myself."

Gyle shook his head. "Sure, if that's what you want?"

I thought about what Susan's party could have been if we hadn't intervened. They would have slaughtered everyone there without question. I couldn't stand aside and watch while Union City was overrun with demons.

"Yeah. I can't just sit by and do nothing," I answered.

Gyle reached his arm out, letting Claudy climb around it and back to his shoulder. "I'm okay with you not staying here. But if you want to get some training in, your mornings are going to start early."

"How early are we talking?" I asked.

Gyle smiled. "I'll be in touch. Don't worry."

25

When I arrived home, Amon greeted me as he managed the defensive ward around the house. I was finally getting used to that whole routine. I went to the fridge and made a quick snack. The TV played in the background as I listened to my thoughts. Nyx found a cool spot on the tile in the center of the living room. He licked his front paw, craning his neck back and forth. When he stopped, he stared at me.

"Thank you," he said.

"For what?"

Nyx refused to look at me as he spoke. "Against that demon... You placed your body between me and him." I hadn't expected Nyx to answer. And even if he did, those weren't the words I ever expected him to say.

"In all fairness, if you would have died, so would I—so it really is a moot point," I said.

Nyx continued to clean himself. "Either way, you have my thanks."

"No problem," I responded. I leaned my head back and stared at the ceiling.

I never imagined I would be the pet guy, but now I had two demons calling my house their home. Something was bothering me that I hadn't been able to put into words until now. "You said once demons become higher-level., They just fight to become the strongest, right?"

"Essentially. Why?"

"Charles, he called out to his king. Then there was the stuff about the 'war.' It was clear his ideas weren't his own." I wasn't sure if my theory would hold any weight, seeing how little I knew about the Otherworld, but I gave it a shot, anyway. "What if the demons are working together as well? You can't win a war alone."

Nyx paused, then resumed cleaning. But even in that split second, I could feel Nyx's heart waver. "And your point is?" he asked. "It is impossible. Demons would never work together. The second one of them turns their back, the other will shove a claw through it."

I shook my head and opened my palms. "I have no point," I said. "I just wish it made sense." I tapped my fingers against my knee. "What do you want? If everything goes Nyx's way, what will happen?"

Nyx stopped. "You're an odd character," he said. "What I want isn't of any importance right now. The main issue is figuring out why and how we were bonded."

The age-old question, and the one I wanted to stay as far as possible from. Nev Nox, what the hell was going through his mind? Over the years I put a few things together, none that would have brought me to this conclusion. I spent the early years of my life wondering about my parents. My mother died while giving birth and my father had taken his own life soon after. I gave myself a few years of wallowing, then I cut the thought of parents from my mind altogether. There was no way I was going fishing for memories now.

"Now's not the time," I said. "Not now…"

Nyx didn't pry. With our bond, I felt the connection between our emotions. There was a silent understanding. I wish I could, but there were still some mountains I wasn't ready to climb yet.

We sat in silence. Neither of us felt the need to add to the world. It felt good—relaxing. After the amount of stress that piled onto my shoulders, I would likely need to see a chiropractor. Or try yoga and meditation. Meditation was cheaper—free. I stayed in a suspended state of mind and watched the ceiling fan go around and around and around.

After half a minute of the spinning, I recharged and got moving again. I grabbed my laptop from my desk and brought it downstairs.

While I connected my phone to the stereo, I got comfortable on the couch with my laptop. A mellow beat played. I opened the word processor and titled the document, *The Book of Nox*. My best work always came from my experiences. First person would work. I needed to be in my own head for this one. Above all, write what I knew, got it.

I almost laughed as I wrote. Maybe the reason I had been feeling so uninspired was because I hadn't lived anything worth writing about. And maybe I was writing in the wrong genre. The words poured out of me. My fingers glided across the keys. Save for the times I had to backspace for a mistake or cut a whole paragraph because I hated it, the work easily found itself brought to life. I would always wonder how authors spoke of writing an entire novel in a night. I never thought it possible to write tens of thousands of words all at once. Yet here I was finishing the first ten thousand. The next ten came just as fast, if not faster. Before long, day turned to night, and the dark hours took the wheel. Then I finished—done. I got all my words and thoughts into something I felt was worthwhile.

I gave the work a quick once-over (I wasn't proud of my lack of editing), then printed it. With any luck, I could get through without changing the cartridge. I went upstairs and put something comfortable on. When I came down the printer had just finished. I clipped the novel, grabbed the car keys, then left.

I parked, then half-walked, half-ran up to Alekka's apartment. I put a black folder with a sticky note that read: *The Book of Nox*. At least with this manuscript, I could be happy with myself, regardless of whether my piece won the fiction contest. I walked down the stairs and went back to the Jetta.

The wind seemed colder than yesterday's. I opened the door to the Jetta, then stopped and looked at the pulsing stars.

"What is it?" Nyx asked.

I got in the car. "What isn't wrong?" I asked. "I'm nervous. Anxious." I couldn't explain the sensation. Pressure, maybe? I wasn't nervous about something attacking us. I was nervous about the future. Everything changed the day I lost my name and encountered Nyx for the first time. I would no longer spend my days going to work and home, going through the same dull routine. My life had become one passive action after another. Now I was in control and that sensation scared me more than ever—but excited me all at the same time.

I put my things away after arriving home and went to my room. "Hey, question," I asked as I hopped in the bed and pulled the covers snugly. "Why *Nexus*?"

Nyx gathered himself at the edge of the bed. He gazed at me. "The name is one I approve of, as my host will be the center of the world." His golden eyes traveled to me, glowing. "But I'm not the one who gave you that name."

"What?" I asked, confused. "What do you mean you didn't name me?"

"I didn't name you," he said flatly.

I rubbed my face. "But I thought the name was given to me when you created the bond?"

Nyx sighed. "My mind is as hazy as yours when it comes to our bond. I don't remember bonding us." He rolled on his side. "I'm sure it'll come to me. I must have bonded us at some point or we wouldn't be here."

I tried not to frustrate myself with the details. There were more questions at every turn. I could barely keep up. "I guess you're right," I said. Nyx knew more than I did on the subject. There was no point in stressing myself over the small stuff, I had enough of that building up already.

I checked my phone, turning my alarms on (yes, I'm one of those people). In a couple of hours, I had to meet Gyle. I would have barely enough sleep to be functional. Looks like sleepless nights were going to be a recurring theme in my life.

I found myself at Fernando's to get a drink and a bite to eat a couple of days later. Their blackened shrimp and fries were the right touch with a cool beer. This bar used to be a place of happiness for me. One I came to when I needed to unwind and smile. With friends that I thought I would know for years to come. I glanced over to Nyx, then rolled my eyes. Maybe I was being a bit melodramatic. Nevertheless, Fernando's meant something to me. And I wasn't going to let that change.

Fernando came over and leaned his elbow against the bar top. "You good, man?" he asked. "Having you over here pouting isn't good for business."

I ate a fry. "Sorry, man," I said. "I never meant to stop coming, you know that, right? You know how much I love this place. I just… at the time, I really didn't know. Then I started looking at everyone differently. And—"

"Relax, man, it's all good. No harm, no foul." He leaned closer. "Between you and me, I wasn't a big fan of everyone in the group, anyway. Some of you guys were assholes." He shrugged, laughing.

I'd spent so many days living in my own head that I had never gotten out to see the world for the truth. Sure, some people chose sides, but that wasn't true for everyone. In this case, Fernando was collateral damage in a situation he wanted nothing to do with. Here I was, having a main character syndrome for a moment, thinking the world revolved around me. The least I could do was give Fernando business as usual. I liked the food, so why wouldn't I? It was time I started doing what I wanted, anyway. I raised my glass to cheer the air, then took a long cold pull of beer.

When I was no longer facing the bottle, Fernando was looking toward the door. His eyes came to me and signaled me to turn around. Alekka held her finger up to Fernando who promptly made her drink, remembering it from the last visit. Damn. I wished I had that good of a memory.

"Figured I'd find you here when you weren't at home," she said. "You know, texting is for quick responses. If I wanted to wait days for an answer, I would've sent you a letter by pigeon."

I checked my phone, seeing several unread messages. "Sorry," I replied. "I've just been thinking a lot lately. Haven't really looked at my phone much at all."

"Trust me, I know. Well, kinda. I was young when I met Eira." Alekka grabbed her drink and handed Fernando her card. "I really haven't had many friends besides Eira since the day we bonded." Eira jumped in her lap. Alekka rubbed behind her ear. "It gets lonely sometimes. But that's also partly our fault. Hybrids tend to isolate themselves, think we're alone, nobody could possibly understand, right?"

"You know, I don't see it like that," I said. I ate more while gathering my thoughts. "Sure, others might not understand. Hell, if we ever said anything to anyone about the Otherworld, we'd be put in an asylum. But I was lonely before all of this happened. I've always been alone." I glanced at Nyx. "Now I feel like I'm surrounded by more people than I've ever had in my life. And whether I like it or not, I'm kind of stuck with it. I guess I'm trying to get used to not being alone."

Alekka wiped imaginary tears from her eyes. "Aww, how sweet of you, Nexus," she said. "Who knew you were such a softy?"

"You're an asshole," I said.

Alekka shrugged. "Comes with it, what can I say? Are we really friends, or am I just secretly judging you? You'll never know."

Another bartender came from the kitchen, handing Fernando a basket of blackened shrimp and fries. Fernando grabbed the food and placed it in front of Alekka with napkins and dipping sauces.

"I didn't order anything," Alekka said.

"This is my bar. I give food to whoever I want," Fernando replied. "If you put up with this guy, you're fine by me. Good to see new faces in here, too."

Now Alekka looked like she really was going to cry. "Aww, thank you. That's so nice," Alekka said, eating a fry. She turned back to me. "I like this place. It's my type of vibe. We should come here more often."

I scanned the bar, listening to the bass of the song kick in the background. "Yeah, we should."

She pulled out the chair next to me and took a seat. "So, what's new?" she asked.

I didn't immediately speak. Then something came over me. I put my hand up a little and got Fernando's attention.

"What can I do for ya?" he asked.

"Let me get two of the Fernando specials," I replied.

He put his hand on his chest sarcastically. "Coming right up." He flipped two shot glasses up and put them in front of Alekka and me.

Alekka narrowed her eyes at me. I turned to see Nyx directly beneath my feet, Eira beneath Alekka's. At least they were acting somewhat peaceful; it was progress. "I don't know how else to say it, besides, we escaped death on Halloween," I said. Fernando mixed a concoction, shook it, then poured it into the shot glasses until they were barely beneath the rim—perfect pour.

I took my glass, holding it up. We clinked glasses. "To life," I said.

We tapped our glasses on the counter before taking sips.

"To life," Alekka repeated.

ACKNOWLEDGMENTS

And let's not forget all the wonderful people that helped me get here, whether one of my mentors, or friends or foes (artistic rivals.) To my family who've help see me here, it's been a long journey, yet it has only just begun. Also, huge, huge, huge shout out to Audrey Fierberg, my wicked cool editor extraordinaire. Oh, and one more, to the entire operations and production team who helped put this together. You're the best!!!

ABOUT THE AUTHOR

Who is Kadeem Locke? Kadeem Locke is a Jamaican-American writer, born and raised in Jacksonville, Florida. I would love to tell you he was out fighting crime or something of the sort. But Kadeem is an avid anime watcher, video game player, a reader, and a slew of other things that take up his time, with writing being the number one culprit. You can catch him at your local restaurant or bookstore doing what he always does— reading, writing. More reading, more writing. He was a second grader when he started trying to write his first story but it, of course, bombed. However, he kept trying and trying and... You get the point. Kadeem graduated from the University of North Florida where he received his Bachelors in English with a Minor in Creative Writing.

-Detective Cirrus